I0763580

The Other Side of Fear

By

Ciana Stone

The Other Side of Fear

ISBN: 978-0-9985808-9-0

Cover art by Syneca Featherstone

Electronic book publication first edition 05/06/ 2022
Print book publication 05/06/2022

DEDICATION

For the love of my life.

Always and forever. I do.

CONTENTS

Prologue

Of all the luck. The storm caught up with them, bringing sheets of rain that cut visibility in half, even with the windshield wipers going at full tilt. Flashes of lightning bright enough to leave white spots in the vision, and thunder powerful enough to rock the ground, made for a night where no one should be on a winding country road in the foothills of Georgia.

Jack cast a fast look in the right-side mirror, then up at the rear-view. *Shit.* At least two more sets of headlights followed him now. He pressed harder on the accelerator, trying to coax more speed out of a car with little left to give. For the tenth time in less than ten minutes, he wished he had his own car.

Yeah, smart move, son. Drive something that shouts hey, look at me.

Wasn't it odd that his conscience sounded exactly like his father? Snorting at his own imagination and annoyance at the present circumstances, he checked the rear-view. His pursuers weren't gaining, but neither was he pulling ahead.

A sudden gust of wind, strong enough to push the car, preceded a downpour that cut visibility down to mere feet. This was getting worse by the moment. Jack focused on keeping the car on the road and ahead of the people in pursuit.

"They're going to catch us."

"It'll be okay, just stay down," he cut a quick glance at the woman in the back seat who'd spoken in a trembling voice. "You hear me?"

Her face was nearly void of color, and her entire body shook like someone caught out in the cold without a coat. "Do you understand?" he asked.

"Y—y—yes." Fear nearly robbed her of speech, and she clutched the toddler tighter to her.

Just as she spoke, the first crack of gunfire sounded, adding weight to the assurance Jack now had that this wasn't a standard "grab the target and go" operation. Not. At. All.

Fine. So be it. It wasn't the first time things had gone south on a job. Not as spectacularly as this, however. The hell of it was he couldn't figure out where he'd gone wrong. It was almost a textbook case. Contact the target by phone, provide proof you're telling the truth and when the target believes you and agrees, pick the target up and drive away. The end.

That's what he did. So why were they being followed by four cars, obviously carrying at least one person with a weapon? Something was wrong, and it wasn't with him. Jack yanked out his phone and stole a glance at it to activate a call.

Rain and now hail slickened the road, making the tires slip and slide. One of the pursuing vehicles gained on them. He could make out someone leaning out of the passenger window, trying to take aim at them. But with what? Between trying to keep his eye on the road, the driving rain, hail and persistent flashes of lightning, visibility was crap.

For the first time, doubt entered the picture. Jack tried to shove it back into the dark. This was no time for doubt. He had to believe they'd see this through.

"Jack?" a deep male voice sounded from the earpiece in his left ear.

"It's a fubar, Dad."

"Tell me."

"Pull up my location and call the locals. Tell them whatever you have to, just get 'em coming at us from every direction."

"It's going to be fine, Jack. Stay on the line."

The calm assurance in his father's voice sliced through the knot of tension holding him prisoner. For the first time since everything went to hell, he could breathe. At least for a split second. That's when the shooting started.

"He's in the system—check his location." Jack's father, Clayton ordered as he paced the floor, holding his phone and speaking into the air.

"We have him, sir."

"Then get him help. Now. Send all of them—city, town, county, state."

"Under whose authority, sir?"

"Mine."

To his subordinate's credit, the order wasn't questioned. "Yes, sir."

Jacob switched back to the call with Jack, just in time to hear a woman scream, rapid gunfire and the shriek of tires on asphalt. "Jack!"

“Dad, we’re screwed.”

It was the tone more than the words that alarmed Clayton. Jack didn’t rattle easily, nor did he back down.

“No. Help is on the way.”

There was no reply. Just the sounds of bullets thunking into metal, the rapid percussion of multiple weapons firing in concert, mixed with the sound of an engine stretched to its limit, screaming like a wounded animal.

“Jack?”

“I love you, Dad.”

The sounds that followed those words would forever be the most horrible, gut wrenching, heart-breaking moments of his life. All notions of strength and fortitude, of power and might—it all just fled. Like a light that is suddenly extinguished.

“Jack? Jack!”

One soul curdling scream accompanied the wrenching shriek of metal just before the line went dead, with Clayton still shouting his son’s name.

And for the third time in his life, Clayton Blackstone was brought to his knees.

Chapter One

Six months. That's how long it'd been since he lost his youngest son. Sometimes the grief welled up so strong and bitter it took his breath. He stared for a moment longer at the small framed photo taken last Christmas. All his boys came home, and Sam took a family picture as they sat on the front porch steps.

He swiped at his face where tears had escaped and worked their way to his jawline. This wasn't the time for reflection or grief. There were matters that required attention. He'd grieve later when the lights were out, and there would be less chance of anyone seeing his tears.

Clayton walked out of the house and onto the front porch. He took a deep breath, moved over to the porch railing, and hitched one hip on the top rail as he listened. When Sam, his business manager, and attorney, finished speaking, he cleared his throat before responding.

"I trust your judgment, Sam. Tell me what you think."

"It's a lot of money, Clayton, maybe more than is wise at present. Are you sure you want to dive in now? The owners have received little interest in the land, so chances are, we could wait, and maybe they'd come down on the price even more."

"Are you saying we can't afford it?"

"No, that's not what I'm saying. I'm suggesting we're stretching the cash reserves, and you specifically said to keep a tight rein on spending."

"You're right, as usual. Do you think you can get them down another twenty percent?"

"One way to find out. Want me to go back to the table?"

"Are you willing to do that?"

"When am I not willing to try and get you what you want?"

Clayton smiled. "Let me think tonight, and we'll talk again tomorrow."

"You're the boss. Have a good night, Clayton."

"And you."

Clayton ended the call and dropped the phone into his left front shirt pocket. He had faith that if he instructed Sam to return to the table with a lower offer, she'd do it. And chances are, she'd walk away from the table with the deed to the land in her hand.

Sam rarely failed. She was intelligent and savvy, one heck of a tough negotiator, but never broke the law or took advantage of folks. That's why he kept her around. Clayton snorted at the thought. It wasn't entirely true. At least the part about why he kept her around. She was all the things he wanted in a manager and attorney, but she also kept him on his toes. Not to mention that she was a woman with a kind heart. He'd developed a fondness for her that went beyond work and counted Sam among his friends.

She was not, however, future wife material, despite what some thought. He'd said it a hundred times if he'd said it once. He would never marry again. Marriage had granted him five fine sons and one daughter, who died young and tore the heart from his chest with her passing.

No, he'd not marry again, but he'd allow himself the pleasure of Sam's company on a professional level and on the rare occasion where he needed a date for a social function. Clayton wondered when the day would come that she'd tell him she was hitching her horse to another wagon, moving away, or getting married. Neither option would make him happy, but he would wish her well if that's what she chose. Clayton would never stand in her way or use their friendship or business relationship to influence her decision.

He knew she had more than a passing interest in him. But she respected his decision not to get involved, so they kept their roles more business than personal.

Clayton was eager to buy the land they'd discussed. White Mountain National Forest covered nearly 800,000 acres across New Hampshire and western Maine. The Speckled and Caribou Mountains represented about 12,000 acres of Maine's portion of the White Mountains.

In the last few years, Clayton had purchased over 5,000 acres of land in Maine and New Hampshire, bordering White Mountain National Forest. His goal was simple. Create a moat that would cut off development around the forest.

Some called him crazy, not that he cared. Most people only paid lip service to the climate crisis. He paid attention and acted in what he considered a responsible manner. He bought as much land as possible, putting an end to deforestation, mining, diverting, or polluting the rivers and lakes on the land he owned and developed. Humans wouldn't survive if they kept stripping and poisoning the land.

How fortunate for him that his great-great-grandfather had come to this country on a whim, an adventure for a prince. What he found was the daughter of a Native American woman and a white landowner in the northwest who wasn't impressed with his wealth but fell in love with him because of the passion he learned for the land.

He promised his new wife that they'd raise their children in her country, according to her ways. Once the children were grown, he'd leave them a kingdom if she'd accompany him home to take the throne once his father died.

She agreed, and he was true to his word. The fortune he left his family was vast. Sadly, he and his beloved perished in a terrible storm at sea, leaving behind two sons and a daughter. The oldest son died of cholera, and the daughter died in childbirth, leaving the youngest son, Job, to inherit the family fortune.

It was Job who amended the family name from Khan, his father's name, to Blackstone, the clan name of his mother. He kept Khan as his middle name, and that tradition still lived today. During Job's adult years, Native Americans were not given due respect by most people in America. During that time, foreigners named Khan were given less.

Clayton walked down the front porch steps, looking out over the land. Of all the family-owned property, this was the place they had called home since the 1800s. He'd done his best to be a good steward of the land and had found another calling. Blackstone Holdings was the parent company for all the family's property and business interests. One of those interests was a little-known and never publicized operation his father started when Clayton was a boy.

James Blackstone, Clayton's father, believed in protecting the land and helping people, particularly women and children. If he heard of a woman or child being mistreated, he made sure whoever was hurting them didn't get another chance. The guilty party ended up in jail or a cemetery, while the victims were rescued and provided with the means to start over. They could get new identities or simply funding. Whatever it took.

Clayton had not only kept that operation alive, but he'd also expanded it. The people who worked for him were hand-picked for their skills and humanity. Now they had a dozen branches across the country.

It was a worthy cause, but had cost him a son. He still had a hard time coming to terms with that. But no matter who'd been assigned that task, someone would probably have lost a son. Clayton had no clue how things went sideways but wouldn't give up until he had answers.

Not only had he lost a son, but someone lost a daughter and a grandchild. The people responsible had to pay, and he'd not rest until that happened. His phone rang, and he pulled it out to look at the caller ID. Now here was a surprise.

"I hope you're calling to say you're headed north to do some fishing."

"I wish," the male voice on the other end replied. "Just thought I'd say hello and see how you're doing."

"Hanging in there. How about you?"

"Okay. Ready to retire."

"Bull."

"No, this time, I mean it. Things are changing since that damn pandemic. People are meaner, kindness and common sense seems to have skipped town, and I'm sick of it. Maybe I'll do like you, retire, pack up the missus, and head for the middle of nowhere."

Clayton chuckled. "I'll believe that when I see it."

"Well, don't be shocked to find me on your doorstep a year from now. But enough about me. How are you? And don't give me that line of BS. I know losing Jack hit you hard. Hell, if I lost one of my kids, I don't know what I'd do. So, talk to me, old friend."

Clayton collected his thoughts. "Some days are better than others. I remember when we lost Rebecca. I thought that would end me, knowing I'd never see her sweet face again—that she'd never grow up and have a family of her own. But in time, the pain dulled enough to be bearable. This time..."

He took a beat. "This time, it feels like I'm responsible. I sent him out there."

"To do a job he has done many other times."

"This time was different."

"Yes, and I still believe this was a setup."

"Maybe," Clayton admitted, since he'd come to the same conclusion a week after Jack's death.

"And?"

"And we're trying to figure it out."

"My offer still stands. If there's anything I can do..."

"You can retire and go to work with me like we discussed."

"Okay."

The agreement took Clayton by surprise. "Are you serious?"

"I am. Eleven months and two weeks from now, I'm turning in my badge. Lena said she's ready for a change, so where do you need me?"

"Take your pick. Run any of the satellite locations. I'll make it worth your while, as promised."

"I never doubted that."

"Then it's a deal."

"Yes, it is."

"This is the best news I've had in a while."

"I hope you feel like that a year from now."

"I'm sure I will. Thanks for calling."

"I'll be talking to you soon, and if you need me..."

"I have your number. Be safe, buddy. Talk soon."

When Clayton ended the call, his spirits were lifted a bit. The man on the phone had been a trusted friend for most of Clayton's adult life. Clayton had been trying to talk him into retiring and going to work for Blackstone for years. It was good to know that his offer had finally been accepted.

Just as he pocketed his phone, it rang again. "Well, dang, I'm popular today," he murmured as he answered. "Hey, son."

"Hey dad," his oldest son, Judson, replied. "Got a minute?"

"Always."

"Good. I want to talk to you about this horse, Whiskey."

"You still want to buy that stallion?"

"I do. He's in the money, and his stud fee has climbed three hundred percent. I believe it will go higher. I'd like to bring him up to the mountains for spring and then to the ranch in Montana in the summer."

"You don't want to keep him in Florida and let Ellis work with him?"

"Ellis said he has his eye on two others and wouldn't have time. I'll take him on."

"If that's what you want, do it."

"The owner wants one-point-two for him."

Clayton whistled. "That must be some horse."

"He is."

"Then make the deal and bring him home."

"Thanks, Dad."

"You know you don't need my permission, Jud."

"And you know I enjoy talking things out with you."

"I appreciate that, son. When are you looking to seal the deal?"

"Next week."

"I'll tell Sam to expect to hear from you, and she can handle the finances."

"Thanks. And tell her I said hey."

"Will do."

"Okay, I need to get on and help Jim finish repairing a section of fence near the lake. Talk to you tomorrow?"

"Sure thing."

When Clayton ended the call, he turned off his phone. What he wanted right now was to take a walk in the fading light of day, watch the stars appear, and remember all the things he had to be grateful for, rather than stewing on all he'd lost.

Chapter Two

Ivy made the turn and then slowed to check her directions. With only a week under her belt on this job, she was mindful of being an exemplary employee. Showing up at the wrong house wouldn't add to that status. She pulled over to the edge of the road and looked behind her. The road sign was just within range. Sure enough, this was the right road, but her new boss at the pool cleaning business had said nothing about the house being in a gated community.

She pulled out her phone and called the office. After two rings, a voice came on the line. "Dan's Pool and Spa."

"Mr. Peters? It's Ivy McCoy. I'm on Westmore Road, but there's a gate, and it looks like guards. I don't have a passcode or resident's name. What should I do?"

"Hold on, Ivy." She heard the phone clank. A couple of minutes passed before he came back on the line. "Tell the Guard who you are and that you're there to take care of the pool at the address I gave you. If they need verification, they can call me or the owner, but the passcode they gave me is 32714."

"Okay, thank you." Ivy proceeded to where a young man in a security guard uniform stood at the curb, outside of what she assumed was a guard hut or whatever such a structure was called.

She rolled down her window and smiled at him. "Hello, I'm with Dan's Pool and Spa service, here to clean the pool at 307 Oak Lane. The passcode they gave me is 32714."

"One moment, please."

The man went into the building. Ivy watched him pick up an iPad. After a few moments, he returned to where she waited. "You're clear, ma'am. Wait for the gate to fully open, please."

"Yes, sir. Thank you." She pulled up to the massive iron gate and waited. It opened smoothly, albeit a bit slowly.

Ma'am. She grimaced as she pulled through. Did she look that old, or was he just being polite? Maybe she was too sensitive about the age issue these days. Let it go. Of all the things in life to get upset about, someone calling her ma'am, ought to be at the bottom of her list.

Ivy turned her attention to the directions and drove slowly. enjoying the ride through the community. All the houses sat on big lots, with lavish landscaping, and most had pavers on their driveways, some in quite intricate patterns.

The houses were enormous, making her wonder what people did for a living to afford these homes. She was barely scraping by, and that was with three jobs. Yes, they were all part-time, but she still worked at least fifty hours a week, and if she worked two hundred hours a week, she couldn't afford to live here.

Ivy almost passed the house, braked, and backed up. What a place. From the tiled roof to the lavish entrance of marble and glass, it was like something out of a magazine. She pulled up to the garage, parked, and got out to walk to the front door.

No one answered the door, even though she rang the bell three times. She peered in through the sidelight and glimpsed someone who quickly skirted out of view. Once more, she rang the bell and waited. When no one came to the door, she headed around to the rear of the house.

Her instructions were to go in through the back entrance if the residents weren't home. There was a keyed lock, but she'd been provided with the code. The lanai and patio surrounding the pool sat on a sloped lawn that was as big as four yards in her neighborhood. The infinity pool was listed as forty by sixty. She was sure she'd never seen a private pool this large.

Also, as indicated on her worksheet, there was a pool house on the far side. Ivy let herself into the screened enclosure, made her way to the pool house, and looked through the French doors on the side facing the pool. She saw what looked like guest quarters, so went around the side of the building and found a side entrance with a metal plate on the door that read "Pool equipment".

She keyed in the passcode she'd been provided and entered the storage area to find all the chemicals and cleaning equipment she'd need. Ivy gathered up the hose, vacuum head, and pole, along with a test kit, and headed back to the pool.

It came as a surprise to discover the depth of the pool. Most residential pools were eight feet deep. This one had to be ten feet in the deep end. She hummed as she worked but didn't dawdle. She still had two other pools to clean after this one.

She gave it a thorough cleaning, double checked the water and made sure the saltwater system was operating with no problems. Just as she finished, her phone chimed, alerting her to a new text. She stepped under the cover of the lanai to make it easier to read the screen. They had given her another pool to take care of today.

Her first reaction was annoyance, which immediately made her ashamed. Ivy knew she should be grateful for the work, but wished it wasn't necessary to do it today. That would put her getting home at dusk, which meant she and her dog, Face, wouldn't be able to go for an evening run. A guy who lived down the street from her had a German shepherd who must have been trained by Nazis. He always came out after dusk and if another dog was around, he'd let the lead out on his dog to provoke or intimidate the other animal.

The thought of Face getting into a fight with that dog terrified her, so she went out before the man walked his beast. Not that she feared it would kill Face. Ivy had no doubt that Face would annihilate the shepherd.

An amiable Irish Wolfhound, Face lived up to his ancestry. He stood three feet tall at the shoulder and weighed one hundred and seventy-five pounds. Falling into the Sighthound category, Wolfhounds were originally used to pursue game, as they're capable of great speed at a gallop. They were also famed as guardian dogs, specializing in protecting against and for the hunting of wolves, thus their names.

She'd fallen in love with Face the first day she saw him and if there was any living creature she'd trust with her life, it was him. He deserved a better life than what she could provide, but she did the best she could for him.

Ivy was tempted to text and ask if someone else could do the job but didn't. She was trying to save enough to take a trip home to the mountains of Georgia, and every extra job she could pick up helped her get a step closer to making that happen.

It took just a couple of seconds to respond. She'd be happy to do the job. After sliding the phone into the holster clipped to her shorts, her eyes moved to the gigantic sliding glass doors that led into the house.

There are things in life that stop you in your tracks, confuse or frighten or make you feel sick to your stomach. What Ivy saw literally made her entire body twitch sharply, then a hot flush of terror engulf her, freezing her in place for the space of a heartbeat.

Her eyes blinked, and she stumbled back, whimpered in terror, and looked again. Had she not been completely terrified, she might have screamed, but her legs went into motion as if they had a mind all their own.

By the time she reached her car, she was panting and close to vomiting. "Oh God, oh God, oh God." She was trembling so badly, she nearly dropped her phone when she tried to remove it from its holster. With shaking hands, she dialed 911.

"911, what's your emergency?" A female voice answered.

"I work with a pool service and when I finished cleaning the pool at 307 Oak Lane, I looked in through the sliding glass door and there's… there's a giant snake in the house and it's eating a man."

"Pardon? Did you say a giant snake is eating a man? Is the man alive?"

"No, I don't think so."

"Are you at the residence now?"

"Yes, ma'am."

"And is there anyone else there?"

"Yes. No. I don't know. When I got here and rang the doorbell, I thought I saw someone inside, but no one ever answered the door, so I used the code they gave me to get into the pool area and did the pool cleaning."

"I'm dispatching to your location now, Miss. Do you think you're in danger where you are now?"

"Uh," Ivy looked around. "No. No, I don't think so."

"Do you want me to stay on the line until responders reach your location?"

"No. Can I wait in my car?"

"Yes, of course, but please don't leave."

"I won't. Thank you."

Ivy ended the call and got into her car. An image of the man on the floor filled her mind. His eyes and mouth were open and there was a look of terror frozen on his face. Only his chest, neck, one arm and head were visible, the rest was inside the snake.

Bile rose in her throat again and she started the car and turned on the AC, trying to push the image from her mind. And not throw up.

She failed at both and barely made it out of the car and to the grass before she spewed. Oh great, now there was puke on the lawn. Ivy returned to her car, fished a cold bottle of water from the cooler she kept behind her seat, and washed out her mouth.

Less than five minutes later, she heard sirens. Their volume increased and within a minute, an EMT truck, two firetrucks and three police cars appeared. The EMT truck and police vehicles pulled into the driveway, while the firetruck parked along the curb in front of the house.

Ivy got out of her car again as police officers emerged from their cars. When one of them drew his weapon and yelled for her to turn around and put her hands on the car, she nearly fainted.

This day was getting worse by the moment.

Chapter Three

The moment she walked into the house, Face was there with his tail wagging and his face turned up to greet her with his customary soft "woof". Had it been a normal day, Ivy would have given him a rub and a hello, then headed to the kitchen to put her bag and phone on the counter.

But today wasn't a normal day. Today, she'd witnessed something she wished she could forget. She sank down and gathered Face to her in a hug. His soft whimper reminded her how empathic dogs were and she pulled back to rub and pet him, seeking to ease his discomfort.

"Hey, buddy," she crooned. "Wanna go for a walk?"

He just turned and raced for the kitchen. Ivy followed, put her things on the countertop and waited until Face emerged from the laundry room that was right off the kitchen, with a harness in his mouth.

Ivy held out her hand, and he dropped the harness into it. She gave him another rub and then fastened his harness on him, made sure the leash was clasped and stood. "Ready?"

As soon as the word left her lips, he was in motion, heading for the door. Rather than getting jerked off her feet by a nearly two-hundred-pound dog, she hurried to keep up. Thanks to her getting home later than normal, rush hour traffic had died down. Most everyone in her community who worked a day shift was already home. As she walked, she could see lights on in the houses she passed, some with blinds or windows open, giving a glimpse of the people inside.

Thankfully, the Nazi with the shepherd was not to be seen, something that filled her with gratitude. She was tired of him taunting her and Face and encouraging his dog to attack.

It made her smile when she heard laughter or the sounds of children playing. This might not be the most affluent community, but it was filled with good, hard-working people and families who loved one another.

Ivy hadn't made a lot of close friends, but she knew most of the people on her block by name. Sometimes she wished she had more friends, but between her job cleaning pools, working three half-days a week at a veterinarian's, bartending on the weekends and trying to finish the last of her classes to get her degree, she had little time to socialize and what free time she had; she spent studying or taking Face out to parks and on nature hikes. He was cooped up all day, and she felt guilty about that. With luck, one day she'd have a fenced yard for him, although she couldn't imagine how tall a fence would be required.

That thought turned her mind to daydreams of having that fenced yard, maybe a little pool, a new or at least newer car and some money in the bank. Thoughts of money stole some of her good mood. When she booted her cheating husband out, he beat her to the punch, cleaned out their checking and savings accounts, leaving her pretty much penniless. To top it off, a realtor showed up a week later with a for sale sign to put in their front yard. When she argued she wasn't selling, the man told her he got his orders from the owner.

Fool that she was, she never bothered to check the deed, but as it turned out, her name wasn't on it. So, along with being broke, she was also homeless.

Didn't that figure? She'd worked as a bartender to put him through undergraduate and then law school, spent her entire college fund on his education and three years after he made partner, he took up with a fellow associate at the law firm. Ivy couldn't forgive him, as much as she wanted to, she just couldn't. So, here she was seven years later, still trying to get her degree and support herself.

That old saying about life never being what you imagine was certainly true. She never imagined herself living this life. Not that it was all bad, she reminded herself. There were people with far bigger problems, so she should count her blessings.

Mostly, she did. As a rule, she was grateful for every day. Today was an exception. What a nightmare. She hated being interviewed by the police, but one of them, an older officer, a detective, Bill Gordon, was very kind and made her feel less ill at ease. He assured her she wasn't being viewed as a suspect, which was a relief.

Her stomach growled, reminding her she missed lunch. "Come on, Face, let's go home and eat."

Anyone who said dogs don't know what you say to them was an idiot in her book. Face yipped and made the turn to head home, practically dragging her behind him. Ivy laughed and broke into a jog.

By the time they got home, she was sweaty and winded. Face dashed to the kitchen as soon as she unlocked the door and practically dove into his water bowl. Ivy did the same, but with a bottle of water, she took from the refrigerator.

After downing half the bottle, she toed off her shoes, turned on her iPad that rested in its stand on the kitchen countertop and turned on her local news feed. She then opened the refrigerator door again, this time to see what kind of leftovers she had to choose from.

Just as she reached for a bowl of leftover lo mein, she heard the word "shootout" and turned to look at the iPad. "Yes, Andrea," the anchorman gave a nod to his co-anchor, then looked into the camera. "Police were called to the scene of what is being called a bizarre murder this afternoon in the..."

Ivy didn't hear the next few words the man said. The plastic storage bowl slipped out of her hands, hit the floor, and exploded lo mein over half the kitchen. Face beat her to the clean-up, gobbling as fast as he could.

That was fine with her. It meant less to clean up. She turned her attention back to the newscast. Her unease grew the more she heard. After being called to the scene of a murder, when police tried to enter the residence, there was a shootout. They found a body inside, half swallowed by a giant anaconda and was later identified as the owner. A suspect who was apparently in the house all along killed two police officers, along with a first responder EMT. Three firefighters sustained gunshot wounds, one of whom was in critical condition, and the shooter escaped. The anchorman gave a description of the man and read a message issued by the police department of their intention to see the man caught and jailed.

Ivy felt like she was either going to faint or heave her guts out. She didn't understand why, but she felt threatened. *That's silly*, she told herself. *It's not like whoever shot those officers knows who you are. No one mentioned your name.*

Repeating those two sentences like a mantra, she set about cleaning up the floor. Face continued to help and by the time she went to the laundry room for a mop, there was nothing left except the vegetables he wouldn't eat.

Within minutes, the floor had a clean shine, and Face's food and water bowls were filled. Ivy's appetite vanished with the newscast, and she didn't expect it would return. She picked up her iPad and went into the family room.

Just as she sat on the couch, her doorbell rang. She checked the time and felt a bit uneasy. It was past eight, and she didn't know anyone who would come to her house without calling first. Had it not been for the fact that Face was merely sitting at her feet, calmly looking from her to the door, she would have traveled from unease to scared at warp speed.

Ivy rose and went to the door. "Yes?"

"Ms. McCoy? It's Detective Bill Gordon."

Ivy cracked open the door and as soon as she got a look, opened it fully. Sure enough, there stood Detective Gordon and another man, one a good bit younger, both dressed in business suits. "Detective Gordon, is everything okay?"

"This is Detective Mitch Burman, Ms. McCoy. Would you mind if we come in?"

"Oh, of course, I'm sorry. Please." She pushed the door open more, moving with it to allow them entry.

He stopped stone cold still, and she looked in the direction of his gaze. There sat Face, looking at the men. "Oh, I apologize." She hurried to close the door and then skirted around them to Face. "Detectives, this is Face."

Ivy then placed her hand on Face's head. "Face, these men are our friends. Say hello."

Face stood and approached Detective Gordon, who held out one hand. "That's one big dog. What breed is he?"

"Irish Wolfhound," Ivy answered and rubbed Face's back. "Someone abandoned him when he was not even a year old. Just dropped him at the pound and walked away. Poor guy, he nearly grieved himself to death. I started working at the shelter the week after he was abandoned, and he was scheduled to be put down. I couldn't stand the thought of that, so I adopted him. I read about the breed, but never imagined he'd get this big."

"Big?" Detective Burman asked. "That guy's gigantic."

"And sweet," she assured him.

Detective Gordon reached out his hand to Face. "Hey there, big fella. I'm Bill."

Face sniffed the hand, then wagged his tail and looked up at Ivy.

"Does that mean I passed the test?" Detective Gordon asked.

"Indeed. Please, have a seat. Can I offer you something to drink? I have bottled water and–and bottled water."

"No, I'm fine, thank you," he replied as he took a seat on the worn recliner.

"How about you, Detective Burman?"

"No, thank you." He chose the rocking chair on the other side of the sofa. "We're here to check on you. What you witnessed today must have been very frightening, and by now I'm sure you've heard what happened after you left."

"I did," she reclaimed her place on the couch and made room for Face, who jumped up beside her. She had to scoot all the way to the end, he took up so much room. Not that she cared. Face lay his head in her lap, and she rubbed him as she talked. "It's horrible. I hope they catch whoever did it."

"So do I. But," he paused a beat. "Look, we think it's possible the suspect saw you. You were there for a good while and he could have been watching. He might even have made note of your car and tag number."

Ivy considered his remark, then asked. "You honestly think someone was inside with that—that giant snake? Doing what? Feeding that man to it? How is that even possible? I mean, how do you feed a man to a… God, I can't even say it."

“I don’t know how it happened, and have trouble even thinking about it,” Detective Gordon said. “What concerns me is the man who shot our officers might have seen you.”

"And what if he did?” she asked. “He couldn't find out who I am, could he?" Fear made her words rushed and loud, which caused Face to whine.

"It's okay, buddy," she ran her hand down his neck and back as she glanced at Detective Gordon. "Right?"

"In a perfect world, yes. But it's not perfect and criminals have ways of gaining information."

"Well, would it matter if he knew who I am? I didn't see him, so I'm no threat to him."

"If he knows that." Detective Burman argued. "There's always the possibility that he isn't aware you didn't see him and can't identify him."

"What are you saying?" Ivy suddenly felt as if she should be concerned. "Exactly."

"I'm saying that for your own well-being and safety, it might be smart if you stayed with a relative or friend until we find the suspect."

"Because you think he might want to what? Kill me?"

"Yes, Ms. McCoy, that's what I think. If he believes you can identify him, he may try to kill you. And he's obviously not hesitant to shoot."

"Oh, God," Ivy's mind was in a whirl. "I–I don't know anyone. My family is in Georgia and none of my friends will let me stay with them because of Face and–and I can't leave him."

"Surely there has to be someone."

"No, sir. There isn't. It's just me and Face. My grandmother used to live here. Right here. This was her house. But she died three years ago and left this house to my mom, who rents it to me to cover the mortgage that's still on it. I–I..." she blew out a breath. "I can't leave."

"I understand and am sorry. At the least, perhaps you could take Face with you when you leave for the day?"

She looked at Face and then at the officer. "I can't take him with me to work. Look at him. You know how people are about dogs this big, no matter how friendly they are. No, I can't leave and won't leave him."

Detective Burman glanced at Detective Gordon, then turned his attention back to Ivy. "I understand. How about this? I'll have a patrol car pass by every hour at night and during the day. You promise to be mindful of the people around you."

"I can do that."

"And I'll check in on you every evening," Detective Gordon offered.

"You don't have to do that," she protested. "I mean, it's very kind and would certainly make me feel better, but you have your own life and—"

"And I'd hope someone would do this for my daughter if she were in a similar circumstance."

"Thank you, sir," she gave him a smile. "You're very kind."

"Then we have an arrangement?" Detective Burman asked.

"Yes, sir."

"Good. Then we'll leave you to enjoy the rest of your evening." He stood and Face sat up, which apparently unnerved the Detective.

"He's not going to attack me, is he?"

"Of course not," she chuckled and patted Face. "Be a friend, Face."

She could tell the Detective wanted to step back by the way his body twitched, but to his credit, he stood his ground as Face got off the couch and approached him. It surprised Ivy that Face merely stared at the man, which apparently unnerved Detective Burman even more because this time, he stepped back. "You're one big fella, Face. Take good care of Ms. Ivy, you hear?"

When Face 'woofed' Burman looked at Ivy in surprise. "It's almost like he understands."

"Because he does," Ivy said and stood to offer her hand. "Thank you, Detective."

"Just doing my job, Miss McCoy."

"Nonetheless, I appreciate it." She then looked at Detective Gordon. "And thank you, sir. You restore my faith in the kindness of people."

"I think that's the nicest compliment I've ever received. Have a good evening, Miss McCoy."

"Ivy, please."

He nodded and smiled. "Thank you, Ivy, and you can call me Bill." He then walked over to give Face some rubs. "You take care of Ivy, big guy. I'll see you both tomorrow."

"Thank you again," she said as she headed for the door.

Once they left, she locked the door and turned to Face. "Well, I think we made a new friend today, buddy. Let's just hope we don't need his services."

As Face wagged his tail and yipped in agreement, she wondered if maybe she should speak with her parents about coming to Georgia for a visit. No sooner had the thought surfaced, she dismissed it. Her mother didn't like Face because he was so big and would never allow him into the house. And her father wouldn't dare go against her. That's just how it was in her family.

Which meant she'd just have to stick it out and hope the police were wrong and the murderer wasn't interested in the woman who cleaned the pool.

Chapter Four

Ivy finished sweeping the kitchen floor and walked out front to sweep the front entrance and short sidewalk. She anticipated Detective Gordon showing up anytime now. The last three days, he'd checked in with her every evening at half-past eight. It was almost that time now.

Had it not been for Detective Gordon, she would have turned in early. Since the day she saw that man being eaten by a snake, she'd had trouble sleeping. She couldn't stop imagining how horrified the man was and what pain he'd suffered, being crushed by that beast.

She'd taken time to research. Based on what she remembered, and what Bill Gordon told her, the snake was a

Burmese python. Typically, they live in marshes of southeast Asia, but during the last twenty years, their numbers had been increasing in Florida. The one they killed at the house she went to weighed in at one hundred and eighty pounds and was twenty-one feet long. Bill said the snake's girth was almost equal to a telephone pole.

Like others of its kind, a Burmese python bites to capture its prey, then wraps its body around it to suffocate the animal, or in this instance, the man. She couldn't imagine a more terrifying way to die and wished she'd never seen it.

Face came out and entertained himself, sniffing around the yard. Two of the neighborhood boys, Juan and Tony, both ten years old, rode up on their bikes. "Can we play with Face, Miss Ivy?"

"Of course," she replied with a smile. Despite his size, Face was a gentle creature and loved playing. Juan and Tony had become his friends and now he was hurrying to greet them.

"I brought a new tennis ball, Face," Tony announced, and pulled the bright yellow ball from the pocket of his shorts.

Ivy sat on the small bench beside the front door and watched the boys and Face play. She got a kick out of watching them throw the ball and then try to race Face to fetch it. They never won, but it didn't seem to dampen their enthusiasm.

As she watched, a car pulled into the driveway. Both boys stopped, watching the unfamiliar car with expressions that belied their unease. "It's okay, guys," Ivy said as she rose and headed down the sidewalk. "This is my friend, Detective Gordon."

"Hello there," Bill greeted them and then called to Face. "Hey bud, you going to say hello?"

Face raced over, reared up on his hind legs, put his feet on Bill's shoulders and licked Bill's face. Bill laughed and gave Face a good rub, then stepped back. "Okay, go play while I talk with Ivy."

Face and the boys resumed their play, and Bill followed Ivy to the front stoop. “You don't have to keep doing this, Mr. Bill," she said and gestured for him to have a seat on the bench.

"Oh, I think I do." he patted the bench beside him and waited for her to sit before continuing. "I have some bad news, Ivy."

"How bad?"

"It doesn't get much worse, I'm afraid."

"I don't want to hear this, do I?"

"Probably not, but you have to. Your boss at the pool place, Dan Peters, was found half an hour ago. Someone ransacked his office, took his phone and shot him."

"Shot–shot him? Is he okay?"

"No, honey, he's dead."

"Oh, god." She stood and called out to the boys. "Juan? Tony? Face needs to come in now."

"Okay, Miss Ivy,” Juan yelled, then hugged Face. "See you tomorrow, Face."

After Tony gave Face a hug, he and Juan waved to Ivy and headed home. Face ran over to Ivy and Bill. "Let's go inside," Ivy suggested.

Once inside, she made sure Face's water bowl was full, then went into the family room where Bill stood at the window with his hands in his pockets. "Are you okay, Mr. Bill?"

"I'm worried, Ivy. If the same man who killed that fellow in his home and shot the others killed your boss, then he might be looking for you. I know you don't want to leave, but this time I don't think you have a choice."

"There's always a choice."

"Perhaps. Can I borrow your phone?"

"Sure," she hurried to fetch it from the kitchen, unlocked it and then gave it to him. "I'm entering a contact into your phone—it's under In Case of Emergency. If anything happens, if you feel you're in danger, I want you to call this number and tell whoever answers that Bill told you to call and that he's calling in that favor."

"What does that mean?"

"It means someone I trust owes me, and if you find yourself in danger, you should call this number and say what I told you."

She didn't intend to call the number but appreciated his concern. "Thank you, Mr. Bill. You're a good person and I appreciate you looking out for me."

"Ivy, I really think you need to get out of here. Tonight."

"I told you I–"

"I know. Just think about it."

"I will." She walked him to the door and watched him walk toward his car. Just as he opened his car door, gunfire sounded. Bill jerked twice, and then again before he fell.

Ivy screamed and ran to him, kneeling beside him. He lay on his back, eyes closed and blood running from his nose and mouth. "Bill? Oh God, Bill?" She put her hand on his chest. "Please wake up. I have to get you inside and—"

"I–vy," his voice was barely a whisper, and a bubbling sound accompanied his syllables. "Go. Ca–call the–"

"Bill, no!" she screamed when he groaned, and his body arched. He coughed and blood spewed her clothing. Ivy didn't know what to do. He was too big for her to move. "I'll call for help. Just hold on, Bill. Please–"

It was then she realized his eyes were closed. A sob escaped her lips. "Bill," she whispered and then jolted as gunfire sounded again and a bullet slammed into the side of the car.

Ivy clamped her hand over her mouth, ran into the house, slammed the door and locked it. She raised her phone, called 911, reported a shooting at her location, then hung up before questions could be asked. After that, she located the new contact and placed a call.

"Yeah?" A man's voice answered.

"Hello. Bill Gordon gave me your number and said if I was in trouble to call you and say that Bill told me to call and that he's calling in that favor."

There was a brief pause before the man responded. "What's your name?"

"Ivy McCoy."

"Where are you, Miss McCoy?"

Ivy gave him her address and waited for what seemed an eternity but was only a minute. "Listen carefully. Here's what I want you to do. Pack a week's worth of clothing and whatever personal items you need into one bag, something you can carry or pull. Once you're packed, leave via your back door. Don't drive. And turn your phone off. Hold on for a sec…"

It felt like an eternity before he spoke again. "Go to this address and wait."

He gave her the address. "Repeat that back to me."

She did, and then he asked. "Do you know where that is?"

"No."

“Do you have a current cell phone?”

“Yes, an iPhone.”

"Good. Put the address into your map app and get directions. If you have a way to print out the directions, do so, or jot them down. Then turn off your phone. Can you do that?"

"Yes, but…"

“But what?”

“Bill is lying shot and bleeding in my driveway.”

“Did you call 911?”

“Yes.”

“Then help is on the way. Do as I told you.”

“He needs help now.”

“Ivy, get off the phone and get moving."

The line went dead. She hurried to the extra bedroom she'd converted into a small office, opened her laptop and keyed in the address she was given. Then she printed the directions and turned off the laptop.

Ivy folded the printout and crammed it into the pocket of her shorts. She'd reached the door when she realized her laptop and iPad might provide clues to her destination if anyone was tech-savvy enough to break into them. So, she retreated, grabbed the laptop and its power cord, then headed back to the family room for the iPad.

After putting the electronics on the kitchen counter, Ivy ran to the bedroom and pulled out her one piece of luggage. She tossed underwear, socks, shorts, jeans and tops into it, along with a zip up hoodie and an extra pair of sneakers. The last thing she did was grab clean jeans and a t-shirt and head for the bathroom.

Scared to delay too long, she refrained from showering but washed the blood from her face and arms. Then she grabbed toiletries, a small cosmetics bag and a towel. Once she had the items in her bag, she backtracked to the kitchen, put in an unopened six pack of water, what was left of a bag of dog food, one of Face's small bowls and his favorite blanket.

The water and dog food made the bag heavy, but not so much she couldn't manage. Ivy put the harness on Face, shoved her phone and laptop, along with her iPad into a big shoulder bag she rarely used, dumped her purse into it and looped the strap over her body.

She reached for the back door-knob and froze. What if the shooter was out there? She almost chickened out. Then the thought of someone breaking in and shooting her or Face, spurred her into action.

The sound of sirens in the distance sent her heart racing. Ivy nearly broke into tears as she opened the back door and followed Face outside. What if this was the last time she saw this place? This was where she brought Face when she adopted him, and she'd watched him grow from a big puppy to a grown dog.

Here was where she'd finally started making real progress toward finishing her degree and learning to let go of the past. Was she really going to lose it because she saw a dead man she didn't know through the pane of a sliding glass door?

Talk about the world's worst luck. Surely this had to rank high on the list. It almost overwhelmed her and had Face not looked back and whined, she might have allowed herself to sink into that pit of despair. But if nothing else, she'd protect Face. That's what she agreed to when she adopted him, to protect, love, and care for him.

"Come on, Face, let's go have an adventure."

She hoped her false positivity fooled him, because right now she wasn't positive about anything except that she wanted to rewind the last week and have a do-over, one where she quit her job or called in sick on the day she saw the dead body.

That wasn't in the cards, so she started walking. Two hours they walked and finally reached their destination, a crossroads with a bus stop bench in the grass beside the sidewalk. She sat and fished out a bottle of water from the suitcase, along with Face's bowl. Ivy poured half of the bottle into the bowl, placed it on the bench, and then tilted the bottle up to her lips and drank.

Face polished off his bowl, and she gave him half of what was left in her bottle. Once his bowl was empty again, she put it back into the bag, along with the empty bottle. Face jumped onto the bench and lay his head on her legs.

Ivy went over everything in her mind. Was she doing the right thing? Detective Gordon must have thought so, or why would he have told her what to do? A vision of his body jerking as he was shot, and the blood spray that hit her when he coughed and went still, had tears gathering.

Unable to hold back, she let the tears come. Face raised up and licked her face and she hugged him as she cried. Finally, she had no more tears. She dried her face with her shirt, gave Face some rubbing, trying to assure him she was fine, and looked up and down the road.

How long should she wait? That thought made her start. She'd forgotten to turn off her iWatch. Did she have the location service turned on? With trembling fingers, she checked the settings and blew out a breath. Thank God. One thing she'd become very careful of since her divorce was to keep her life private, including where she went and what she did.

Right now, she felt grateful she'd adopted those habits. Two and a half hours had passed. Should she turn on her phone and call the number again? Just as she reached for her shoulder bag, a black Mercedes stopped at the curb.

She stood as the back door opened. A handsome man with dark hair and eyes that appeared black in the dim light stepped out. In his hand was a handgun. "Get in the car, Ms. McCoy."

Ivy froze. A menacing growl came from Face, and the gun swung in his direction. "No!" Ivy screamed and stepped in front of Face. "No," she repeated. "I'm not going anywhere with you. I don't even know who you are."

"Unfortunately, you do now, and I can't have loose ends, so I suggest you get into the car. I promise you'll die quick."

"No," Ivy tried to sound defiant, even though what she wanted to do was beg for her life and hope he'd comply.

"Then we can do it here."

“Face, run!” Ivy shouted.

But instead of running, Face lowered his head and growled menacingly. The man with the gun took a step back, clearly scared of Face, and raised his weapon. “I’ll kill you both.”

Ivy saw no way to fight. He had a gun, and she had nothing. She knelt and put her arms around Face's neck. If they were about to die, at least she could hold him. "I'm so sorry," she whispered, then waited for the pain.

But instead of a gunshot, what she heard was the sudden roar of an engine. She looked up just as a big, black, double-cab Dodge truck rammed into the back of the Mercedes, making it lurch forward a good five feet. The man with the gun scrambled for the car, shouting at the driver to "Go!" as gunshots from the truck slammed into the car.

Ivy nearly burst into tears as the car raced off. Thanks to dark windows, she couldn't tell who was inside the truck. The passenger door opened. "Ivy?" A male voice asked.

"Who's asking?"

"The man repaying a favor to Bill. I'd suggest you hurry."

His answer satisfied her. She wiped her eyes, rose, looped the strap of her bag over her shoulder and lifted the suitcase. "Come on, Face," she took hold of his leash.

He didn't hesitate, and they walked to the truck. "Put your bag and dog in the back seat."

Ivy opened the rear door and set the bag on the floor. "Come on, Face. Hop in."

That's exactly what he did. With little effort. She closed the door and then climbed into the front passenger seat. Face already had his head over the back of the seat, getting some affectionate petting from the driver.

That sight made her weak with relief. People could fool or hurt her because she was mistaken about their characters, but Face wasn't. He was far more intuitive than any person she'd ever known, and she'd trust his judgement over a human any time.

"His name is Face?" the man asked.

"Yes."

"What kind of dog is he?"

"An Irish Wolfhound."

"He's something." The man stopped rubbing and spoke to Face. "You need to sit down now."

The man looked from Face to Ivy in surprise when Face complied. "You have him well trained. Who was that in the Mercedes?"

"I'm guessing the man who killed Detective Gordon." Ivy crossed her arms, rubbing her hands up and down them, not because she was cold but to try to stop her body from shaking like she was about to have a seizure.

She noticed the look the driver gave her and wondered what he was thinking. "You mean you don't know who's trying to kill you?"

That was a fair question, and she bet he was thinking she had to be a fool not to know who was trying to shoot her. "No. And until this moment, I guess I didn't want to believe that someone would actually try to kill me."

"Then it's a shame you saw his face."

Ivy ignored the comment. "Just who are you and where are we going?"

"I'm Judson Blackstone."

"Are you friends with Detective Gordon?"

"Not exactly."

"Then why are you here?"

"Because he saved my father, and we owe him."

"Oh. Well… well, where are we going?"

"To my father's ranch."

"And where is that?"

"Ever been to the Appalachians?"

"I grew up in the Blue Ridge Mountains."

"Where?"

"Blairsville."

"Any relatives or friends in the Clear Lake, North Carolina, area?"

"No, I don't think I've ever heard of it."

"You have now."

"And that's where we're going?"

"It is."

"How long will it take to get there?"

"Nine hours if we don't stop, more if we do."

She nodded and was silent for a few minutes, staring out of the window. Then she turned to look at him. "And what happens when we get there?"

"That's up to you. My job is just to see you get there safely."

And with that, he fell silent.

That's up to you. She heard that over and over in her mind and each time she asked herself what part of this was up to her? She made no decision to be part of any of this. For the next half hour, she stewed on it and her driver didn't say a word.

Finally, she couldn't stand the silence. "You're wrong. None of it's up to me."

"Sure, it is," he glanced at her. "You called the number Bill Gordon gave you. I'm assuming no one held a gun on you and made you do that. Am I right?"

"Yes but–"

"And you obviously packed some things to bring with you. So, you knew you'd be gone for a while, right?"

"Well, yes but–"

"But nothing. You chose to follow his advice, and here you are. With luck, whatever you're running from won't find you, and depending on what or who you're escaping, maybe one day you can go back. But that'll be up to you as well. So, yeah, it's always your choice, Ivy. Life is a series of them, and this is another one on your journey."

"Is that how you see it?"

"I reckon it's as good a way as any."

She nodded and looked away. As much as she hated to admit it, his words carried the ring of truth.

Funny thing, though, it didn't make her feel better.

Not one little bit.

Chapter Five

"Isn't this the long way?" Ivy asked.

"No," Judson answered.

"Yes, I'm pretty sure it is. This way goes out tohe coast around Melbourne. It would be quicker to take I-4, wouldn't it?"

"No."

"But I thought we were headed for North Carolina?"

"We are. I have to pick up a horse."

"A horse?"

He glanced at her. "Are you hearing impaired?"

"No. I just don't understand why we're picking up a horse?"

"Because I have to take him to North Carolina."

"Oh!" She felt a bit foolish, since he'd told her he lived in North Carolina. "Why are you getting a horse?"

"To make money."

"How?"

"Shows and stud fees."

"So, it's a performance horse?"

"You know what that is?"

“Yes. Do you work with the horses personally?”

“Yes.”

Ivy latched onto the curiosity that statement provided. Anything was preferable to fretting over why she was in this mess, on the run with a man she didn't know while a police officer lay dead in her driveway.

"That's interesting. How did you learn to do that?"

"From my father."

"And you do that professionally? Train performance horses?"

"Not exclusively."

"I'd love to learn about that—what's involved, I mean."

"Well, if you're gonna be at the ranch for any length of time, you can watch what goes on."

"You wouldn't mind?"

"Not as long as you don't interrupt," he cut a look at the back seat where Face was snoozing. "And as long as that big guy doesn't chase horses."

"I don't think he's ever seen a horse, so I don't know."

After that, there was a good half hour of silence. He pulled a cell phone from his shirt pocket and made a call. "Almost there and we're coming in hot." He looked in the rear-view mirror as he listened. "Good idea. Yep, will do."

Ivy wanted to ask who he was calling and what he meant, but the way his jaw was clenched changed her mind. When he made a turn onto a small asphalt road with no markings, she looked around. It seemed they were in the middle of nowhere. That made her nervous, but she told herself that right now everything made her nervous so not to read too much into it. Still, she felt a bit of relief when lights shown through the old oaks that lined the road.

Judson stopped at a closed gate, reached in his pocket and pulled out his phone. "I'm here," he said after he placed a call. "Will do."

He pocketed the phone and looked at her. "Can you drive the truck through the gate?"

"Sure, but why don't you do it?"

"Someone has to open the gate."

"I can do that."

"If you get out, your dog will want to follow."

"Good point."

He got out, and she slid over into the driver's seat. As soon as he had the gate open, she slowly pulled through, noticing the road changed from asphalt to gravel. After putting the truck into park, she climbed into the passenger's seat. Judson closed the gate and got back into the truck. In minutes, he stopped beside a paddock.

A man walked out of the barn carrying a rifle. Judson exited the truck and had a conversation with the man before returning. He opened the passenger side door, reached into the glove compartment and took out a handgun. Now Ivy was scared. "Why do you have a gun and why is that man carrying a rifle?"

"Because someone followed us, and I'm betting it wasn't to steal a horse."

"Then what–" it suddenly hit her. "You think that man who tried to kill me followed us?"

"It seems likely."

"Well, damn, this just gets worse by the minute. What do we do?" She looked into the side mirror but saw only darkness. "Do you think they'll come here?"

"I reckon we'll see. Right now, I want you to get Face and take him into the barn."

"But–"

"Ivy, do as I say. Now."

It both hurt her feelings and made her angry to be dismissed and bossed around, but at the moment, fear was stronger than hurt feelings, so she got out, grabbed Face's leash and harness, opened the back door, and put it on him.

Judson closed the door once Face hopped out of the truck, then took Ivy's arm. The man with the rifle walked ahead of them and opened a regular sized door on one side of the barn. "You'll be safe in here. The walls are block and the door is metal."

He turned and walked back to Judson's truck, staring into the darkness. Ivy looked at Judson. "What are you going to do?"

"That depends."

"On?"

"On what the person or people in the car following us do."

"I don't understand. How did anyone know where we were?"

"My guess is whoever followed us is a backup for the man in the car who stopped and wanted to shoot you."

"But he drove off when you ran into his car and shot at him."

"Yes, but that doesn't mean he didn't have someone tailing him for protection."

"This is insane. What are we going to do?"

"You're going to wait in the barn with Face and not come out until you hear me say I think Face needs a pit-stop."

Ivy thought that was a silly thing to say and opened her mouth to argue, but Judson stopped her with his next sentence. He pulled out his phone and handed it to her. "That way, no matter if it is me, if I don't say those exact words, you use this phone and call 911. Tell them where you are and that someone is trying to kill you. Then stay in the barn until they show up."

She took the phone, wishing tears were not suddenly flooding her eyes. "But I don't know where I am."

"The phone's GPS is on; they can figure it out."

"Well, can't we just call them now?"

"No, Ivy, we can't. If we don't stop them, we won't make it to North Carolina. It has to end here."

"Fine," she agreed and put her hand on Face's neck when he whined and looked up at her. "It's okay buddy, it's okay." Then she looked again at Judson. "It *will* be okay, won't it?"

"I hope so. Now, go in and lock the door."

She did as told. This was apparently some kind of office. There was a desk, one chair behind it and one facing it. Aside from that, there was a wall of shelves bearing labeled boxes. Ivy tried the chair in front of the desk, changed her mind, and sat down on the floor beside the door. Face lay on the floor beside her, with his head on her leg.

Ivy checked the time on Judson's phone and prayed that whatever was about to happen, he didn't get hurt and she would soon hear him say the sentence he'd given her as the code for all was well.

Because if he didn't, it would mean she'd cost another man his life for trying to protect her and she didn't think she could live with that.

*****

Judson walked back to his truck and spotted his friend and ranch foreman, Jim Eastwood, standing off to one side in a stand of trees with Judson's brother, Ellis. They were almost invisible in the darkness. Judson strode over to join them. "I didn't mean to bring trouble here, brother, and apologize if I have."

"I remember bringing trouble to you a time or two," Ellis responded.

"And I know I have," Jim added.

"Yeah, well, ex-wives and crazy girlfriends are a far cry from men with guns."

"You have a point," Ellis agreed. "What the hell did this gal do to have people trying to kill her?"

"Hell, if I know. When I found her, a Hispanic man had a gun on her, and she'd run away from her home with a police officer shot and bleeding in her driveway."

"Wonder why that guy had a gun on her?" Jim asked.

"Maybe whoever shot the officer thinks she saw him commit a crime and could identify him."

"What do you think?"

"Like I said, when I went to get her, someone in a Mercedes got there before me and tried to kill her."

"Did you kill anyone?" the question came from Ellis.

"No. Just rammed the car and added a little lead to it. I got the tag number."

"You want me to get my buddy the state trooper to run the plate?"

"Thanks, but no. We'll let the guys at Blackstone handle that. I'll text it to Pop."

“Sounds like a plan. So, what's your next move?"

"Depends on whether the car following us shows up."

A soft buzz had Jim pulling a phone from his pocket. "Perimeter alert," he said as he activated an app on the phone. We're about to have company. How do you want to play this?"

"Fast and final."

"Let me take the lead?"

Judson looked at Ellis, who shrugged. “Works for me.”

"Then have at it,” Judson agreed.

"Good, just make sure you follow once they're after me. I see lights."

"I'll take the other side."

“On your six,” Ellis said.

Judson and Ellis hurried to the other side of the drive, stepping into the deep shadows of the trees a few seconds before Judson heard tires crunching on gravel. Whoever was driving had already turned off the headlights, which told Judson this wasn’t their first rodeo.

A dark 1990s model car rolled up and stopped behind Judson's truck. The front doors opened, and two men got out, armed with automatic weapons. One of them yelled. "Send the woman out and no one has to die."

"Not gonna happen." Jim's voice rang out.

"Kill him," the speaker ordered.

Gunfire opened up and when it ended, Jim's voice came again. "You'll have to do better than that."

"You're a fucking dead man," one man yelled before he took off in the direction of Jim's voice, leaving the leader to follow. Jim made a hell of a lot of noise running through the brush and trees, obviously to make it easy for his pursuers to keep on his trail.

“And away we go,” Ellis said too low to be overheard.

They followed close enough to keep an eye on the men, cognizant of the sound of loud grunts ahead. Judson wasn’t a native Floridian, but he’d spent enough time at this ranch to recognize the sound. Alligators.

"Son of a bitch," Judson mumbled as he realized Jim's plan. “Is he doing what I think?”

“If I were a betting man, I’d put money on it,” Ellis answered.

Taking care to stay on the high ground where the alligators rarely nested, they made their way to the swamp. Spires from the roots of cypress trees crested the water, standing like sharp tipped fingers, reaching out of the dark water. Downed limbs from the trees created perches for the myriad breeds of birds and snakes who fished these waters.

Judson could hear the men ahead of him and see the crisscross of light beams from flashlights. There was also a lot of cursing as they splashed through the water. If he was right, Jim was leading the men right into the nesting area. There was a wide swatch of shallow water and marshland leading to a peninsula in the lake. The marsh was a place the alligators had claimed for their own.

Moving fast but cautiously, he and Ellis drew in closer to the men until he could see them in the dim light of the moon filtering in through the cypress. Their voices carried in the night, bringing a halt to the grunts of the alligators.

"What the fuck?" One man, the tallest of the two, blurted and jumped, pulling one foot free of the water.

"What?" the shorter man turned, shining his light around.

"Something touched my leg."

"It was probably just a vine or rotten piece of wood." The short man replied as he moved his light around in a circle. "Oh shit. Oh, shit!"

"What?" the tall man asked in a clearly scared tone.

"What the fuck is that?"

"What?"

"Look!"

He moved his arm, shining the beam of light around them. Judson would have smiled, but even he felt revulsion flavored with fear skitter down his spine as red eyes glowed in the light. Alligators. And more than a few.

“It’s about to get ugly,” Ellis whispered from behind him.

A split second later, it did. "Holy shit, man," the tall man turned one way and another. "Holy fucking shit, they're all around us."

"Look!" the short guy directed the light toward a fallen tree that rested above water level. "They can't get us there."

Both men splashed hurriedly to the tree and stepped onto it. "What the fuck are those spikes?" the tall man asked, pointing his light at the spires of cypress roots sticking up out of the water.

"Fuck if I know or care. Keep moving."

Judson followed carefully, with Ellis on his heels. Despite his knowledge of the land, he felt the stir of unease, that message stemming from the primitive part of the brain that still existed and warned of danger. He knew the feeling it evoked, had felt it more times than he wanted to remember.

First your body heats, sweat begins to ooze from the pores, sending out the scent of fear. Then the shakes begin, the almost incontrollable reflex of jerking or jumping at every sound, every touch of a leaf or tip of a branch against you.

Fear swells, becoming more dominant with each heartbeat until you lose the ability to access the situation. And that's when you truly become prey.

He knew how to control it but was certain the men ahead of him didn't. It was obvious in the way the man in the rear moved his feet only inches before shining his flashlight around, wobbling on the log and breathing hard enough to be heard in the still of the night.

The short man was either braver, or had walked through a swamp before, because he kept moving slowly but steadily, placing one foot on the log, testing to see if the wood was rotten and would support him, and then taking another step.

A loud grunt close by had both men freezing. The tall man swung his light around and red eyes glowed in the murky water. He screamed like a girl, wobbled and fell face first. The next sound was one Judson wasn't likely to forget. A howl of agony as the man fell onto one of the sharp spires of cypress reaching out of the water.

"Raul!" the short man yelled and jumped off the log, landing in a splash in the waist deep water.

His partner was impaled on the cypress spire like a discarded cloak. "Oh God," the short man touched his partner and then withdrew his hands. "Oh God." He looked around with wide eyes. "Oh, no. God, oh, God."

He tried to lift his partner, but to no avail. There was a good foot of the spire protruding from the man's back. "Oh shit," the short man looked around. "Shit. Raul, man, I'm–"

Then he screamed, and a split second later, Judson knew why. An alligator had hold of him, just below the elbow. Judson could hear the crunch and break of bone, even with the howls of pain coming from the man.

There was nothing he could have done for either man, even if he was so inclined, which he wasn't. Within moments, the water was churning with alligators, dismembering the men and fighting over the meat, which they'd take below and tuck away to tenderize.

"I guess the gators took care of the job," Ellis commented.

“Leaving no trace,” Jim's voice came from ahead.

Judson looked to see Jim easily walking along the log toward him. "Bad way to die."

"Yep."

Once Jim reached them, they all headed back toward the barn. "What do you want to do with the car?" Ellis asked.

"Drive it back to the main road, pull off the side, and leave it."

“Doable,” Ellis agreed, then asked.

"You still taking the horse?"

"I am."

"Then let's get him loaded."

They walked in silence for a few minutes, then Ellis asked. "Is she worth all this?"

"Hell, if I know," Judson replied. "I never set eyes on her before tonight."

"Strange times, brother. I hope this doesn't come back to bite us in the ass."

"Nah," Judson cut a look over his shoulder. "The gators will finish those two, and no one will have reason to suspect anything. We'll punch a hole in a hose in the engine of their car and it'll look like they broke down. The police will think it's abandoned."

"I hope you're right."

Judson felt the same because this situation had become far more dangerous than he imagined.

Chapter Six

It was so quiet that when Face's ears perked up and he raised his head, Ivy jerked. Her heart raced and palms grew moist. He sat completely still and focused on the door. Ivy rose and walked over to the door, then looked back at Face. He hadn't moved. She placed her ear against the door. How long had she and Face waited here in the barn? She'd not paid attention to the time when they arrived at the ranch, but it felt like they'd been in the room for a long time. Horrible visions of Judson and his friend being killed played in her mind, along with fears of the door bursting open and men rushing in with guns.

How did an ordinary woman, struggling to support herself, end up in such a mess? Was she going to survive this and if she did, would her life be nothing more than looking over her shoulder every day, waiting on the next assassin the man who killed Detective Gordon would send?

That wasn't living, and maybe she should just walk out the door and face her death with as much bravery as she could muster. She didn't want to live in fear every moment, and she didn't know how to move beyond that fear.

When the door opened, she jumped back with her heart hammering in her chest and her hands tightened into fists. She felt a little short of breath and suddenly cold, even though the temperature hadn't changed. Then she looked at Face, who stood beside her. His tail was wagging.

Relief flooded her as Judson walked in and, without considering her actions, she launched herself at him, wrapping her arms around his neck. "Oh, thank God, you're okay."

To her surprise, when his arms circled her and held her firm against him, a feeling of safety claimed her. It was the first time she'd felt safe since she saw the dead man on the floor being eaten by a python.

"Everything's okay," Judson assured her.

"It is?"

"It is," he released her and gave Face a rub.

"How?" she asked. "How is it suddenly okay? And what does that even mean? Are we safe? Are those men going to just leave and–" Insight struck like a fork of lightning. "Oh, God. You didn't kill them, did you?"

"No, I didn't."

"Then they're still alive?"

"No."

"No?" Ivy stepped back, raising both hands, palms toward him. "They're dead?"

"Yes."

"But you didn't kill them?"

"No."

"Did your friend?"

"No."

"Then how did they die?"

"Alligators."

As someone who'd spent a lot of years in Florida, she was familiar with the dangers of alligators. Most people didn't realize how deadly alligators are, in or out of the water. On land, they can reach speeds of thirty-five miles per hour and in the water, up to twenty miles per hour. In other words, it's hard to outrun or out-swim them.

They can also climb. If there's enough of an incline, they can haul themselves up and over chain link fencing or even up trees. And then there is the fact that their bite is one of the most powerful on Earth, delivering over two thousand pounds of pressure.

Alligators are not to be taken lightly, and Ivy was smart enough to never try to get close to one. It horrified her to think of someone being attacked by an alligator.

"I don't want to know any more." It reminded her of her father's old cliché: *Ignorance is bliss*. In this instance, she agreed and almost wished for ignorance. But she knew and needed to figure out what that meant to her and her situation.

"So, now what? We're safe?"

"We will be. Ellis will going to follow Jim, who will drive their car, leave it ten miles down the road with a hole in a hose and the hood up. Whoever finds them will think the car broke down."

"And then?"

"Then nothing. There's nothing to link them to this place and no one would walk ten miles to a ranch you can't even tell is there from the road."

She considered it. "Then you think we're safe?"

"As long as you stay off your phone and don't let anyone know where you are, yes."

"But my parents–"

"I told you we'll let them know you're safe."

"Okay." She didn't see the point in arguing. If he didn't live up to that promise when they arrived at his ranch, she'd find a way to do it herself.

"So, get in the truck and we'll get the horse loaded and hit the road."

"Okay."

It took all of ten minutes to get the trailer hooked up to the truck and the horse into the trailer. Judson spoke with Ellis and Jim for a minute, then shook hands and climbed into the truck.

"Isn't this a long way to haul a horse?" Ivy asked.

"It's done all the time."

“Oh, here’s your phone,” she fished the phone from her pocket and handed it to him.

“Thanks.”

That ended the conversation. For the next three hours, there was silence. She wished Judson would say something, just the sound of his voice would be better than sitting there, prisoner to her own thoughts and fears. She was saved when Face sat up and whined. "Oh oh,” she looked back at Face and then at Judson. "I think he needs to make a pit-stop."

"That makes two of us," Judson commented. "We'll take the next exit."

There was a convenience store at the next exit. Judson pulled up to the pump. "I'll fill up. If you need to hit the bathroom, now's your chance. We'll pull over after I gas up and let Face do his business and stretch his legs.”

"Okay. Want anything from the store? Soda, water, coffee, snacks?"

"Coffee and a large water would hit the spot. Let me give you some cash."

"I have some. I'll get it. And I can pay for the gas on my debit card."

He looked at her for a second with a slight frown on his face. "I don't know what has you on the run, but I'm guessing it might be smart not to use a card that can be tracked."

"What do you mean, tracked?"

"I mean if someone can hack into your account, they can tell where you are by the places you use the card."

"Oh, I didn't think of that. Still, I have cash so I can pay, and I'd like to."

"Fine. Thank you."

"It's the least I can do." She turned and gave Face a rub. "I'll be right back, buddy."

Ivy went into the convenience store, looked around, and when she spotted the sign for the restrooms, headed for the ladies' room. As soon as she cleaned her hands and washed her face, she went in search of water.

They had gallons of drinking water for sale, so she bought one for Face, got four bottles of cold water from the cooler for Judson and herself, then grabbed a box of crackers with peanut butter, four apples and three big beef jerky sticks.

There were three people in line ahead of her. Ivy watched out of the door to see if Judson was still pumping gas. He was talking on a cell phone.

She watched as she waited, wondering who he was talking to.

Judson glanced at the store. Ivy was in line. "It'll probably be daylight before we get there."

His father responded. "Did she say why Bill gave her the number?"

"No."

"It's strange that he didn't let me know he was calling in that favor."

"It's strange that he called it in for a woman and a dog."

"What kind of dog?"

"Irish Wolfhound. Big guy. Healthy. Friendly."

"And the woman?"

"Mid-thirties, I guess. Could be older, it's hard to tell. Seems intelligent, curious and friendly, but I think that's just a cover to hide her fear."

"We need to know what she's afraid of, son. If trouble's going to come our way because of this, we need to know what kind of trouble."

"I hear you. I'll see if I can get her to tell me. Oh, and I'm texting you the tag number of a car. Someone found her at the meeting place and tried to take her out. I scared them off, but they must have had backup because we were followed to the ranch."

“And?”

“They won't be following anyone else.”

"Do I have to ask?”

“Best you don't.”

“Fine. Drive safe. See you in the morning."

"Will do. Get some rest."

The pump turned off, and he removed the nozzle, giving the store another glance. Ivy was now at the register.

Ivy indicated Judson's truck as she spoke to the cashier. "I'm paying for the gas on that black truck, too. And can I get a large coffee? Biggest you have."

It was far more than she imagined and took nearly all her cash, but she wouldn't complain. Judson was doing her a big favor. The least she could do was pay for the gas. She grabbed a handful of sugar packets, four creamers and a wad of napkins, then headed outside.

"Here you are," she handed Judson the coffee when she reached the truck. "There's cream and sugar in the bag, some snacks and water."

"Black is fine," he said. "Hop in and we'll pull over to the edge of the parking lot, out of the way."

Once they were parked, Judson got out to check on the horse. Ivy fished Face's bowl from the luggage, hooked his leash onto his harness, then grabbed the gallon of water. "Okay, buddy, let's go find you something to pee on."

Face didn't need coaxing. The moment she opened the door, he hopped out. She walked with him to the grassy area beyond the parking lot and after a few minutes of sniffing, he did his business and returned to her. She poured water into his bowl, and he lapped it up.

"More?" She poured just a bit more into the bowl.

He looked at it and then away, signaling he was done, so she tossed the water and headed back for the truck. Judson was already behind the wheel. She put Face into the back seat and then climbed in the front.

"Jerky?" she asked as she pulled out the two sticks.

"No thanks," Judson declined.

"Do you mind if I give one to Face?"

"He's your dog."

"But it's your truck."

"Well, as long as he doesn't puke it up, it's fine."

"I doubt he will." She unwrapped a stick and reached back over the seat. "Want a treat, Face?"

His answer was to take the jerky and start gnawing.

"Ready?" Judson asked.

"As I'll get, I guess."

"You don't have to go, Ivy."

"I think I do."

"Okay then."

Aside from Face chewing, the only sound as they rode was the hum of wheels on the road. An hour passed in silence. With nothing to occupy her mind, Ivy's thoughts turned once again to the events that led her to be riding in a truck with a stranger.

She turned her head to the side, pretending to look out of the window, when in reality she wanted to hide the fact that tears were streaming down her face. Try as she might, she couldn't stop seeing things play out in her mind. Bill Gordon was probably dead because of her.

What she couldn't figure out was how anyone found out about her. The police were the only ones who knew she found the dead body, so how did the bad guy find her?

It felt like a nightmare, and she wished it was. At least you can waken from bad dreams.

And what about her folks? When the police showed up at her house, they would find it empty and then what? Would they figure out who lived there and then use that information to figure out who her parents were and where they lived?

That sparked more worry. Her parents would be frantic. She was going to have to find a way to let them know she was okay. She couldn't let them worry.

"Ivy?"

She wiped her face with her hands and turned her head to look at Judson. "Yes?"

"We need to talk."

"About?"

"About why you're sitting in my truck, why Bill Gordon gave you my father's number and why that man at the bus stop had a gun on you."

"It's kind of a convoluted mess."

"I've got time."

Ivy gathered her thoughts, then started the tale, beginning with finding the dead man at the house where she cleaned the pool. Judson was silent throughout the entire story and when she finished, he nodded, rubbed his forehead, and blew out a breath.

"I have to say I've never heard of anyone earning the label of murder victim from being eaten by a python. I'm guessing Bill thought the killer would try to find you to keep you from identifying him."

"But I never saw him. I told Mr. Gordon that."

"But the killer didn't know that. And he obviously was determined to find you if he killed the man you worked for and then Bill. What concerns me is that he knew where to find you. Do you have a phone on you?"

"I do, but it's not turned on."

"Make sure it stays that way until we can get it checked out."

"Checked out? By whom?"

"A friend."

She nodded and despite her best attempts not to, started crying again. "I'm so sorry about Mr. Gordon. He was so kind and I–I didn't mean for this to happen. I don't even know why it is."

"I know, but it has, and Bill was smart to give you that number. As long as you don't tell anyone where you are, you'll be safe."

"But I need to tell my family I'm okay. They'll be sick with worry when they find out what happened."

"We'll figure something out when we get home."

"We don't have a home anymore," she looked back at Face, and then at Judson. "Will we be able to go back?"

"I don't know, Ivy."

"Well, at least you're honest," she said, almost wishing that he was not. Right now, what she needed was someone to tell her that everything was going to be okay.

The trouble was, even if Judson spoke those words, she wouldn't believe him, because she was pretty sure, life was not going to be okay for a long time.

Chapter Seven

Ivy jerked awake, at first unsure where she was. Her heart raced as she looked around. Face immediately stuck his head between the seats to nuzzle her. Ivy leaned over, put her cheek on top of his head and rubbed his neck. "Hey buddy. How's my big guy doing?"

"He's been asleep almost as long as you," Judson said.

"What time is it?"

He pointed to the display on the dashboard. "Almost dawn."

"A new day, doodle bug," she said softly.

"Pardon?"

"It's something from my childhood. In the mornings when I was little, one of my parents would come into my room to sit on my bed and wake me. "It's a new day, doodle bug." That's what they always said."

"Doodle bug?"

"Yep," she smiled as she remembered. "Back then, I thought every new day was something magic."

"When did you stop thinking that?"

"Probably about the time I found out my husband had been cheating on me for a long time. He planned on leaving me for an associate who worked at the law firm with him."

"You're married?"

"Divorced. When I discovered what he was doing, I waited for him to go to work one morning, called in sick and cleaned out everything that belonged to him. I piled it all in the driveway, changed all the locks and canceled every credit card with his name on the account."

"That's cold."

"He deserved it. And he got in his own shots. After I canceled the cards, I logged onto our banking app and discovered he'd cleaned out our checking and savings, so it was fair."

"I'm guessing he didn't see it that way."

"Probably not," she felt a bit of guilt over admitting her animosity toward a man she'd sworn to love and hold dear. "But I was angry and felt betrayed – and he made me feel unworthy."

"How so?"

"Well, we were both college freshmen when we married. I dropped out of college and put him through undergrad and law school, working two to three jobs. Once he got a job, I was supposed to be able to go back to college, but we were in debt, and he pleaded with me to give him time to make partner before I quit. Like an idiot I agreed. When I found out about the other woman and finally was able to talk to him without being so angry, he said I didn't fit into his world. She had a law degree, and I didn't even have a college education."

She shook her head, as if the act would shake off the bad memories. "It hurt and I felt humiliated, which was what he wanted, but I sucked it up, enrolled at the University and started taking two classes a semester. Once I finished my undergraduate degree, I started taking veterinary classes."

"You're a vet?"

"I wish. It's always been my dream, but I still have two classes left and then I need to intern and…and well, now, who knows if that will ever happen. I'm not exactly a kid anymore."

"You're not too old to get your degree."

"I guess not. But enough about me. If you're going to show that horse we're hauling, then you must know something about performance horses, right?"

"I spent a little time on the circuit. Pop started his career in rodeo. Broncs and bulls, then roping, then moved into training and breeding."

"Does he still do it?"

"Nope."

"But he still rides? For pleasure, I mean."

"Yep."

"I'd love to be able to ride."

"Do you know how?"

"Yes. So why did your dad give it up?"

"He took a bad fall from a bronc and broke his back."

"Oh, how awful. That rehab must have been long and painful."

"He says it saved his life."

"Really? Why?"

"That's how he met my mother. She was a nurse at the facility he was placed in to learn to walk again."

"Oh, that's romantic, isn't it? So, tell me about your father...I'm sorry what's his name?"

"Clayton Blackstone."

"What kind of man is he?"

"A good one."

"What does he like?"

"The quiet of the forest, animals, the mountains and apple pie. He isn't keen on technology but does own and use a cell phone, even though he'll swear he hates the thing. He'd rather read than watch television, hates crowds but loves kids and dogs. Someone once described him as the last of his kind and I reckon that's fitting."

"Or not."

"Pardon?"

"From the way you talk about him, I think maybe you're a lot like him, which would make you the last of his kind – unless you have children, or siblings."

"A sister who died young and four brothers. No, sorry three."

“You don't know how many brothers you have?”

“We lost our youngest brother six months ago. I reckon sometimes I forget.”

“I'm sorry. That must be difficult.”

“Yep.”

"So, what about your mother?"

"Nosey much?"

"I'm sorry," she felt a bit hurt at the question. "I don't mean to pry, I'm just trying to get a feel for who you and your family are, since Mr. Bill sort of forced me on all of you."

"He didn't force you on us. And my mother's dead."

"Oh, I'm sorry for your loss. How long ago did you lose her?"

"The day my youngest brother was born."

"She died in childbirth?" Ivy thought that was horribly sad.

"She did."

"Do you have a stepmother?

"No."

"Your dad raised you all by himself?"

"He did."

"And he never remarried?"

"No."

"Wow, did he ever say why?"

"Yep."

When he let it go at that one word, she complained. "Oh, that's just mean to say yep and not tell me the rest."

"He said it seemed disrespectful. She died giving birth to what he wanted more than anything in the world. Another child. How could he let another woman raise her children?"

"Oh god, that's..." She trailed off, searching for the right words. "That's powerful love."

"Yep."

"But once you were grown, he could have remarried."

"He could, but he didn't. And I don't reckon many women would be content with the life he lives. Too quiet, not enough frills."

"Some women like quiet. What about you? Are you married?"

He snorted. "What woman would want me?"

"Probably a lot."

"I doubt it. I'm ornery, not particularly easy on the eyes and too much like my father."

"I think you're selling yourself short."

"I doubt it but thank you. You know, there's an extension of NC State not far from the ranch, and they have a school of veterinarian science. Just in case you're not able to get back to Florida for a couple of months. Do you have a contact there with the police?"

"Bill introduced me to a detective working the case."

"Then you should be able to get information."

"I guess."

"Guess?"

Ivy chewed on that thought for a few minutes. "Bill thought it wasn't safe for me to be in Florida, so is it wise to reach out to the Detective? Should I keep my location a secret?"

"Good point," Judson agreed. "And it's not like you have to decide right this minute."

"True. But I need to let my parents know because if I'm not making the mortgage payment, they need to make arrangements for the house."

"Do you have savings?"

Ivy laughed. "I work three jobs to afford rent, food and tuition, so no, I don't have savings."

"I can give you a job while you're staying at the ranch."

That shocked her. "Seriously? Doing what?"

"As an intern."

"Okay, color me confused. An intern for what?"

"Vet intern."

Ivy opened her mouth, closed it and then opened it again. "You're a vet?"

"Large animals for the most part. Primarily horses, but people do bring in their pets or hurt animals they find that need rehabbing."

"Oh my gosh, are you kidding? Thank you, Judson. That's– well it's not just kind, it's amazing. I'll work hard, I promise."

"I'm sure you will."

Face stuck his head through the opening in the seats and leaned against her. Ivy gave him some rubbing and after a few minutes he settled back down. She stared out of the window, thinking about the strange turn of events in her life.

Here she was, on the run from someone she didn't even know his name, scared of being murdered for something she didn't see. And in the middle of the fear and uncertainty, the opportunity she'd prayed for appeared.

She didn't know how to react or what to make of it. Conflicted was an apt description of how she felt at the moment. Thinking about her little house made her sad. It wasn't much and was furnished with things she'd purchased at consignment shops and garage sales, but it was home.

Ivy was confident her folks could either sell or rent the place, but someone would have to get rid of her things and get the place ready. What if the man looking for her showed up? Would he hurt her parents?

She couldn't stand that thought and quickly turned her mind to the positive. Thanks to Bill Gordon, she might get a chance to intern with a Vet. If she could find a way to take some classes, she just might move forward with her plan on becoming a Vet herself.

If, if and if. Ivy realized how many ifs were governing her life but had no clue how to get rid of them. At present, her choices were limited. She would go to North Carolina and hope she wasn't walking into something she would want to escape.

She cut a quick look at Judson. He seemed like a decent man. The fact that Face liked him made her feel comfortable. Animals were intuitive about people. Had Face not liked Judson, she probably wouldn't have gotten into his truck to begin with.

So, maybe she'd hang onto that bit of positivity for a while and try not to come up with too many more *what ifs.* Right now, she was pretty sure she wasn't mentally or emotionally prepared for more fear or danger.

For the moment she just wanted to feel safe and figure out what her next move should be.

She leaned back and closed her eyes, not intending on going to sleep, but just to rest her eyes for a bit. When the truck stopped, she jerked awake and quickly looked at Judson.

"What's wrong?"

"Face needs a pitstop. He's been whining the last five miles. And I could use a break to stretch my legs. There's an all-night diner up ahead if you're hungry."

"That sounds good, but I don't want to leave Face alone."

"Then let's see if they'll give him a seat."

Ivy didn't believe for a moment he would do that, but after Face relieved himself, Judson asked if he could take the leash. She saw no reason to refuse, so handed it to him. He walked up to the door, tapped and when a waitress behind the counter looked up, Judson motioned for her to come to the door.

"Yes sir?" She said when she opened the door.

Ivy saw the reaction on the woman's face when Judson put two fingers to his hat in a cowboy gesture and smiled. "Good evening, Miss. Any chance you'd let my service dog come in and sit while we eat?"

"He's very big."

"Maybe you could ask your manager. We'll take that booth in the back where there aren't any other customers."

"Let me go ask." She gave him a smile and hurried inside to speak to a heavyset man working at the griddle.

When she returned, she wore a brighter smile. "He said if it's a service dog it's fine."

"Thank you, ma'am," Judson put his finger to the edge of his hat in another little salute.

Once they were seated with Face taking up one booth seat, leaving Judson and Ivy sitting side-by-side, the waitress brought menus and a big steak bone for Face. "Can he have this?"

Judson looked at Ivy and she gave an almost imperceptible shake of her head. "I wish I could say yes, but I'm scared he might be too enthusiastic and get it stuck in his throat."

Judson smiled at the woman. "I'd be happy to order a couple of New York strips for him."

"How would you want that cooked?"

"Not at all."

"Oh, okay, I can do that. And what will y'all have?"

"I'll have the steak and eggs, with hash browns, biscuits and coffee. And make that steak medium rare."

"Got it. And you, Miss?" she turned her attention to Ivy.

"Same as his but medium well."

"You got it. I'll be right back with your coffee."

Ivy angled on the bench to better face Judson. "For a man who claims to have no appeal, you sure charmed that lady."

He shook his head. "Nah. She was just being polite."

"For a seemingly smart man, you sure are dumb about women. Her smile was an invitation if I ever saw one. But what do I know, right?"

"Exactly," he agreed around a smile.

Ivy shook her head. "It was nice of you to get them to let Face come in."

"He would've been upset if we left him in the truck."

"Yes, he would. He's handling all this pretty well, but he has to sense that things just aren't right."

"Yeah, he does. But you're doing a fair job of keeping it together and that helps."

"A fair job?" She arched an eyebrow. "Fair?"

"Yeah, fair. See?" he pointed across the table to Face who was watching her. "He's making sure to keep his eye on you. He knows you're upset."

"I don't quite know how to make him feel I'm not."

"By looking at things another way."

"Here's your coffee," the waitress returned with two cups and a platter with two steaks on it. "You want me to put this on the floor for him?"

"Sure, that'd be great," Judson answered.

She set the plate down and backed away as Face sniffed at the meat. "Your order will be up soon."

"Thank you," Ivy replied at the same time Judson said "thanks."

Once the waitress left, Ivy reopened the conversation. "So how do I look at things another way?"

"Easy. Gratitude."

"Gratitude?"

"Yes. Let me ask you something. Aren't you grateful to be alive? That Face is alive and well and whoever the guy is who's looking for you doesn't have a clue where you are?"

"Well, yes, but–"

"But what? Isn't that enough?"

"Well, yes. No. I mean, it's good but I'm still running away from home and some person who wants to kill me and all I have is a week's worth of clothes, my dog and twenty-six dollars in cash. So…"

"So, it's enough. You'll have a bed to sleep in tonight, be in a safe place and if you're serious, I'll put you to work and help you move toward getting that degree. Face will be safe with space to run, and we'll make sure your folks know you're safe. If you had to run to stay alive, then this has to be better than hiding in a run-down motel or sleeping on a park bench."

"Well, when you put it that way…"

"There you go. Look at the positive."

Ivy nodded and turned her attention to doctoring her coffee. Judson made sense. This wasn't what she wanted, but life had thrown her a curve ball and her old life was no longer an option. So, like he said, she needed to focus on the positive.

If only she could get a clear vision of what that was.

Chapter Eight

Mitch grimaced as the last swallow of tepid coffee hit his belly. Whoever made that pot must have added battery acid to the mix. Or perhaps his sour gut was a result of the last six days. Bill Gordon was being buried today, and the entire department would be attending. It was the last thing Mitch wanted to do. No matter how many times he told himself that Bill's death wasn't his fault, he knew different.

If he'd just been able to talk Bill out of trying to protect Ivy McCoy, Bill would still be alive and Mitch wouldn't be scared to go home at night for fear of finding the man who ordered Bill's death, waiting for him.

Mitch scowled at his computer monitor and ran his hands over his face. He should have stayed in bed, but he needed time to do some digging and before five in the morning, there weren't many detectives around.

There was an APB out for the McCoy woman who was presumed missing. Speculation was that she'd been kidnapped, probably killed and her body dumped somewhere. Thus far there was no evidence to back up such speculation, but with Bill shot dead in her driveway, and bloody clothing found in her home, it was a reasonable assumption.

The only one in the department who knew the fallacy of that theory was Mitch and he wished to God he didn't. But he'd made his mistake. Rafael Martinez was the biggest drug kingpin in Florida, bringing in shipments daily while the Coast Guard turned a blind eye and the authorities at the ports pretended not to see.

They were quite happy to look the other way and collect the bountiful gratitude Martinez offered. Most of them would now retire rich thanks to their fealty to Martinez. Mitch was in that boat with them, but at present his position could be in peril. He had to tread carefully and make sure no connection could be made between him and Martinez. He'd never be arrested. Martinez would have him killed. A dead man can't tell tales, after all.

He didn't plan on ending up dead in a ditch, so while everyone else was searching for Ivy McCoy's body, he was looking for where Ivy McCoy may have gone. There was no evidence at her home as to where she might have gone, and he knew for a fact that Martinez failed to grab her at a bus stop. She was definitely on the run.

Mitch believed Ivy's statement that she hadn't seen anyone at the house on Oak Lane except for the dead man. She thought she saw movement in the house when she first arrived and rang the doorbell but couldn't be sure.

He'd tried to assure Martinez she wasn't a threat, but Martinez didn't like loose ends and as far as he was concerned, Ivy McCoy was just that. So, he went after Ivy. What puzzled Mitch was how Martinez was able to find her.

Moreover, who came to her rescue? According to Martinez, it was a black pickup truck. That's all he could tell Mitch, aside from demanding that Mitch find the woman. So, it was up to Mitch to find her, whatever it took.

That was proving to be a very difficult task. Without cause, he couldn't have her phone records subpoenaed. It stood to reason that if she had left her car behind and met someone in the black truck, she was being cautious and might not be using her phone.

At first, he thought maybe she'd try to get a bus or train ticket. But, the fact that her giant beast of a dog was gone as well, muddied the water. She couldn't get on a bus, train or plane with that creature, so that ruled out public transportation. He'd canvassed her coworkers and even called her parents in Georgia, pretending to be her boss.

No one had spoken with her or had any idea about someone who drove a black pickup. Her parents were frantic and on their way to Florida to see about Ivy's house and talk with the police. They would appear at a press conference after the service with the Chief of Police and Mayor to appeal to the public for any information about their daughter.

Thanks to the attention the case was given in the media, the powers that be in the department and city were focused on making themselves look good. Which meant they wanted their people working round the clock. They, like Ivy's parents, wanted her to be found.

So did he, but for very different reasons.

*****

Clayton Blackstone rose and went into the kitchen. He took a glass from the cupboard and stuck it under the faucet. As it filled with cold water, he stared out of the window above the sink. When he made the pact with Bill Gordon, he never imagined repayment would come in the form it'd taken.

He'd turned on the news as soon as he woke and was dismayed to hear about Bill's death and the feared murder or kidnapping of Ivy McCoy. Even more disturbing was that it made national news. There would be a memorial for Bill, and Ivy's parents would be present at a press conference being held by the Mayor and Chief of Police.

That meant people all over the country would see photos of Ivy. That might make it more difficult to keep her safe. Clayton would feel better if he knew more about the people who wanted her dead, but to secure such information meant him calling in favors from people he'd rather not become indebted to.

Noticing that his glass had overflowed, he turned off the water and lifted the glass to his lips. Nothing ever tasted as good as the water that came from his well. Naturally filtered through three hundred feet of coal and granite, it was as cold as if it had just come from the refrigerator.

Clayton finished his water, rinsed the glass and turned it upside down in the dish draining rack. He then headed back into the den, sank into his recliner and reached for the cell phone on the table beside his chair.

Judson answered after one ring. "It's kind of early, even for you. Everything okay?"

"Good morning, son. I hate to tell you, but the story about what happened at Ms. McCoy's house hit the national news."

"I was hoping it wouldn't."

"Her parents are on their way to Florida for Bill's memorial, and they're taking part in a press conference afterwards."

"Then the killer…"

"Yep, he's likely to make a move on them."

"What do you want me to do?"

"Just get back here and we'll figure it out."

"We should be there in about two hours."

"I'll have a fresh pot of coffee waiting."

"Thanks, Dad. See you soon."

Clayton walked outside and sat on the back porch swing, staring at the predawn sky. The situation with the McCoy woman came out of the blue. He'd always assumed the debt would go uncollected. When that marker was called in, it shocked him.

And brought back a memory.

Clayton guzzled down the remainder of his beer, pushed back from the bar and clapped his buddy, Tommy Nash on the back. "Guess I better head on back to the hotel. My bus leaves at daybreak."

"Eager to get back to the ranch?" Tommy asked.

"You know it."

"I hear ya," Tommy smiled. "My bus is due to leave around two in the afternoon and I can't wait to get on it and head home. I've seen enough blood and death to last a lifetime. This is it for me. I'm ready for civilian life."

"Same here," Clayton agreed.

"Stay in touch, my friend," Tommy stood and offered his hand.

"You know it," Clayton shook his friend's hand and then pulled him in for a back pounding hug.

"Oh look, ain't that sweet? The Marines boys are butt buddies."

As if possessed of one mind, Clayton and Tommy turned at the same time. A muscle-bound white guy with a confederate flag tattoo on one arm leaned an elbow on the bar, smirking at them.

"Ignore him" Clayton said as Tommy took a step toward the guy. "He's not worth it."

"Says the chicken shit queer," the guy taunted.

"Oh, hell no," Tommy said, grabbed his empty beer mug and headed for the guy.

The man stood and took a swing, but Tommy dodged to one side, raised the mug and clobbered the man over the head with it. The guy went down like a sack of brick.

And that's when the shooting started. After all the bloodshed he'd seen overseas in Vietnam, he'd have thought he was immune to the sight of it but seeing Tommy's body jerk three times and blood blossom with each movement, had nausea bubbling in Clayton's gut and rage overshadowing his judgment.

He caught Tommy, lowered him to the floor and then rose, planning on launching himself at the man wielding the weapon. The man pointed the gun at Clayton and in that moment, Clayton accepted that he was about to die.

Only the shot that rang out didn't hit him. It hit the man trying to shoot him. A hole opened in the man's forehead, and he toppled back like a felled tree as blood and brains billowed from the back of his head.

"Nobody move!" A male voice rang out.

Clayton froze and heard footsteps behind him. A tall, stocky man walked by him holding a badge in one hand and a handgun in the other. He barked an order at the bartender who peered over the bar. "Call 911." Then he looked around. "The rest of you sit your asses down. If I see a weapon, I'll shoot first and ask questions later. You got it?"

Clayton was the first to sink to the floor with hands raised. It wasn't long before the place was swarming with police. The man who'd saved him from being killed walked over to Clayton. "I'd appreciate you giving a statement Mr.....?"

"Blackstone," Clayton replied. "Clayton Blackstone. Do you want me to do that here?"

"Or you could ride to the station with me and do it there."

"It's your call, sir. After all, I owe you my life."

Clayton leaned back in his chair and closed his eyes. The police officer who saved him was Bill Gordon. Before Clayton left the station that night, he told Bill that he was in Bill's debt and asked for his phone number. He promised to call and give Bill his number as soon as he was home.

He'd kept his word, and despite the passage of time, always made sure Bill Gordon had the correct phone number for him. If ever Bill needed to call in a favor, he had only to call, and Clayton would drop everything to repay the debt he owed.

Surprisingly, he and Bill ended up being friends. They'd only seen one another a dozen times over the years, but they spoke often, and Clayton trusted and respected Bill.

Now he felt sadness well up inside him for the man who'd saved his life, and the life of the woman Judson was bringing home with him. He'd protect the woman to honor his debt to Bill, but right now would take some time to grieve the passing of a man so willing to put his life on the line for another.

So, he rocked and let the tears come.

There was a good hour of silence before Ivy's voice sounded softly. "Who was that?"

"My father."

"Is everything okay?"

"No, Ivy, I don't think it is. Your parents are on their way to Florida. They'll attend Bill Gordon's memorial service and then join the mayor and chief of police in a press conference."

"They can't do that!" She reached for his arm. "Judson, we have to stop them. If the killer sees them, he might decide to–oh God, what if he kidnaps them to try to find out where I am? What if –"

"Ivy, stop." Judson peeled her hand off his arm and captured it in his, holding tight. "Listen to me. The police have sense enough to know the killer might make a move on them, so they'll make sure your parents are protected."

"But what if they don't?"

"They will. It's their job."

"Oh God," she tore her hand free of his and put both her hands over her face. "I have to do something. If anything happens to them, it'll be my fault."

"No, it won't, and you've got to stop expecting the worst. Let's just get to the ranch, sit down with Dad and we'll figure something out."

"What? What will we figure out?"

"What we need to do next."

"Why doesn't that comfort me?"

"I don't know. I reckon because you don't know me, so have no reason to believe what I'm saying is true."

She fell silent and for the rest of the drive, remained that way. When he turned onto the drive leading to the ranch, she looked at the sign that read Blackstone Ranch. It'd been a long time since she'd been in the mountains. The towering hardwood trees, mixed with the pines and evergreens made her feel a bit like being on home soil. "We're here?"

"Yep."

"It's beautiful."

"Yes, it is."

"I'm sorry I was impolite."

"You weren't. You're just scared."

"I'm afraid that evil bastard will hurt them to get to me."

"Maybe we can stop that from happening."

"How?"

Judson couldn’t answer that question but hoped he and his family could come up with a solution to the situation. Before someone else got killed.

Chapter Nine

Clayton looked up from tightening the cinch, listening. Some would scoff if he spoke it aloud, not that he'd care. He could tell the difference between the sound of Judson's truck and any other. If asked, he'd not be able to put his finger on anything specific, nonetheless, he knew the sound.

"Eddie, finish saddling this sorrel and the blaze face bay for the Finch couple. They're riding with Greg and Taylor and the Booker party."

A tall, thin man with blond hair cut high and tight, hurried over. "Sure thing, Mr. Blackstone."

Clayton relinquished the task and headed for the corral closest to the barn. The horse Judson hauled home would need to be walked, watered, fed, and brushed. Just as he reached the corral, Judson's truck stopped beside the gate.

As Clayton watched, the passenger door opened. Expecting to see the woman Judson had rescued, Clayton was surprised to see an enormous wolfhound jump out. The dog paused, sniffed and then looked back at the woman getting out of the truck.

He'd not had any expectations on the woman, so found it interesting that her looks surprised him. She was of medium height, slim, with long honey brown hair, pulled back into a low ponytail.

Just as she looked his way, Judson's voice rang out. "Where you want me to put him?"

For a split-second Clayton thought Judson was referring to the dog. Then Judson opened the rear of the trailer. "Put him in the east corral and let him stretch his legs."

"Will do."

"And welcome home, son."

"It's good to be back," Judson said, then added with a look at the woman. "Dad, this is Ivy McCoy. Ivy, my dad, Clayton Blackstone."

Clayton tipped the front of his hat marginally in Ivy's direction. "Pleasure to meet you, Ms. McCoy."

"Ivy," she said and after cutting a look toward Judson who was backing the horse from the trailer, she hurried toward Clayton with the giant of a dog pressed to the side of her leg protectively.

"It's an honor, Mr. Blackstone." She offered her hand, and he was impressed at the strength of her grip, and the way she met his gaze. He could see the sincerity in her eyes when she said, "I'm sorry for the inconvenience and I hope I don't bring any trouble to you or your son."

Clayton released her hand. "It'll be fine, ma'am. Now, who's this fine fellow?" He extended his hand to Face.

"This is Face," she put her hand on the dog's neck and the dog looked up at her. Clayton regarded the look of love she gave the animal and the adoration in its gaze as it looked at her. "Face, say hello to Mr. Blackstone."

Face turned his head and sniffed Clayton's hand, then took a step closer, sniffed again and wagged his tail. Clayton rubbed the broad head. "You're one fine fella, aren't you?"

Face's tail wagged more enthusiastically, and he moved closer to Clayton, sniffing his legs and boots. Clayton didn't mind and wasn't concerned. It was clear the dog was friendly. He turned his attention back to Ivy. "I imagine you'd like to get clean, eat and rest up after that drive."

"Actually, I'd like to take Face for a run if that's permitted." She looked around again and Clayton noticed the way her gaze followed Judson. He wondered if there was an attraction between them. On the one hand, he'd like for Judson to find a good woman to build a life with. On the other, he wasn't sure he'd be happy for that woman to be Ivy McCoy. At least not until he figured out what kind of mess she was in and whether it was her fault.

Dismissing those thoughts, he answered. "That'll be fine. Just keep him away from the livestock until we figure out how he'll get along."

"Oh, yes sir, I understand, completely. Would it be okay to take him on the driveway?"

"That'd be fine," Clayton agreed and pointed to a section of pasture beyond the house. "And that pasture's empty if you want to let him run there."

"Thank you, Mr. Blackstone."

"You're welcome."

Ivy turned away, calling to Face. "Come on Face. Let's go run."

Clayton watched Ivy and Face as they broke into a run. Face kept pace with Ivy, sticking close to her side. Just as they reached the gate to the pasture, he'd indicated they could use, he heard a yell.

"Oh hell." Clayton took off in a jog. One of the new ranch hands was trying to stop at least a dozen cows from breaching a fence line and having no luck. The cows were headed straight for Ivy and Face.

He expected Ivy to be scared, had no clue what to expect from the dog and was shocked at what happened next.

Face had just cleared the gate when Ivy heard shouts and cows mooing. "Oh shoot." She hurried through and closed the gate. "Face, with me," she patted her thigh and he obeyed immediately, moving close to her side.

It'd been a while since she helped her father with his cows but hadn't completely forgotten what to do. She ran out into the pasture, waving her arms and shouting at the cows "Hey, hey! Back! Back!"

The cows slowed, but kept coming, so she kept at it, hoping they'd either stop or turn back. A yell from behind her had her glancing over her shoulder to see Clayton running toward her. He was shouting at a ranch hand who was running alongside the herd, waving and shouting. "Turn them east!" he yelled.

Ivy wasn't sure which way east was until Judson appeared on horseback, galloping alongside the small herd. "East!" he pointed off to one side.

She slapped her thigh and called out "Face!" Less than a second later, Face was beside her. "Come on, buddy," she patted his back. "Let's turn these cows."

Ivy had no clue if she could, but figured it was worth a try, so she shouted and waved at the cows. A few seconds later, Face seemed to figure out what she was doing. He ran, barking at the cows, his long legs eating up the ground.

If she'd had the breath, Ivy would have cheered. Face accomplished what she couldn't. As if possessed of one mind, the herd turned east. "Face, come!" Judson yelled as he raced by.

Face fell in beside Judson and Ivy watched in amazement as they finished turning the cows. Clayton ran up and reached her as she stopped. "That's some dog," Clayton said.

"Yes, he sure is," she managed to say between breaths, still watching. Until this moment she hadn't really noticed, but now, watching Judson, it hit her. Big, and strong, he rode like he'd been born in a saddle and had those pale hazel eyes that either drew you right in or made you step back in fear.

She cut a look at his father. Judson was an attractive man, and he favored his father. Clayton was, in her book, one hell of a good-looking man. No sooner had the thought registered than she felt ashamed. Her life was a real mess, she'd survived possibly being murdered but even that escape brought problems. Now her parents could be in danger and here she was, thinking how appealing her host was.

"Mr. Blackstone, do you think there's any way we can let my parents know I'm okay without putting them in danger?"

Clayton looked at her for a moment and then away. "Well, I don't know, Ms. McCoy. I reckon that's something you'd need to speak with Judson about. I'm just an old rancher whose expertise lies in training a horse, tending livestock and the land and trying to mind my own business."

"Somehow I don't believe that."

"Oh? Why?"

"Something in your eyes. And why Judson? Isn't he a rancher, too?" The question popped out before she could stop it.

"That's a question for Judson."

"Fair enough," she conceded. "I'll ask him when he's not busy. For now, what can I do to help out around here?"

"You know about ranching?"

"Farming. My folks raised goats and cows, chickens and ducks and we had horses. I guess I'm qualified to feed animals, clean out stalls and brush down or wash horses. Have a need for any of that?"

"Always, and we'll put you to work soon enough. For now, though, maybe we should get you settled. Do you have any belongings in the truck?"

"Just one suitcase and my shoulder bag."

"Then let's get them."

"Okay."

After a quick look across the pasture where Face was sticking close to Judson as he and another hand herded the cows, she turned to follow Clayton. "How long have you lived here?" she asked as they walked.

"My family settled here in the late 1800's. When I came back home from Vietnam and married Judson's mother, we moved into the foreman's house." He pointed off to his right. Halfway up the side of another hill sat a wooden house, large and constructed of whole logs.

"Who lives there now?"

"Judson, when he's not in Florida or the place in Wyoming. He spends most of his time in Wyoming."

She nodded. "This is a beautiful place. I don't think I've ever felt happier or more at peace than when I lived in the mountains."

"Why'd you leave?"

Ivy shrugged. "Life, I guess. I fell for the wrong guy, became the one who made it possible for him to follow his dream, and somewhere along the way, lost sight of what I want or need."

"And what is that?"

Ivy considered the question for a few moments before answering. "To become a vet, have some land and lots of animals, a husband who loves me and kids running around in the yard, playing in the creek and learning to ride."

"A family."

"Yes, sir," she looked at him. "Only I think maybe that ship has sailed."

"You're not too old."

"Maybe not, but you don't always get what you want, so now I'm just trying to make sense of what life throws at me and pray that no one I care about gets hurt because of me."

"Sound sensible – making sense of things, that is. The rest of it? Well, I'm trusting there will be solutions."

"I sure hope so."

They reached Judson's truck and Clayton opened the back door. "This yours?" He lifted the suitcase from the floorboard."

"Yes, sir," she replied and then opened the front passenger door to get her shoulder bag.

"Anything else?"

"No, sir."

"Then let's take this to the house."

"Which house?"

"That one," he pointed to the main house. "We have a fair to middling guest suite that Judson and one of the hands, Marvin helped me fix up a few years ago so Judson's fiancé would have a place to stay when she visited."

"Judson's engaged?" She wondered why Judson hadn't mentioned that. And why she felt so disappointed. She'd known the man less than a day. She couldn't be falling for him.

"Was."

"Was?"

"As in past tense."

Ivy got the message. Clayton wasn’t going to discuss it. Probably just as well. As soon as she figured out how to avoid being killed, she'd return to her life, and this would be nothing more than a trauma she survived thanks to the help of strangers.

The funny thing was how sad it made her feel to contemplate never seeing these people again once she returned home. Were her feelings all mixed up because of the fear and uncertainty she'd experienced? Ivy wished she knew the answer and hoped that once it came to her, it didn't involve her being infatuated with a man who only saved her out of duty.

Chapter Ten

Mitch stood off to one side, barely paying attention to what the Chief of Police or the Mayor had to say. Something was off and had been since the night Ivy McCoy disappeared. The shooting of a police officer wasn't a crime that went unnoticed. A fatal shooting raised enough ire to worry the powers that be. That old saying about police "taking care of their own" was not just a saying. It was gospel.

It didn't surprise Mitch that the very next day a task force was created from men and women within the department. Their job was to uncover who shot Bill Gordon and why. What troubled Mitch was that he wasn't invited to be part of the task force.

That brought another troubling tidbit to mind, one he'd dismissed until now. Bill's wife, Lena, had not taken his calls.

Mitch must have called her a dozen times and she hadn't answered or acknowledged his texts. Today, he hadn't been invited to the dais, nor had he been asked to speak about Bill Gordon. What the hell was going on?

That question precipitated the onset of acid reflux, and he fished a roll of antacids from his pocket as his gaze moved over the assembly. Mitch hated the little tickle of fear that accompanied his gaze landing on a handsome Latin man, impeccably and expensively dressed. He sat near the back; his dark eyes unblinking as he watched the others in the room. His gaze met Mitch's and held.

Martinez. Damn. Of course, he'd show up. Mitch didn't know whether to admire his audacity or worry that something nasty was going to go down before the press conference ended. Mitch silently cursed and looked away from Martinez.

Just then, the parents of the missing woman, Ivy McCoy were ushered to the dais. The room fell silent as the father leaned in toward the microphone.

"Hello. I'm Ed McCoy and this is my wife, Helen. We'd just like to ask that anyone who has seen or knows of the whereabouts of our daughter, please call your local authorities and report it. I'm betting all of you have someone you love and would be terrified if that person just vanished.

"That's how we feel right now. I know we have no right to ask, and you have no duty to say yes, but still – here we stand, asking anyway for your help. We just want to find our daughter.

"Thank you."

Mitch despised the sharp snap of alarm when a low voice spoke from over his left shoulder. "Poor people."

Alarm morphed into the heat of hatred, yet still he nodded deferentially at Martinez who stepped up beside him. "It would serve you well to find a way to join the task force," Martinez's tone was amiable, but Mitch was smart enough to recognize the implied threat as Martinez continued. "If there are any leads from the heartfelt plea of the father, there just may be one that is viable and if so, we need that information first. Am I clear?"

"Yes." Mitch didn't see the need to say more. They both knew he'd do whatever it took to get on the taskforce because what Martinez had on him would not only see him lose his badge, but his freedom and possibly his life.

"Excellent," Martinez smiled and extended his hand. "I'll expect daily updates."

Mitch wasn't sure which was worse, being afraid to ignore the offered hand or being afraid someone would notice him with Martinez. He accepted the hand, but only briefly. "We'll talk soon."

"Of course," Martinez made a move as if to turn away, then stopped. "Oh, and I need you to get me into a room with the parents of the missing woman."

"Are you nuts?" The words spilled out before Mitch could consider the consequences.

"No, I am quite sure I am not. Just as, I assume, I do not have to repeat my order."

Mitch couldn't bring himself to do more than give a tense nod of acknowledgement. Martinez smiled but it wasn't a smile of friendship. It was one that promised he'd exact more than his pound of flesh if you crossed him. And he'd enjoy doing it.

*****

Clayton turned off the television and placed the remote on the coffee table as he stood. If he was a betting man, he'd put money on the police being inundated with calls. Particularly considering that the city offered a reward, since Ivy McCoy was their only witness to the shooting of Detective Bill Gordon.

A sudden thought had him breaking stride on his way to the door. Why hadn't Lena Gordon attended the press conference?

Wouldn't she have been asked to attend, to accept the thanks of a grateful city on his behalf?

Something was off. If pressed, Clayton wouldn't be able to tell anyone *how* he knew. He just knew. It was a talent he'd possessed his entire life. Well, as far back as he could remember. He could look at a set of events and tell if something was missing or concocted. Clayton was good at connecting the dots in a way that lit the path towards the truth of things.

Right now, he was convinced nothing about this situation was as it appeared. With a shake of his head, he snatched his hat off the rack, crammed it on his head and was just reaching for the doorknob when his phone rang.

He pulled it from his pocket and for the second time this morning, stopped dead in his tracks. The caller ID read Bill G. Reason intervened and he scoffed at his own reaction. Lena must have found his number in Bill's phone.

"Lena?" he answered.

"Try again."

Stunned didn't touch what Clayton felt at the sound of Bill's voice. Or was it, Bill? That thought raised ire he was quick to act upon. "Who the hell is this and how—"

"It's me, Clayton."

"You were reported dead."

"Yep."

"Care to tell me why?"

"I'd rather show you. Are you near your computer?"

"I can be." Clayton turned and backtracked through the house to his home office. He went straight to his desk and activated his speaker mode. "Okay, I'm ready."

"Okay," Bill cleared his throat. "Sorry, still a little scratchy."

"How bad was it?"

"Bad enough they put me into a medically induced coma."

Clayton thought that made sense from a medical perspective, but something bugged him. "That makes sense. But why report that you were killed? What's the game, Bill?"

"Nasty business, my friend. I was working the case of the dead guy Ivy McCoy found. Oh wait – let me summarize."

Clayton listened as Bill told him about Ivy finding a dead man while cleaning the pool. It was good to know more about what had transpired, but he needed more. "And?"

"And I got a break in the case."

"Did you tell her?"

"No. I only told one person. Someone I trust. That's where I screwed up. Anyway, the man responsible for the death of the man in the house found out what I knew and ordered a hit on me."

"So, you know who did it?"

"Sadly yes. The person I trusted. He pulled the trigger. I saw him."

"What other proof do you have?"

"None. That's why I'm calling. Now, I'm sending you a photo. Tell me when you have it."

Clayton watched and a few seconds later his messenger app activated. He looked at the image. "Got it."

"Okay, remember that face and find a copy of that press conference."

That was easy enough. "Okay, got it, what now?"

"In the beginning, before anyone starts talking, the cameras are not in tight, and you can see people lined up on either side of the room. Police officers and plain clothes cops. Do you see?"

"Yes."

"Then watch and tell me what jumps out at you."

Clayton watched the video for five seconds. Nothing. No, wait. He rewound and started again. There! On the left side of the screen, a man stood near the corner of the stage. Every few seconds he looked back, behind him or over the crowd.

"I see."

"And you see who it is?"

"The man in the photo you sent."

"Bingo. Mitch Burman, my partner."

Clayton considered the question before he asked. "And what exactly do you want me to do with this knowledge?"

"Help."

"How?"

"First, take care of Ivy. If they find out where she is, the man in charge, whoever is controlling Mitch, will send someone to kill her."

"We'll keep her safe. What else?"

"Help me nail the man who betrayed me. My partner. The minute he finds out I'm alive, he'll come gunning for me again."

"And what steps are being taken to ensure he can't get to you?"

"I'm in a secret location and will remain so until we get the evidence that connects Mitch to whoever he's working for."

"I'm in – on one condition."

"What?"

"That you let the company see to your safety. We have locations far more secure, and I won't rest easy until I know you are, in fact, somewhere safe."

There was a second of silence before Bill responded. "Fine."

"Good. I'll make the arrangements and will talk to you before noon."

"Thank you, Clayton."

"Friends help friends."

He ended the call, leaned back in his chair and regarded the paused video. What had Mitch Burman spooked during the press conference? Was his boss in attendance or was Mitch just nervous that his superior might show up, and others would notice and question the man's attendance?

More pieces to a puzzle that didn't yet make sense. But maybe he could uncover another small clue. Clayton headed for the guest suite, but noise from the kitchen drew him in that direction. He found Ivy standing at the counter, pouring a cup of coffee. Face sat beside her.

At a soft "woof" from Face she turned and saw him. "I hope you don't mind if I helped myself."

"Not a bit." He crossed the room to the bar that separated him from where she stood on the other side. Clayton called up the photo Bill sent and turned the phone toward her. "Have you ever seen this man?"

In mid-motion of turning toward him, Ivy jerked so hard, coffee splattered every which a way, especially on her hands. Her stifled sound of pain had him abandoning the phone on the bar top and hurrying to her. Face whined and licked her arm, trying to comfort as best he could.

"It's okay, Face." Clayton spoke in a calm tone as he took the cup and set it aside. "I've got her," he put his hands on Ivy's shoulders and guided her to the sink. "It'll sting," he said just before he took hold of her wrists and pushed her hands under the cold stream of water.

Two bright spots of color bloomed on her cheeks, standing out sharply against skin that had gone pale. Her eyes filled with tears, but she just nodded and bit her lip a little harder. At length he felt some of the tension ease in her wrists. "You recognized the man?"

"Yes. He's a police detective, why?"

"Just curious." Clayton wasn't ready to dive into the information he'd gotten from Bill. First, he needed to speak with his sons and decide how much of their family business they wanted to commit to this investigation. It was important to Clayton, because Bill was his friend, but he wouldn't ask his sons to become involved unless they felt it warranted.

And even then, Clayton wasn't sure he wanted either of his sons to be personally involved. He'd lost one son. He didn't intend to lose another.

Chapter Eleven

"Want me to order you something else?" Ed McCoy asked as his wife, Helen, pushed back from the table in the hotel suite.

"No. I'm just not hungry."

When she rose and crossed the sitting area to the bedroom, Ed followed. She opened the sliding doors of the balcony and stepped outside. "I never did like it here."

"Which is why we don't live here."

"I wish Ivy had never moved here."

There it was, the pinprick in her armor. Helen had held it together since they were told Ivy had disappeared. Now, after too many sleepless nights, not enough food and having to hear about and speak about Ivy with strangers, her strength was depleting. "Ah, babe," he reeled her into his arms and enveloped her in a hug.

"She's okay, babe. I swear, she's okay."

"You can't know that," she argued against his shoulder, fighting back tears.

"But I do. I know she's alive and you have to believe me on this."

"I want to," she said and then sobbed. That one, led to many more. It took nearly half an hour for her to cry out her fears, then she clung to him like someone seeking rescue.

Just as Ed opened his mouth to tell her to keep trying, there was a knock at the door. "Wait in the bedroom," he said and hurried inside to peer through the peephole of the door. Mitch Burman stood in the hallway.

Ed cracked open the door. "Can I help you detective?"

"Can we speak inside?" Mitch asked.

Ed considered it, but only briefly, then opened the door. The two officers who'd been flanking either side of the door, were not at their posts. "Where are the guards?"

"I sent them down the hall to watch the exit," Mitch said.

"Oh," Ed moved out of the way for Mitch to enter. Once inside the suite, Mitch looked around. "Is your wife here?"

"I am," Helen stepped into the room. "What can we do for you, Detective?"

"Mrs. McCoy," Mitch acknowledged her and then turned his attention back to Ed. "Sir, we believe your location may have been compromised and so we're moving you to a secure location. If you'll quickly gather up your things, we can be on our way. I have four cars with undercover officers as our escort."

Ed didn't know what to say. He looked at Helen and she extended her hand to him. "Could you excuse us, then, Detective? It shouldn't take long to pack."

"Certainly," Mitch agreed.

Helen held onto Ed's hand until they were standing in the bathroom. She closed the door and leaned in close. "I don't want to go with him."

"Why?"

"Because he won't look at you when he talks to you. His gaze always slides away, and because the Chief of Police told us to stay in this room until he arranges for a protective detail to escort us home. If he'd wanted to change the plan, he would have called or at least told Detective Burman to tell us. Instead, he shows up with nothing more than a "we have reason to believe" line, and not one word about his Chief. No. We shouldn't go with him, Ed."

"Honey, he's with the police." Ed wanted to discount what she'd said, even though his gut told him she was right.

"There are such things as crooked cops."

"But no evidence to suggest he's one."

"My gut tells me this is a bad idea. Let's just get in our car and head home."

Having spent most of his life with Helen, Ed knew she wouldn't play the "feel it in my gut" card, if she wasn't dead serious. Helen's gut feelings were right ninety percent of the time. The fact that his gut was screaming the same, made up his mind.

"Fine, come on. We'll tell the detective."

They returned to the sitting room to discover two more men in the room, both Latin. Ed had never seen either of them before. He didn't acknowledge them and addressed Mitch. "We're not leaving. We'll stay here as the police chief directed. If he wants us to leave, tell him to inform us personally."

Before Mitch could respond one of the other men spoke up. “Mr. McCoy, I’m Carlos Morales, Agent in Charge. We wouldn’t ask you to make this move unless your safety had been compromised. It has, and so it is our duty to move you to a secure location.”

“No,” Ed replied.

“No?” Mitch asked.

“I didn’t studder. Once more – if the Chief feels it is necessary tell him to come see me. Otherwise, please get out of my room.”

“I’m afraid you have no choice, Mr. McCoy,” Morales argued in a placating tone.

“Oh, but I do, sir. Now if you’ll excuse me.” With that, he turned, took Helen’s arm and went into the bedroom.

“Let’s get packed.”

“What about those men?” Helen’s concern was apparent on her face, but to her credit she went right to work, getting luggage from the closet.

Ed grabbed the few things they’d put into the dresser and plopped them onto the bed. When Helen rolled the two carry on pieces of luggage to him, he lifted each onto the bed.

“Do you think they’ll just let us go?” Helen asked softly, cutting a quick glance over her shoulder toward the sitting room.

“We’re not criminals, babe. They can’t stop us.”

“I’m afraid we can, Mr. McCoy.” The Hispanic accented voice had Ed reaching into his luggage as Helen looked back at the man.

“Oh my god, he’s got a gun.”

“So do I.” Ed said and raised his handgun as he turned to face the man calling himself Agent Morales. “No one has to die, you know. You can turn and leave.” He hoped he sounded convincing, even though he felt like his heart was beating loud enough that they all could hear it's pounding pace.

"No, actually, I cannot. Put down your weapon."

"Not going to happen."

"Then your wife can watch you die."

Ed saw the way the man's gun hand rose and he pulled the trigger. The man's weapon went off a split second later and had there been time Ed might have blinked. By the time he realized the man had fired, he also became aware that he'd hit the man in the center of his chest. As the man toppled over Helen grabbed his arm.

He turned to see her on the bed, holding onto her arm, just above the elbow, her face white with fear and pain. Just as Ed reached for her, Mitch ran in with the other agent behind him. "Put the gun down!" Mitch yelled.

Ed turned and trained the gun on Mitch. "The two of you need to leave. Now."

"Can't do that," Mitch held his arms up, slightly and walked closer. "Let's just all calm down."

"I am calm," Ed replied, wanting to look back to make sure Helen was okay, but not about to take his eyes off Mitch.

"We just want to speak with your daughter," the other Latino man spoke up.

That statement put the situation into an entirely new light. Why would the guy make such a statement? Everyone knew Ed and Helen were desperate to find Ivy, so why would an undercover officer, say that?

The only explanation was that these guys weren't who they seemed. Which meant he and Helen were in deep shit. He didn't act on his suspicions with his response. "Clearly, so do I, but neither of us can do that right now, so get out. Both of you."

That's when Mitch made his move and lunged at Ed. Unfortunately for Mitch, Ed was bigger and stronger. Ed clobbered him on the side of the head with the gun and at the same moment Mitch staggered, grabbed him and hauled him in.

With Mitch's arm wrenched up behind him and the gun pointed at his head, Ed faced the last man. "Get out."

The man didn't answer, he just pulled his weapon and fired. It was fast and fluid and before Ed could react, Mitch's blood and brains doused him, and the body went limp. Ed struggled to keep Mitch's body in front of him as a shield as he fired.

He staggered under the weight of Mitch's body and that's when he realized he'd hit the Latino man in the upper right shoulder. The man turned and fled, and Ed let Mitch's body fall. He rushed to Helen who was now sitting on the bed with one of her t-shirts he'd tossed onto the bed, pressed against her arm. It was heavily stained with blood.

Ed gathered his wits, called 911 to report a shooting and request an ambulance, then fished out the card the Chief of Police had given him and placed a call.

It took less time to tell the Chief what had happened than it did for the police to arrive. Ed fully expected to be taken into custody. Instead, they escorted him and Helen to a waiting ambulance and told him the Chief would be paying them a visit soon.

Ed waited until they were in the back of the ambulance and Helen had been checked out before he slid closer to her. "We need to get out of this place."

"How?" she asked. "We're not exactly prepared. All our stuff is at the hotel."

"I know. We'll figure out something."

"I hope so." She was quiet for a minute and then added. "There's more to this tale than we've been told, Eddie. We do need to leave, and we need to find Ivy."

"And that's what we're going to do, babe. I promise."

Silently, Ed added, *I hope,* because he had no clue at all how they were going to achieve that the way things were at present.

Chapter Twelve

Clayton stood on the front porch, one hip hitched up on the railing, sipping coffee and staring out across the valley. The atmosphere in the house had been a little tense since his conversation with Ivy. She pled fatigue and skipped supper. He saw her slip out with Face and return a couple of hours later, but she went straight to her room.

This morning she was up and gone when he rose. He thought about going out to look for her but decided against it. She had a lot to think about and come to terms with. He fully understood her being desperate to contact her parents but knew that would be a mistake. Bill had assured him the McCoys were under police protection and for now that was the best that could be done.

Clayton had a decision to make and needed to talk to his sons before making it. He planned on doing that today. As his thoughts turned to that, the ring of his phone interrupted. He pulled it from his pocket and smiled at the name on the caller ID.

"Good morning, Bill. You're up early. How's it going?"

"I'm doing fine, but others aren't."

"I don't like the sound of that."

"And you'll like what I have to tell you even less. Last night there was a shootout at the hotel where Ivy's parents were staying. A detective was killed, along with a man identified as Carlos Morales, who is thought to work for a drug cartel operating out of Miami. Two police officers who'd been assigned to guard the McCoy's room were found shot dead in their cruiser in the parking deck."

Bill halted and the length of the pause cause a quick prick of unease. "Helen McCoy was shot, but in the arm and is fine. Ed McCoy was not injured but he shot and killed Morales, who claimed to be an undercover agent. A third man, who never gave his name, shot and killed Mitch Burman then tried to shoot McCoy, but was shot himself—not fatally. He fled and police have an APB out to all hospitals in a hundred-mile radius.

"Christ, this thing keeps getting worse, doesn't it?"

"Sadly yes. I know it's pushing the limits, Clayton, but the McCoys need a haven. It's clear that whoever is out to get Ivy now knows who they are and where they live. There's been one attempt on their lives and if I was a betting man, I'd put money on there being another before it's over."

"I agree. Let me talk with the boys and I'll get back to you. And speaking of haven, when are you going to be mended enough to be released? I want to get you and Lena transported and settled as soon as possible."

"I'll check with the doctors and the Chief and let you know the next time we talk."

"Which will be later today, so get on it. Talk to you soon."

"Yes, sir."

Clayton pocketed his phone and stared out for a few moments, then carried his cup into the kitchen. As he refilled it, he called Judson. There was no answer, which meant he was probably already working. With the fresh cup of coffee in hand, he headed out to look for his son.

It was no surprise to find him in the barn, but he was shocked to find Ivy with him, both focused on a mare who was trying to foal and in breach. Ivy had both arms inside the mare, almost the full length, trying to guide the baby out without damaging the mother. Judson had hold of the mare, crooning and stroking, directing Ivy in her efforts.

When the foal slid free it was sudden enough to send Ivy tumbling backwards with the foal.

"We did it!" she was awash in amniotic fluid and blood and her face lit with unmistakable exhilaration. In that moment, Clayton was certain he saw Ivy – the real person, and he liked what he saw.

"Well, look what we have here, a fine new filly."

She looked up at him and grinned. "Judson let me help. It was amazing."

"Indeed," he agreed, then added. "And seeing as how you helped this being into the world, I think it only fitting that you name her."

"Really?" She got to her feet and made room for the mare to get to her foal.

"Really."

She turned, looked at Judson, the mare and then the wobbly legged foal. "Gia."

"Gia?" Judson asked. "What does it mean?"

"God's gift. Is that okay?"

"It's perfect," Clayton replied.

"She's perfect," Ivy looked at the foal again and tears streamed down her face. "A miracle."

She then turned her attention to Judson. "Thank you. I will never forget this. Never."

It was only then Clayton noticed Face lying just outside the stall door, calmly watching. "He watched?"

"He guarded," Ivy corrected. "That's what he does."

"Amazing," Clayton walked over to give Face a rub. "You're something, aren't you?"

"He sure is," Ivy agreed. "And wow, I just realized I must look a mess."

Judson chuckled. "Let's just say you could use a shower."

"Then I guess I'll go do that. Thank you again, Judson. This was one of the most remarkable things I've ever experienced."

"You're welcome."

She eased her way out of the stall, but paused when Judson spoke her name, and looked back.

"You did well," he said. "You'll make a fine vet."

Clayton saw the smile of delight that lit her face. "Thank you. That means the world to me. I'll be back. Come on Face."

Both men watched her and the dog leave, then Clayton turned his attention to Judson. "We need to talk about this situation."

"Then let's talk."

"Walk with me."

They headed out of the barn and took the driveway that led to the string of guest cabins they rented to tourists. At the fork just before the entrance to the cabins, they turned onto the road that led to the equipment sheds.

"Bill Gordon is alive."

Judson stopped dead in his tracks. "Then why was there a memorial?"

"To catch a killer."

"Or a bad cop?"

"That too."

"And?"

Clayton gestured and they fell into step with each other. "Bill finally accepted my offer. As soon as he's fit, he and Lena will leave Florida."

"To work here?"

"I told him I'd set him up wherever he wants. If it's here, that's fine."

"I'm glad he's not dead and bet Ivy will be, too."

"I reckon so. There's more. Bill's death was faked because his partner was the one who pulled the trigger on him. Bill was trying to help discover who his partner was working for or with, and so they staged his death."

"And?"

"And the partner was killed in a shootout – at the hotel where Ivy's parents were staying."

Again, Judson stopped. "Were they killed?"

"No. Her mother caught a round in the arm but is fine. She and her husband are being guarded 24/7 and were taken to a hospital out of the city. We can have them transported in a medivac, but I don't think they should return home."

"Then where should they go?"

"How long are you staying here?"

“I plan on heading back to Wyoming at the end of the month. I want to be there before spring. But I can go sooner if you want to send them there.”

“And what about Ivy?”

“What about her?”

Clayton considered for a few moments before responding. “Will you take her with you?”

“If that’s what she wants, and I imagine she’ll want to be wherever her folks are.”

“I imagine so.”

“Just let me know what you want done. Like I said, I can leave early if they opt for Wyoming or stay here and help you get ready for the spring tourist season.”

“Thanks, son. I appreciate that and I’ll let you know.”

“And who’s going to tell Ivy about her parents?”

Clayton cocked one eyebrow. “Well seeing as how you and Ivy are on friendly terms, I reckon you’d be best suited for that job.”

From the scowl on his son’s face, Clayton got the impression that giving Ivy bad news was not high on Judson’s list of things he’d like to do. But in this situation, he was the best man for the job.

Judson obviously hadn’t noticed, but Clayton saw the way Ivy looked at Judson. She might not be looking at him as a potential mate, but she trusted him, and he’d given her the chance to bring a life into the world. She’d dreamed her entire life of being a vet and today Judson made her feel a bit like one.

Yes, he was most definitely the best choice for delivering the news and dealing with her reactions to it.

“Then I reckon I’ll go deal with that now.”Judson nodded and turned back the way they’d come.

Clayton watched him for a moment then continued toward the equipment shed.

Chapter Thirteen

Judson gathered his thoughts as he walked. He tried to put himself in Ivy's position, imagining how he'd feel if someone gave him the news he was about to give her. It didn't help. He would react in a manner that was bound to differ from her simply because of the differences in their life experiences.

He felt he could expect her to be upset, probably cry and possibly ask him to help her get her parents somewhere safe. So far, her behavior suggested she'd put more energy into saving someone else before she saved herself. It had not gone unnoticed that when she thought Face was going to be shot, she'd put herself between the shooter and her dog.

Judson admired her for that, but still dreaded delivering the bad news. He entered the house and called out her name. When there was no reply, he went in search of her. It wasn't until he looked through the glass of the back door, onto the porch that he saw her. She sat on the steps of the back porch with Face, her ever-present guardian, sitting beside her.

Funny, but until now he'd not noticed the way the highlights in her honey brown hair made her appear more of a blonde when the light was bright. He'd spent little time looking at her, partially because he didn't want her to think he was creepy, and because he'd been focused on the task he was assigned—to keep her safe and deliver her here, to the ranch.

Now, he faced another task, and one he dreaded more than the last.

Ivy sat on the steps of the back porch with Face close enough beside her that he rested against her thigh. His presence was always a comfort. She ran her hand gently over the top of his head.

She was grateful the coffee she spilt hadn't blistered her hands. Had that happened, she might not have been able to help Judson deliver the foal, and even now the excitement and wonder of that filled her with longing to do more, to realize her goal.

Ivy reminded herself to be thankful for what she had now and smiled at the thought. What had Judson said? To change her attitude and practice gratitude? She supposed if there was ever a time in life for her to do that, it was now.

So, she gave thanks that her hands no longer hurt and while red, there were no serious burns. She appreciated the kindness Clayton showed her but thought it odd that he'd be so gentle and caring over spilled coffee and then so dismissive when she wanted to get answers about things that really mattered.

That thought wiped out musings of gratitude and turned her mind to fears. Where had Clayton gotten that photo of Detective Burman, and what did Mitch have to do with someone trying to shoot her?

Obviously, there was something going on she wasn't aware of, and she wondered if Clayton or Judson would tell her if she asked. She'd like to think so, but then she didn't know either of them. They appeared to be decent, honest people, but sometimes people pretend to be what they're not.

She put her hand on Face's neck and reflected on the events that'd led her here. Ivy realized she was fortunate to have people willing to help, but one of the things she needed the most, she didn't know how to make happen.

What she needed was to know her parents would be safe. That need was great enough to have her pushing her hesitancy to the background. She turned to go back inside and found Judson leaning one shoulder against the door frame. He stepped out onto the porch.

"Take a walk with me?" he asked.

Ivy was surprised, and a little apprehensive. His expression was somber. Still, she couldn't say no. "Okay. Can Face come?"

"Absolutely."

They headed out across the back lawn. Built on a hill, the house boasted of a large yard, with an enormous fire pit in the back, surrounded by sturdy wooden chairs. Judson skirted around the area to a well-worn path of dirt and flat rocks that led down to the lake.

Judson tried to gather his words so that when he gave the news, it came through as gentle as possible. It took him until he reached the cleared beach on the lakeshore. In summer, guests kayaked, fished, swam and soaked up the sun here. At present, the air was too cool for swimming or boating, so he and Ivy had the place to themselves.

He jammed his hands in his pockets and blew out a slow breath before turning his head to look at her. "Dad got some news."

"About?"

"Bill Gordon."

He could see confusion in her expression but to her credit she remained silent, waiting for him to continue. "He's alive, Ivy."

"Alive?" Shock gave way to relief, and then happiness. "Thank God."

She'd make a terrible card player because every emotion was clear on her face. Now confusion set back in. As soon as it did, Face edged closer to her. "I don't understand."

Judson explained, relaying the information his father provided. She was quiet for a few seconds. "And he's going to be okay?"

"He is. As soon as he's released, he and his wife, Lena, will be leaving Florida. Bill's taking another job."

"Where?"

"We'll get to that later if you don't mind. The point is, he's okay."

"And the police think there's a traitor in their midst?"

"That's my understanding."

Ivy caught her bottom lip between her teeth for a few seconds, then looked at him again. "Then maybe they should look at detective Burman."

"What makes you say that?"

"Because he's the only one who knew about me other than Bill. He knew Bill checked in on me every evening on his way home. He had to know Bill would show up at my house that day."

"I'm sure others in the department knew about Bill checking in on you."

"Maybe, but Mitch Burman was the only one to ever come to my house."

Judson nodded. “Well, that may be true, but Burman isn’t going to factor into this much now.”

“Why not?”

“He’s dead.”

“Dead? How did he die?”

Having told more than one person a loved one was gone; Judson had learned that people tended to stop listening as soon as they heard the news. So, he practiced a technique that often worked. “I’m going to need you to promise that you’ll let me finish what I have to say before you ask any questions. Can you do that.”

“Sure.”

“Good. Detective Burman was killed in a shootout at a hotel in Florida – specifically in the suite where your parents were staying. Another man, claiming to be a detective was also killed and your mother suffered a superficial gunshot to her left arm. A third man escaped after being wounded by your father. Your mother was treated and is doing fine. She and your father are in the same hospital where Bill Gordon is being cared for.”

He waited a beat and then asked. “Any questions?”

“Lots.”

“Fire away.”

“Will Bill be safe once he leaves the hospital? Will my parents?”

“We’re going to try and make it so.”

“And how will you do that?”

“As I understand it, once Bill is released, he’s officially retiring and taking another job, with a private security company. He and his wife, Lena, will be selling their house in Florida and moving.”

“And my parents?”

“We’ll offer them a place to stay until this situation is resolved.”

“You will? Why would you do that?”

“Because it’s the right thing to do.”

What happened next, was the last thing he expected. Ivy flew at him, wrapping her arms around his neck and plastering herself to him in a tight hug. “Oh god.” He could tell she was crying by her voice, and a moment later, by the way her body trembled and quaked. Face whined and she lowered one arm to pull the dog close to them.

“Thank you,” she managed to get out.

Judson held her close, letting her cry and when she finished and pulled back, she looked him in the eyes. “I’ll never be able to repay you, but I’ll never stop trying.”

“You don’t have to repay anything.”

“But I do,” she argued. “You saved me and now are saving my parents.”

Judson heard the sincerity in her voice and saw the truth of what she spoke in her eyes. Her gratitude didn’t surprise him, but his own actions did.

Without a thought for the consequences, he cupped her face with his hand, leaned in and kissed her softly.

Shocked at his own behavior, he ended the kiss and was delivered another surprise, this time from her. She reached behind his neck and pulled him back. This time the kiss was infused with emotion, and he didn’t think it was all gratitude. There was passion there and it awakened an answering desire inside him.

A desire that wasn’t wise.

Then why didn’t he break away?

That's a question he didn't want to answer because it revealed something about himself, namely that he was attracted to Ivy McCoy.

Chapter Fourteen

Ivy heard voices as she left the guest suite and headed for the kitchen with Face by her side. After the kiss the day before, Judson had made himself scarce and given her a new worry. Had she made a big mistake? Maybe she shouldn't have kissed him, maybe his chaste kiss was nothing more than one of comfort and she had completely misread it and now he thought she wanted more from him.

She wasn't sure what to think, but if he avoided her today it would be a clue that pointed to her screwing up and making him uncomfortable. She hoped that wouldn't be the case. She'd logged onto the internet on her laptop, using an incognito browser window. Two hours later she'd amassed quite a store of information she wanted to share. Now, she turned her mind to the topic to occupy her thoughts and keep from obsessing about the kiss and her parents' safety. Needing more distraction, she followed the sound of the voices.

As she made her way down the long hallway that led to the other side of the house, she saw Judson leaning against a door frame, listening to someone inside the room. He noticed her approach and she stopped. "Am I intruding?"

"No, Ivy, it's fine. What can I do for you?"

His tone was pleasant enough despite the lack of a smile on his face. "Tell me how I can be sure my parents will be safe."

"Come on," he motioned to her and when she reached him, he gestured toward the room beyond the door frame.

"Can Face come, too?"

"Of course, he can," Clayton's voice came from inside the room.

She walked in to find Clayton standing behind a desk with his hands on the top of the desk chair. "I understand your concern, Ivy," he said.

"Thank you, and no offense, but understanding doesn't do much to keep my folks safe."

"No, it doesn't. And it's something we need to discuss. Please have a seat."

She looked around and at a gesture from Judson, took a seat on the sofa. Face sat at her feet while Judson took a seat on the opposite end of the couch.

"First, let me introduce you to my sons, Calvin, Ellis and Brady." Clayton said, then added as he sat and typed on his keyboard. "I'm putting them on the television."

Sure enough the flatscreen mounted above the fireplace mantel lit to display a Skype meeting with three windows showing three very handsome men.

"Can you still hear me?" Clayton asked.

"Yep," one of the men responded.

"Ok," Clayton gestured to Ivy. "This is Ivy McCoy."

"Pleased to meet you Ms. McCoy, but sorry it's under these circumstances," the same man responded. "I'm Cal, the good looking one, and second oldest."

"You wish," another of them men spoke. "I'm Brady, obviously the handsome one, and the next to the youngest."

"Sorry but I'm the most handsome and the smartest," the third man said. "I'm Ellis."

"It's nice to meet all of you," Ivy responded. "And I thank you all for your kindness."

Clayton addressed Ivy. "We've been discussing your situation and it's unanimous. We'll commit the weight of resources of Blackstone Security to the apprehension of the man who ordered Bill Gordon's death and the man who tried to kill you. We suspect it's the same man in both cases."

"That's…" she paused, looked from Clayton to the men on the screen and then Judson. "That's very generous, but I have no clue what it means. What exactly is Blackstone Security?"

"It's part of Blackstone Holdings and its purpose is to help people in need."

"You mean housing and food, that sort of thing?"

"No, he means kidnapping, hostages and other nastiness," Ellis answered the question.

"So, people hire you for that?"

"No." This time it was Clayton who responded. "We never take money from people we're trying to save."

"Then why do you do it, if I may ask?"

"Because someone should."

She saw no need to ask more at this time. "That's very commendable and I'm sure there are a lot of people who owe you a huge debt of gratitude. Not many people are willing to help others unless there's some reward or advantage to themselves."

"Sadly, so," Clayton agreed. "Where we are now, is step one, which is to get Bill Gordon, his wife and your folks to safety. I'm waiting to hear from Bill where he and Helen want to go. To the ranch in Wyoming, where Cal is now and Judson calls home, or here where I can give them a place to stay. Where your parents go will be their choice, but we will get them to safety as promised."

"They'll want to go home," she said, hoping she didn't sound ungrateful.

"Home isn't an option if they want to be safe. With your permission, I'll reach out to them with the offer and then have Bill speak with them to assure that we are who we say and not someone trying to fool them into more peril."

"Thank you, Mr. Blackstone. I don't know how I'll ever repay this kindness, but I'll find a way."

"No repayment required. Now, once we have everyone moved to where we can be assured they will remain safe, we start the search for the man responsible. For that, we'll need to ask you a lot of questions."

"About what?"

"Everything that happened from the moment you saw the dead body," Judson said, and she finally looked in his direction. "You may have overlooked something, something you saw or heard – something that if you think more about it, may come to mind."

"To try and find the man responsible, correct?"

"Yes," Judson replied.

"Then I may already have something for you."

"What?"

"Can I run get my laptop?"

"I thought we told you to stay off that?"

Judson's tone irked her, and she retorted faster and sharper than intended. "I'm not an idiot, you know. I didn't log into anything and used an incognito browser window."

"I stand corrected," Judson said as his brothers laughed. "Go get your laptop."

Ivy hurried to her room, grabbed the laptop and headed back. It wasn't until she reached the door, she realized that Face hadn't followed. She found him sitting with his head on Judson's knee, getting scratched and looking like he was in doggy-bliss.

Before she let herself travel down the *why can't I find a man who would love Face like that, and me too* path, she hurried inside and opened the laptop, talking as she did so. "There are videos starting to surface on social media. Some of the scene where I saw the murdered man, a couple of the aftermath of Bill's shooting and the police on the scene and of a press conference – the one my parents attended."

She looked up to find the others watching her. "Okay, I guess it sounds crazy to you, but I think there are clues in these videos."

Clayton gave her what she interpreted as a placating smile. "They may well be a nugget, but it's also as possible that we could do nothing more than waste time. watching videos in an attempt to find them."

"But I've already done that," she argued. "I can show you."

"Please do," Judson spoke up.

Ivy shot him a grateful smile and queued up the first video. "This one was shot at the press conference, probably with a cell phone." She turned the laptop around for them to view. "As you can see, it clearly shows Mitch Burman and a handsome Latin man who approaches and stands close to him talking. What is interesting is coming up."

She turned up the sound so everyone could hear a male voice saying, “What the hell is Rafael Martinez doing in Orlando? Doesn’t the King of Cocaine prefer Miami?”

Ivy quickly turned the laptop and paused the video on Mitch and Martinez. “This man, the one identified as Rafael Martinez is the man who tried to shoot me. That must be the man who ordered the hit on Bill, and he’s obviously connected to Mitch. I’m no investigator, but it seems to me there’s a connection that should be investigated.”

“You’re right,” Cal replied and then addressed his dad. “When can we get Bill and the McCoy family moved to a more secure location?”

“I’ll talk with Bill today.”

“Just let me know what you need from me.”

“Will do, son. Talk to you later.”

“Later, bro,” Judson added.

“Good to meet you, Ms. McCoy,” Cal said. “Talk to you all soon.”

“Looks like I need to make some calls,” Clayton said when the screen went dark on the television, indicating Cal had signed off.

“We’ll get out of your hair.” Judson stood, then looked from Face to his father. “How about I take Ivy for a ride? She said she’d like to get back on a horse.”

“Sounds like a good idea.”

Ivy looked at Judson in surprise. “Are you sure you have time?”

“I’ll make time. Come on.”

She rose to follow him from the room as he put his hand on Face’s neck. “You too, big guy. Let’s go run.”

Face didn’t have to be asked twice. He bounded up, tail wagging and the dog equivalent of a grin on his face.

They headed outside and started walking toward the barn. Ivy smiled as Face ran ahead of them sniffing and exploring. “Is Cal your younger or older brother?”

“Younger,” Judson answered. “He was the middle child with me the oldest and Jack the youngest.”

“Would it be too painful to talk about Jack?”

“No, I don’t suppose. What do you want to know?”

“What did he do – in life I mean?”

“He went to work for the family business last year after he left the military.”

“He was in the military? Which branch?”

“Marines, like the rest of us.”

“You were in the Marines?”

“Twenty years.”

“Seriously?”

“Yep.”

“What did you do?”

“ACE.”

“Ace? What’s that?”

“Marines Compartmented Elements.”

“I’ve never heard of that. What is it?”

“Ever hear of Delta Force?”

“Yes, of course. There must be a million romance books with heroes who are Delta Force. You did that?”

“I did.”

“So, you’re a genuine badass.” She’d not admit it for a hundred dollars, but she found that exciting and sexy as well.

"You've read too many romance books."

Ivy sniffed. "One cannot read too many romance books."

Judson gave her the side-eye. "No?"

"Single and no time to date – not to mention no one asking, so no, I get my thrills where I can find them."

"I don't believe that for a minute."

"No? Why?"

"No woman who looks like you gets ignored."

"Oh, now you're just being flattering to make me feel better."

"I don't do that."

His tone told her more than his words, and she believed him. Maybe it was relief that his family was going to help her parents get to safety along with Bill Gordon, but at the moment she felt better than she had in a long time. She felt as if hope had been restored to her life.

It made her almost giddy, and a little careless because she spoke without thinking. "You'd make a good romance book hero."

Judson barked a laughed. "Not in a million years. I don't have what it takes."

"Oh yes you do."

"Name one thing that qualifies me as a hero."

"You saved me and Face from being shot at the bus stop," she held up one hand and counted off one finger at a time. "Then you save us when those men followed us to the ranch, and you got the manager at the diner to let Face come in, and –" she paused, not quite sure if she could say what was on her mind.

"And what?" he prodded.

"And you are a very good kisser."

Judson stopped and looked at her. "Ivy McCoy, are you flirting with me?"

"Well, obviously I'm doing a sorry job if you have to ask, Judson Blackstone."

This time he smiled. "I think you're doing just fine."

"And I think you'd make a good romantic hero."

He just shook his head and resumed walking.

Chapter Fifteen

Rafael Martinez saw his lieutenant Juan Carlos Lopez headed across the dining room toward him with a curvaceous blonde woman beside him. Her outfit told Rafael several things. First, she had no class, and second, she was here to try and seduce him. No widow showed up anywhere wearing a skin-tight white leather skirt, red leather thigh high boots, and a red halter top.

No, indeed. This woman was on the hunt. He didn't care what her motives were. He'd promise her the moon if necessary and deal with her after he got what he wanted.

As soon as they reached Rafael's table, he stood and extended his hand to the woman. "Mrs. Burman, my condolences for the loss of your husband. I'm sure you're devastated and appreciate you taking the time to meet with me. Please, sit. Would you care for a drink?"

"Thank you," she sniffed as she sat "And yes, a skinny martini would be lovely."

Rafael nodded to Juan Carlos, who hurried off. It didn't go unnoticed the way Barbie faked a little sob and sniffled. Rafael was certain the oversized dark sunglasses she hadn't bothered to remove were left on to cover the fact she shed no tears.

That didn't surprise him. Burman had been married to his current wife for less than a year. She was one of the primary reasons Burman was eager to work for Rafael. Americans liked to refer to women such as her as "high maintenance". Having now gotten a good look at her, that was obvious.

There wasn't much authentic about her. The slight growth of dark roots belied any chance of her being able to claim herself as a natural blonde. As a matter of fact, the word natural would never be used in a description of Barbie Burman. No woman as thin as Barbie, had breasts that large. Then there was the fact that her face had little movement, giving testimony to regular Botox injections.

What topped it all off were her lips. They were so full of whatever women had injected into their lips to make them plump, they looked almost comical. She removed her glasses, placed them on the table, and heaved a little sigh.

"I still can't believe he's gone. I – I don't know what I'm going to do."

That's when Rafael saw the first genuine thing about her, the gleam of avarice as she cut her eyes at his watch and the large diamond and gold ring he wore on the middle finger of his right hand.

Now I have you. He smiled and extended his right hand across the table to place it on top of hers. "If there's anything I can do…"

"You're so kind." Her voice took on a bit of a whine, something that made him want to grit his teeth. He released her hand and picked up his drink to take a sip.

"Your drink, Mrs. Burman," Juan Carlos returned to the table.

It annoyed Rafael that she neglected to thank Juan Carlos, but it didn't surprise him. Mitch had complained more than once about his demanding, spoiled wife. According to him, the only thing she was good for was making other men jealous and giving a world class blow job.

Rafael wasn't impressed with either, but then he didn't need a woman to make people envious and being talented at fellatio wasn't unusual for women who were only looking for what Americans called a "sugar daddy."

"I hope your husband's death benefits will be sufficient for your living expenses," Rafael decided to set his plan into motion.

"Hardly." Her voice lost its whine and became shrill, the syllables a sharp staccato.

"I'm sorry to hear that. Perhaps I can help."

The expression that came on her face told him more clearly than words he'd hooked her. "Oh, Mr. Martinez, that would be such a blessing. Are you sure?"

He had no doubt she'd asked the question to secure a promise from him. Now the uppermost thing on Barbie's mind would be walking out of the private dining room with a guarantee that her lifestyle was about to improve.

"Absolutely," he assured her with a smile.

"You're an angel and if there's any way I can repay your kindness…" The look she gave him was an invitation, but one he would not accept. Still, he could use her interest to his advantage, as planned.

Rafael smiled. "There is one thing, and perhaps it is silly, but I'd love to find the woman he and Detective Gordon were protecting, you know, the woman Mitch was having the affair with."

"The what?"

"Oh, I apologize. I thought you were aware. Please, forgive me. I should not have—"

"He was screwing that woman?"

"I'm afraid so."

"That bastard." She lifted her glass and downed the contents then looked around. "Hey, you—" she barked at Juan Carlos who stood near the door. "Get me another."

Then she turned her attention to Rafael. "Well, at least I don't have to try and mourn the bastard. I can't believe he cheated on me. His pension isn't going to be shit. If it wasn't what he made doing security work for you, I'd have left him months ago. Shit. That bitch really screwed things up."

"And I fear she may have had something to do with his death, but I won't know until I find her. If only I had a lead, then perhaps I could help bring her to justice and give you closure."

Barbie stared at him for a long moment, and he could almost hear the gears turning in her head. Finally, she spoke. "Well, I know one of the detectives Mitch worked with—Kyle Howard. He always had the hots for me, so I could probably reach out to him—tell him I'd like to have a drink and talk about Mitch or something. Maybe he's heard something."

"That would be incredibly kind. When do you think you might be able to do that?"

"Well, I suppose I could give him a call today."

"Yes, please do. And if you manage to get any information from him, give me a call."

He noticed the look of suspicion, and quickly added. "After all, we do need to get things set up for your assistance. I'll need your banking information in order to wire you the funds."

"Oh, I don't want anything going into my and Mitch's joint account," she quickly responded. "Taxes, you know. And I don't want anyone asking questions. Isn't there another way?"

"Would cash be preferable?"

"Well, I don't know. How much cash are we talking about?"

"More than you can imagine if you can get the location of Ivy McCoy."

That's when Barbie dropped the pretense of being a grieving widow. "I can imagine a lot, Mr. Martinez, so tell me what number you have in mind."

"A million if you lead me to Ivy McCoy."

Her eyes narrowed and the long false fingernails of her right hand tapped on the tabletop. Juan Carlos appeared with another drink for her, set it down and retreated.

As before, she neglected to show appreciation, picked up the glass and sucked down half the drink. "A million down-payment and a quarter of a million per year for the next four years," she said.

"That's a considerable sum."

She shrugged. "It takes time to … bounce back from the loss of a spouse."

"Yes, I imagine so. Very well, it's a deal. If, and pay attention, if you deliver the location of Ivy McCoy."

"Oh, I'll deliver," she said and tossed back the rest of her drink.

Rafael pulled a cell phone from his pocket and slid it across the table. "There's one number programmed in. When you have the information, call and we will arrange to meet and finalize our arrangement."

Barbie slid the phone into her purse, put on her sunglasses and stood. "I'll be talking to you soon, Mr. Martinez."

"I shall look forward to it." He didn't bother to rise. There was no need for politeness now. He had her.

And as soon as she delivered what he wanted, he'd send her to join her husband.

Barbie Burman handed her parking stub to the attendant and stepped out onto the sidewalk to light a cigarette. She knew, without question that Rafael Martinez was a dangerous man, and a smart one. Mitch had told her all about Rafael and his operation. She knew he'd amassed hundreds of millions of dollars in drug money and had a loyal Marines to protect him.

Not that she wanted to harm him. No. She wanted a chunk of his money, and she'd take him as well. He'd probably be a lot better in bed than Mitch. But he also looked like a man who'd not think twice about slapping a woman around and she wasn't about to have her looks destroyed, so she'd forget about seduction and focus on being an asset to him and get her share of his fortune.

She pulled out her cell phone and placed a call to Kyle Howard. He answered on the second ring. "Detective Howard."

"Hi, Kyle, it's Barbie." She tried to sound weak, sad and still a little sexy.

"Barbie, hi. How are you?"

She could hear the squeak of his chair and then sounds from people in the office. "Hanging in as best I can. I was wondering if maybe you could stop by after work. There are some of Mitch's things – his fishing gear, golf clubs—that sort of thing and I need to get rid of them. I remember him mentioning that you are a sportsman, so thought maybe you'd like to take a look at them."

"Ah, well, ah, I–uh, I guess. I mean I don't really need—"

"And I could really use a friend right now. Someone who knew and loved Mitch, you know?"

"Oh, well, yeah, I get that and—and sure, I'll stop by after work."

"Oh Kyle, thank you. Would you like to stay for dinner?"

"Uh, yeah, sure, that'd be great."

"Wonderful. See you later."

"Sure thing."

Barbie smiled and slid the phone into her purse. She saw her car being driven to the curb and tossed her cigarette into the street. She had a couple of stops to make before going home. Kyle was going to get one nice surprise when it came time for dessert.

Barbie au naturel. In her book, that was the one dessert no man could refuse.

Chapter Sixteen

Judson had just rinsed out his coffee mug when Ivy walked into the kitchen. "Your dad said that Bill is going to be released in a few days and has decided to come here for a while so he can learn about the business while he's convalescing."

"Yep." Judson placed his mug in the dish drainer and turned toward her. It came as a shock that as soon as he looked at her, he felt a bolt of heat that warmed his entire body. Today her hair was down, cascading over her shoulders in a shining wave and for the first time since he met her, the shadows beneath her eyes were gone.

She was stunning.

Judson shoved the rush of desire aside. This wasn't the time or place. "I'm drenching horses this morning if you're interested in helping. And after, I'm going to start working with the horse we brought up from Florida."

"I'm definitely interested. Are you ready to start now?"

"Good a time as any. Where's Face?"

"With your father. Clayton said he wanted to take a ride and invited Face to accompany him."

"He and Face are becoming friends."

"They sure are. Let me put my hair up and I'll be ready."

"I'll meet you outside."

As she dashed back out of the room, Judson watched, thinking about his reaction to her. If she'd been a woman he met in a bar or a restaurant, he may have already made a move on her, but she was different and the way they met was far from ordinary.

Ivy wasn't over the fear, even though she tried hard to conquer it. He was willing to bet that before they made it to the barn, she'd be asking about the plans to get her parents moved somewhere safe. Hopefully, once that happened, she'd be able to relax. Until then, he'd try to keep her busy – and keep his hands off her.

It was the second part that concerned him.

He turned and went outside and a few seconds later, she walked out. With her hair pulled back into a long braid, wearing a pair of faded jeans and a t-shirt, she looked like a sexy country girl. His weakness.

Judson shoved aside thoughts that tried to take root and gestured to her. "Okay, let's go."

"What's your ranch in Wyoming like?" she asked as they walked.

"Beautiful. Quiet. Cold as heck in winter and perfect in summer. Clean water, clean air and a night sky that will take your breath away."

"Lots of snow?"

"Sometimes. You can see the milky way at night. It's breath-taking."

"I've seen pictures online, but I'd love to see it in person. And I miss snow."

"Come for a visit and we'll take a ride in the snow and star watch at night."

"That sounds wonderful. Are you sure you wouldn't mind?"

Judson almost passed the question off with a glib response, but at the last instant his mouth appeared to have developed a mind of its own and words he hadn't intended to speak, poured out.

"I'd love to have you spend time with me there, Ivy."

She stopped and gaped at him. "Seriously? I'm not driving you crazy?"

He realized the innocence with which she asked the question and could have simply said that she wasn't a bother, but the attraction he felt for her overrode reason and he reached out to take her hand and pull her to him. "Would it offend you if I said yes?"

The hurt expression that came on her face quickly disappeared as she realized the meaning of his question. "It would thrill me."

"Then, yes, you're driving me crazy."

"I think that's the nicest thing anyone has said to me in a long, long time."

"I can think of a few more, if you're in need."

She smiled and leaned in, standing on tiptoe to give him a soft kiss. “You have no idea how much need I’m in, Judson Blackstone.”

“Well, we’ll have to see what we can do about that, won’t we?”

She smiled and pulled away. “I sure hope so. But first, horses to drench. And I’ve never done that so this will be a great learning experience.”

“You’re serious about becoming a vet, aren’t you?”

“Absolutely. I love animals. When I was a kid I had a dozen pets. Dogs and cats, birds, guinea pigs, hamsters, a lamb, a goat, an adorable donkey and my own pony. It was fabulous.”

“Your parents must have been very indulgent.”

“They were wonderful.” The smile that’d risen on her face faded. “When do you think I’ll be able to see my folks?”

“Soon.”

“How soon?”

“I don’t know, Ivy. As soon as we can arrange it.” The moment the words were out of his mouth he regretted the sharp tone of his voice. “I’m sorry, it’s just that I don’t have a day and time. When I do, you’ll be the first to know. Until then, all I can tell you is they’re in protective custody of the Orlando Police Department and we have Blackstone operatives on the scene as well.”

She was quiet for a few moments, then asked. “So, why can’t I call and talk to them?”

Judson stopped. Why had no one thought about that? “There’s no reason I can think of.”

“Then I can? Are you positive?”

“I’ll make sure of it, but right now I have to take care of these horses and I could use some help.”

"Then pick up the pace, big boy." She grinned and marched ahead with a bounce in her step that had her long braid swinging.

Judson smiled and picked up his pace to catch up. With luck, he hadn't overstepped, but even if he had, he'd find a way to ensure that Ivy got to talk with her parents before the sun set on another day.

*****

"It's completed sir."

Rafael looked up from the report on his laptop to the man standing in the doorway. "And the login credentials?"

"All the pertinent account information has been texted to you, sir."

"Excellent. Thank you, Miguel."

"Yes, sir." Miguel nodded his head and backed out of the doorway.

Rafael picked up his phone and accessed his text messages. As he read the text containing the information, he paused to open a browser window on his laptop and keyed in the site address.

As promised the login information he'd been provided opened a new profile for his review. He smiled as he stared at the screen.

Rafael was a man who always had a multilayer plan. While he had no doubt Barbie Burman would do everything she could to get him the information he wanted, he wasn't going to do as the Americans liked to say and put all his eggs into one basket. If she secured the information he wanted, it would be only part of the plan.

Another aspect of the plan was already enacted. One thing he learned early on was that perception had a major impact upon people's lives, and if you can control perception, you can control the people involved.

With that in mind, he had his people hack Ivy McCoy's social media to determine if any of her family interacted with her online. What they discovered was that she only had a Facebook page and hadn't been active on it for nearly a year. There was little on the page aside from photos of her dog, and some of herself with the beast, or with friends.

That revelation worked to his advantage, and he immediately instructed his team to set up an Instagram account for her. She was in the age range that favored that particular social platform.

Along with setting up the account, he ordered all her photos from Facebook to be downloaded and altered.

Now he accessed her profile and felt a measure of delight at what met his eyes. Where once she was alone in photos, on the new Instagram page, she appeared with him. The same thing applied to photos of her and friends or her with her dog. Rafael was inserted into every image.

He'd also had new ones created by posing for photos with a woman who matched Ivy's size and shape. Then he had the woman's face replaced with Ivy's. The result was a profile with many photos of Ivy.

One delighted him. It showed him down on one knee, to all appearance, proposing to her. The artists had done a magnificent job making it appear that the woman being proposed to was, in fact, Ivy.

The final step was to have fake text messages created and sent to him from her. That took his people a bit of time because it required hacking into her phone account and building a new text message history. The texts were intimate, loving and contained more photos of the two of them.

All in all, it painted a convincing story of a couple in love. All that was left was to discover the whereabouts of Ivy's parents and contact them. Rafael was confident he could sell the tale he'd created and find out where Ivy McCoy was hiding.

As he contemplated his upcoming performance, his phone rang. Barbie Burman.

"Hello there, beautiful lady," he greeted her.

"Hello yourself, handsome," she responded in a flirtatious tone. "I have something you want."

"Is that so?"

"Indeed."

"Then tell me."

"Hmmm, no, I think this needs to be done in person. And when we meet, there's a little matter of payment you need to have arranged. I'm ready to get out of this state and am thinking New York or Los Angeles. It won't be cheap, and I do like luxurious surrounding, so…"

Rafael felt anger flare. This bitch had crossed a line, thinking she could extort him. He tamped down the anger, keeping his tone congenial. "Indeed. Then we should meet in person. Somewhere …special. How do you feel about having dinner with me on my yacht?"

"I feel just fine about it as long as you have a cashier's check as my dessert."

"Darling, I promise, this will be the most eventful night of your life. I'll have my driver pick you up at nine."

"I'll be waiting."

"Until then." Rafael ended the call and considered his next move. He needed whatever information Barbie had secured, if indeed she had. But he didn't intend to pay her a dime. She'd get her reward, but it wouldn't be what she expected.

That thought prompted others. He felt the first stirring of excitement as dark imaginings filled his mind, the kind of thoughts that made a man who found the taking of a life to be the most delicious aphrodisiac of all. He made a mental note to have his people secure several young girls for the after party. Barbie was just the appetizer, and his appetite would require far more.

Chapter Seventeen

"Well, hello there buddy," Ivy turned from the mirror as Face bounded into the bathroom. She'd heard people say that dogs don't have real expressions. The look on Face's sweet face would prove them a liar. He was as giddy as a puppy, practically dancing.

"I'm guessing you had a very good time with Mr. Clayton, eh?" Ivy sat on the edge of the tub and hugged Face, who leaned in toward her and licked her face.

She laughed and he bounded off. Already he and Clayton had become friends. That wasn't a surprise. Face always seemed to know who needed consoling, befriending or protecting. She wondered which category Clayton fell into. Consoling would be her guess. After all, he'd lost a son six months ago. That's not something a parent would recover from quickly.

After combing her hair, she dressed in clean jeans, and a long-sleeved t-shirt. While the days had been nice, the evenings were chilly, and it would only be a few hours before sunset. Since she'd left her shoes on the steps of the back porch, she padded in sock feet through the house and nearly collided with Clayton as he stepped out of his room, followed by Face.

"Oops! Sorry," she apologized. "Almost ran into you."

"No problem," he gave her a smile. "Judson mentioned that you wanted to speak with your parents."

"Very much."

"Well, you can. In person. They'll be here this weekend. We're sending a plane for them and the Gordons. Since they've become friends of sorts, they decided they'd all stay here until spring. Wyoming isn't a picnic in the winter, and Florida probably isn't the safest location."

"Oh, thank you!" Without considering her actions, she threw her arms around Clayton. "Thank you so much, Mr. Blackstone."

"It's Clayton, and you're welcome."

She released him and he gestured for her to accompany him.

"Is there anything I can do to help before they all get here?"

Clayton waited for her to enter the kitchen ahead of him. "We're going to get the cabins closest to the house tidied up for them. Being close to one another, they'll have company nearby and be close to the main house. I'll get Dianne, the housekeeper to get things squared away."

"I'll do it."

"No, I have staff to—"

"Please? They're my parents and Mr. Bill is – well, he almost died trying to take care of me. It's the least I can do. Please?"

"Please what?" Judson asked as he entered the kitchen from the back door.

"I asked your dad if I could get the cabins ready for my folks and the Gordons."

"Drenching horses wasn't work enough for you?"

"Are you kidding? That was amazing. It's almost like they're getting candy."

Judson and Clayton both laughed. "Yeah, they don't mind it at all."

"You get 'em all taken care of?" Clayton asked.

"Sure did. I was going to grab a sandwich and then start working with the stallion."

"How 'bout you and Ivy get some lunch and tackle the cabins. I'd like to spend some time with the stallion before you start working with him."

"If that's what you want."

"Only if I'm not stepping on your toes."

"Couldn't happen. And I'm happy to help." He looked at Ivy. "Want to grab some food first?"

"Yes, please. I could eat a buffalo."

The men laughed, which puzzled her. "Why is that funny?"

"You'd know if you'd ever tasted buffalo," Clayton said, then headed for the door. He stopped when he reached it. "You taking Face with you?"

"You want him to go with you?" Ivy asked.

"I'm curious to see how he is around the stallion. If you don't mind."

"Of course not. He obviously loves being with you."

"Then let's go, big guy," Clayton said to Face.

Face looked from him to Ivy. She smiled and gave him a rub. “It’s okay buddy, go with Mr. Clayton and have fun.”

He bounded to the door and off they went.

Ivy watched them with a smile on her face, then turned to Judson. “I guess it’s just us, big guy. Anything we need to take with us? Cleaning supplies, clean sheets or …”. She let the question trail off.

“The cabins are stocked with everything. All that’s needed is elbow grease.”

“Then lead the way.”

They headed down a small, graveled drive that branched off the road to the main house. As they walked, she asked questions about working with horses. Judson answered every question and didn’t seem to mind her asking. “Here we are,” he said as the path through the trees opened into a small clearing.

“Oh, it’s beautiful,” Ivy stopped and looked.

Two wooden houses stood in the clearing, each with a wraparound porch, dormers in the roof and inlaid rocks forming a path to the front door from the driveway. In between the two houses was a sizeable area that housed a rocked firepit, six weathered Adirondack chairs circling the fire and behind that, a gazebo with a picnic table.

“Your family doesn’t do anything halfway.”

“What would be the point of that?”

She looked at him and could see the love he had for this place shining in his eyes. “Did you grow up here?”

“We all did.”

“I bet it was a good place to grow up.”

“It was.”

“Why did you leave?”

He shrugged. “Seemed like the thing to do. This family’s had its share of hard knocks over the years, but we’ve been luckier than most. Despite losing Mom and our sister, we had a happy childhood. Dad served our country, and it seemed like something I should do. Give a little back.”

“And your brothers felt that way, too?”

“Every one of them. Come on.”

He led the way to the cabin on their right. It wasn’t locked. That surprised Ivy and her surprise bothered her a bit. She’d grown up in a place where the doors were rarely locked. When had she become so mistrustful that she had to live behind locked doors?

Judson stepped aside for her to enter. Ivy walked in and looked around. “It’s really nice,” she said as she wandered through the living area. There was a large fireplace with a flatscreen television mounted on the brick above the mantle, deep cushioned furniture, plush warm rugs and windows that flanked the fireplace, providing a view of the expanse of grass that led to the cover of trees.

A table large enough to seat six people sat behind the sofa and beyond that a long bar which separated the living area from the kitchen. It was the kind of place Ivy would have liked to call home.

“This place is as neat as can be,” she commented as she wandered down the hall. There were three bedrooms and two baths, one clearly a master suite, and the other Jack and Jill arrangement with the second bathroom between the bedrooms with access from each.

“What is there for us to do?”

“Make the bed in the master, put out towels, make sure there’s plenty of firewood. We’ll find out what they want from the store and have someone make a run for supplies tomorrow or on Saturday morning. They won’t be here until afternoon.”

"Okay, then let's get to it."

It took only minutes to get towels from the linen closet and place them in the bathroom. Ivy did that while Judson stripped the bedspread and extra blanket from the bed. She walked in just as he was shaking out the fitted sheet.

She helped and in just a couple of minutes the bed had fresh sheets and pillowcases. Just as Judson rounded the bed with an armload of sheets to go into the laundry, she grabbed one of the pillows off the bed and walloped him.

"Oh, hell no," he dropped the sheets and made a dive for the bed.

Ivy went after him as he grabbed a pillow and when he turned and retaliated, she squealed and evaded, running to the other side of the bed.

Judson pursued and for a few moments they swung the pillows at one another, laughed and taunted. Ivy ditched the pillow and made a break for the living room. Judson caught her, lifted her off the floor and swung her around.

Ivy laughed, squealed and squirmed until he released her. She turned toward him, brushed the hair from her face and put her hands on her hips. "Okay, big boy, you're asking for trouble."

"Am I?" He closed in on her.

She stepped back, ran into a chair and stumbled backward. He caught her and for a moment they simply stood there staring at each other. "Judson—" she didn't know what she wanted to say. Well, maybe she did, but she wasn't about to tell him she wanted him. She'd had enough rejection to last a very long time.

"What?"

"Nothing."

"Tell me."

He started to pull her to him, but she put both hands on his chest, pushing back. "No."

"Yes."

She opened her mouth to argue, but the expression on his face changed her mind. "Fine. I was thinking this…"

She fisted her hands in his shirt and pulled him to her. To her shock, the civility he'd demonstrated since she met him, vanished. One moment he was looking at her and the next he had her snug up against him, one hand wrapped tightly around her body and the other behind her head.

Ivy couldn't boast of having been with a lot of men, and sure couldn't claim to ever feeling this aroused. Judson wasn't hesitant, or timid as he claimed a kiss. Nor did it take long for his fire to ignite an answering blaze in her. Within seconds they were breathing faster, the kiss was increasingly demanding and soon their hands joined in.

Judson pulled, tore and tugged anything barring his hands from her skin. It didn't take long before she was down to her bra and panties. She didn't care, her attention was on stripping off his clothes.

By the time his jeans were bunched around his knees they were both past the point of caring about anything except the liquid silk between her legs that was becoming more wet with each stroke of his fingers.

Ivy felt a moment of panic and would have pulled away if he hadn't crooned against her lips. "Let it go, baby."

That was all it took to send her tumbling over the edge into climax. "In me," she panted before the orgasm could subside.

The wolfish smile he flashed her was all the time it took for Judson to lift her up, supporting her with his hands firmly gripping her ass. Ivy wound her legs around him and he carried her to the bed, laying her back and then sliding into her in one fluid motion.

It had been a good while she'd been with a man and it took her body a few seconds to begin to adjust to the sensation of being so full. A few seconds was all she allowed. Hanging onto his shoulders, she bucked against him, the motion driving him deeper. Judson's breath hissed, his eyes locked onto hers and everything around them vanished.

It wasn't wise and could possibly be unsafe to indulge in unprotected sex but that was something she'd deal with if the need arose. Now there was only him and the tension building inside both of them. She could feel him getting close and it drove her higher. So high that safety was the most remote thought from her mind.

A freefall of overwhelming sensation claimed her as she rode out the storm. When at last reason returned, she lay down on him, feeling the rapid beat of his heart and the sweat damp skin hot against her own.

Judson circled her with his arms, holding her close and for several minutes neither of them moved.

Finally, Ivy rolled away and sat, slinging her hair back over her shoulders. Judson traced his fingers along the underside of her breasts. "You're beautiful."

"Flatterer." She didn't see herself that way and couldn't imagine that he did, either. Not really.

"Not at all. Just telling it like it is."

"Well, in that case, let me state for the record that you are wrong about yourself. If this is any indication of your—talents—then add that to being kind, strong, brave, generous and sexy and there's no doubt that a lot of women would love to get their hands on you. And not let go."

"Does that include you?"

Fear of rejection almost had her opening her mouth and speaking a lie, but this moment meant to much, so despite her fear, she spoke the truth. "Oh, God, yes."

"That's all that matters."

“Really?” She could barely believe he said that. They’d only known one another for a short time. Was it possible to fall for someone that fast?

He pulled her over on top of him and she felt the reaction of his body beneath her as she sat, straddling his body. Most men she’d been with needed a bit longer to get back in the saddle.

Not Judson. And while she’d never have believed it if someone told her it would happen, this time was even better than the first. He took her into a well of pleasure that had her reeling.

When they were depleted, lying on the bed with her head on his chest, she realized that it didn’t matter how much time they had known one another. She was crazy about Judson.

Completely hooked.

Chapter Eighteen

Barbie marveled at the lavish yacht as the speedboat pulled up to the rear and two attendants hooked it to cleats. One of the attendants offered his hand, and she gladly accepted the assist.

She'd no more set foot on the deck than the speedboat took off again, apparently headed back to the mainland. "This way, ma'am," the attendant gestured.

"Ma'am?" she sniped at the man, insulted by the appellation. That didn't, however, stop her from following him.

The yacht was like a floating hotel, outfitted expensively. Barbie could picture herself spending time in such luxury, and before the night was over, she fully intended to seduce her host and have him begging for more.

She'd dressed for the occasion in a barely there short black dress that was essentially little more than a tube of stretchy fabric with sparkles that lit when light hit them. Her stiletto heels added six inches to her height and helped draw attention to her legs.

The attendant led her to the bow of the yacht, where Rafael was seated at a table. A chilled bottle of champagne sat in what appeared to be a gold bucket with two glasses flanking it. He didn't move or even turn his head as they approached. Barbie assumed that was because he didn't hear them.

"Your guest has arrived, sir," the attendant announced.

Rafael looked in their direction. "Excellent," he said with a smile, then rose and pulled out the chair next to his. "Please, have a seat."

Barbie sat and crossed her legs, fully aware that the action made her dress rise high enough to expose most of one buttock and leg. It annoyed her that Rafael didn't bother to look. Instead, he lifted the champagne from the ice. "May I pour you a glass?"

When she saw the label, her ire dampened. Roederer Christal. Anyone who could afford nearly four thousand dollars for a bottle of champagne could be forgiven an oversight. "Only if you're joining me," she replied in a sexy tone.

He smiled, poured two glasses, and handed her one. She took a sip and smiled. "Delicious and the perfect drink to celebrate."

"Are we celebrating?"

"We are."

This time when he smiled, he leaned toward her. "I am breathless in anticipation." He was one hundred percent honest. If she'd secured the location of Ivy McCoy or her parents, then he would have everything he needed to take care of that loose end.

"Well, I told you I'd get you what you wanted, sugar. The only question that remains is what is it worth to you?"

“Didn’t we have an arrangement?” It took a bit of effort to keep the ire from his tone. He didn’t like Barbie and was eager for their association to end. But he would be civil until she gave him what he wanted, and he verified the authenticity of the information.

“I think we can do better, don’t you?” She drank down the entire glass of champagne. “I’m just parched. Pour me another?”

Rafael had a vision of cramming the entire bottle down her throat and watching her drown in champagne, but he couldn’t. Not until she gave him the information. So, he poured her another glass and smiled. “I’m sure we can come up with an equitable arrangement.”

“Define equitable.”

“Let me rephrase. Tell me what you want, and I’ll tell you if I’m willing to pay.”

“Fine,” she drank half the glass. “I want to be Mrs. Martinez, share your yacht, your homes, planes and finances.”

“Seriously?” He was taken aback by the boldness of her demand. “We scarcely know each other.”

“Then why don’t we go to your stateroom and get more familiar with one another?”

Rafael considered it for a moment. “That’s quite tempting, but first, we have a small matter to conclude. Do you have the location of Ivy McCoy?”

She hesitated, polished off her glass of champagne, and smiled. “I have the location of her parents.”

“Tell me.”

“Do we have a deal?”

“That depends.”

“On?”

“On the veracity of your information.”

"It's solid."

"I'm afraid I can't go on your word alone. Give me the location and if it checks out, we have much to discuss."

"Pour me another glass and I'll tell you."

He complied and watched her guzzle the expensive champagne like a teenager drinking a soda. When she placed the empty glass on the table, it would have fallen if he had not caught it and moved it out of her reach. He needed to get that information fast, or she was going to be so drunk she'd be incapable of speech.

"I'm waiting."

"Fine," she sighed dramatically, then gave him a smile he took to be flirtatious. She opened her clutch and withdrew a slip of paper. Rafael took it from her and read what was printing in neat block letters.

"Are you certain about this?"

"Absolutely."

He nodded and pulled his phone from the inside pocket of his jacket. After reading the information to whoever was on the other end of the call, he ordered them to check out the information immediately and get back to him.

"Now what?" Barbie asked.

"Now we wait."

"And what shall we do while we wait?"

"What do you want to do?"

"I have a few ideas." She pushed herself up, wobbled a bit, but righted herself and moved close enough to step one foot over his legs and lower herself onto him. That required her hiking her dress up, as she was straddling his lap.

"Oops, don't look. I forgot to wear panties."

He knew that was supposed to tempt him, or at the least, inspire him to look, but he wasn't in the mood for anything she had to offer. But he'd humor her until he knew if she'd double crossed him with the information.

"You're a naughty one, aren't you? Perhaps I should turn you over my knee and give that bare bottom you're trying to seduce me with a good spanking."

He could tell from the look in her eyes and the flush that rose on her skin, she was interested. How unfortunate that he wasn't. But he could pretend for a while longer, so rather than say more, he did just as he suggested.

Barbie squealed as he pushed her off his lap and then jerked her down on his legs with her rear in the air. Sure enough, she wore nothing beneath the dress.

At first, she squealed softly at the slap of his hand on her flesh, but soon the squeal turned into a protest, accompanied by her wiggling to free herself. That was the first thing she'd done since he met her that roused him.

Which caused him to strike her harder, refusing to release her. It wasn't long before her protest turned into screams and kicks, her arms flailing in a failed attempt to stop him. Rafael grinned, relishing the bloom of red on her flesh that got deeper with every slap of his hand.

"Sir?"

The voice of one of his men had him stopping. Barbie quickly rolled off his legs, landing in a heap on the deck. Rafael ignored her and stepped over to his man. The man cut a look at Barbie before speaking softly. "It's genuine. I sent a delivery of flowers. The McCoys are not the only ones admitted to the hospital. So is Bill Gordon."

Rafael's surprise must have shown on his face because his subordinate quickly added. "Apparently, he was near death when he was found in Ms. McCoy's driveway."

"And why did the police announce his death?" This news gave Rafael a moment of consternation. Why would the police lie about detective Gordon's condition? He needed to recruit someone in the department quickly. Not having all the facts could prove inconvenient.

"We do not know, sir. Shall I have our people investigate recruitment?"

"Absolutely."

"And what about this..." the man glanced in Barbie's direction, who was, at present, standing at the railing looking out to sea, to all appearances, ignoring them.

Rafael considered it for a moment and an inspiration hit, one that filled him with delight. "Could you bring me a sturdy plastic bag?"

"Yes, sir," the man nodded and hurried away.

Rafael walked the few steps back to the table, lifted his glass, and swallowed half the contents. He watched Barbie who had her arms outstretched, with hands on the railing, leaning forward slightly like she was watching the water.

He suspected what she was doing was pouting. Her attempt at seduction had not netted the expected results. Only a few seconds passed before his subordinate returned, holding a large plastic bag, the type that has the plastic zipper at the top. It was quite large, more than big enough for his needs.

Rafael walked up behind Barbie and leaned in over her right shoulder. "Shall we continue?"

She turned her head away, refusing to acknowledge him. "Come now, darling," he crooned. "Didn't I give you want you wanted?"

"Not even close, asshole."

Her tone of voice alone was enough to provoke a flash of anger. Her choice of words only amplified it, and that suited him just fine. He was stronger when enraged and since he was ready to be rid of Barbie Burman, stronger worked in his favor.

She didn't know what was happening when he suddenly slid the bag over her head. "Hey, what the hell?"

It became clear when he tightened the bag around her neck and twisted it tightly, keeping it clenched in his left hand as he swatted away her grasping hands with his right. Within two seconds, she was fighting for her life, trying to scratch and claw his hands to break free. She kicked, squirmed and thrashed, wasting what little oxygen she had left.

To no avail.

Within moments, her movements grew weaker and soon all she could do was claw feebly at the bag. Rafael grinned, reveling in a sudden erection. It didn't take long for the moment to culminate in a climax for both. For him, it meant sexual release. For her, it meant release from life.

He released her and stepped back. "Juan!" he shouted as he turned and headed across the deck.

Juan appeared and Rafael gestured toward Barbie's body. "Toss that trash overboard and set a course for Miami. Make sure the records show we were docked since last night and have not moved."

"Yes sir."

Rafael cut one glance back at the dead woman. He had no feelings of remorse or guilt. There was no one who would miss her and if he'd let her live, there would have come a day when she'd try to extort something from him.

He didn't need that kind of annoyance or inconvenience. Barbie had served her function; she'd provided him with the second element he needed to make his plan work.

Smiling to himself as he headed for his stateroom to change, he imagined what he was going to say to the McCoy's, and then the look on Ivy McCoy's face, when her parents led him straight to her.

His smile grew wider. Rafael loved it when a plan came together.

Chapter Nineteen

"Knock knock."

Ed McCoy turned in his chair, looked toward the door and smiled at the man standing in the doorway. "Well, look who's up walking around." He stood and walked over to the door. "Looking good, Bill. Do the doctors know you're wandering around the hospital?"

"They basically said it was time to get off my ass, so here I am. Lena ran out to pick up some subs. I told her to get you guys something. I hope you like turkey and cheese."

"I wouldn't say no to it," Ed replied. "Come on in and take a load off."

"Still have three laps before I can sit. Want to walk with me?"

Ed looked at his wife, Helen, who sat on the bed playing a word game on her phone. "Do you mind, hon?"

"Not at all. Scoot."

"Then let's hit the bricks," Ed said.

Helen watched them leave and smiled. That old saying about blessings rising out of good and bad was obviously true. What led them all to be in this hospital was horrible, the stuff of nightmares, but the good that had resulted was she and Ed had found new friends.

"Hello."

The voice from the door had Helen looking up. A young Hispanic nurse smiled at her. "Hi, I'm Isabelle."

"I haven't seen you before. Are you new?"

"Just filling in. How are you today?"

"Fine."

"That's good to hear. Are you texting with family?"

"No, just cruising social media and thinking about how important family and friends are."

"That's very true. Do you have children?"

"I do. A son and a daughter. Our son is in the military, currently stationed in Germany, and our daughter…" she trailed off, uncertain what she could safely say. "Well, you know, kids off on their own lives and all that."

"Do you keep up with them on social media?" The nurse checked Helen's vitals as she talked. "Do they have TikTok, Twitter or Instagram accounts?"

Once the nurse removed the blood-pressure cuff, Helen responded. "I thought my daughter had an Facebook or Instagram account, but now I can't seem to find either."

"Want some help?"

“Yes, please.”

The nurse sat on the bed and took Helen’s phone. “So, what name does she use for her account?”

Helen thought about it. “Ivy’s Face.”

“That’s unusual.”

“And if it’s correct, you’ll see why.”

The nurse entered the name. “No, that’s not it. Ivy with an apostrophe s and then Face?”

“Yes, I think so.”

“Let me try a couple of combinations.”

After a few moments, she smiled. “Got it. Is this the one?” The nurse handed the phone to Helen.

Sure enough, there was Ivy’s face, side by side with her dog, Face. But it listed the profile name as IvysFace, without the space. “That’s the one.”

“She’s pretty. Is that her dog?”

“It is. That’s Face. He’s an Irish Wolfhound and weighs almost two hundred pounds.”

“That’s a very big dog.” The nurse glanced at the screen. “She’s engaged?”

“No,” Helen immediately responded.

“Well, she’s wearing an engagement ring. And—oh my God, do you know who that man is?”

“No, who?” The shock had Helen feeling a bit mentally dull.

“Roberto Nieves. He’s a wealthy developer from Puerto Rico who moved to Miami a few years ago. From what I hear, he’s dated a lot of celebrities. Here, let me see your phone. Maybe we can find his account.”

She diddled on the phone for a minute, then smiled and bleeped out an “ah ha!”

Helen was shocked when the nurse returned the phone to her, and she got a look at the screen. There were countless photos of Ivy and the man Roberto, and it was clear from the pictures they were close, smiling at one another like people in love.

She went back to Ivy's account and saw many of the same images. How could she not have known? And why would Ivy keep something like this a secret? It made little sense. She wished she could talk to Ivy. Heck, she'd settle with talking to the man. Maybe he knew where Ivy was.

"I wonder if I could get in touch with him?"

The nurse shrugged. "I know a woman who works for an attorney who does legal work for him. Maybe I could see if she could put you in touch."

"That would be so kind, thank you."

"No problem, Mrs. McCoy. I'll let you know if I make any progress with that."

"Thank you again."

Helen stared at the screen of her phone, studying the images. How had she and her daughter grown so far apart that Ivy wouldn't tell her she'd fallen in love? Sudden memories filled Helen with remorse over all the less than kind things she'd said to Ivy when Ivy's marriage fell apart. Tears seeped from her eyes, and she prayed God would give her the chance to make amends with her daughter.

Just then, Ed and Bill Gordon returned. Helen swiped at her eyes and set her phone aside. "How are you feeling now?" she asked Bill.

"Pretty good," he cut a look at Ed. "You want to tell her, or should I?"

"Go ahead," Ed replied. "As soon as you take a seat."

Bill took the seat beside the bed, and Ed sat on the end of the bed. "Well?" Helen asked.

"We're all headed for North Carolina this weekend," Bill announced.

"We are?" Helen looked at Ed. "Why?"

"We'll be staying there for a while until everyone's sure it's safe." Bill answered, and then added. "But that's not the best part." He looked at Ed. "Go on, tell her."

"That's where Ivy is." Ed said and reached for Helen's hand.

"Oh, God," Helen fought back tears. "She's okay?"

"She is," Ed assured her. "We spoke with Mr. Blackstone. That's the man who runs the security company who's protecting her and soon, us. He said she's fine and she'll call you later in the day. At present she was helping get the cabins ready where we'll be staying."

"Thank God," Helen blew out a breath. "I've been so scared."

"Same here," Ed squeezed her hand.

Helen nodded, thinking about the photos on Ivy's Instagram account. She wasn't ready to tell Ed about it and couldn't figure how she was going to speak with Ivy about it on the phone. Ed was sure to want to talk to his daughter and the chances of being left alone to talk in private were slim. If she asked for that, Ed would want to know why.

Lena Gordon entered the room with bags of food, so Helen set that dilemma aside for the moment. With luck, she'd find a way to speak privately with Ivy or perhaps the nurse could contact Roberto Nieves. If Ivy was really engaged, Helen intended to find and speak with the man who'd put a ring on her finger.

But that was another thing she wasn't ready to share. She tried to stop thinking about it and got out of bed to join the others at the small table that'd been set up for them. They often shared meals, and she and Ed already thought of Bill and Lena as friends.

Just as they were finishing, Isabelle returned. Helen got up as soon as Isabelle entered. "Is everything okay?" Ed called out.

"Yes, I just asked Isabelle if she would ask the doctor if this bandage could be removed. It itches like mad."

"He said maybe tomorrow, but I can change it now and put some cream on it."

"That would be wonderful. Let's go into the bathroom so the gang can finish their lunch.

Isabelle picked up the tray of bandages and antiseptic and followed Helen into the bathroom. "Do you want me to change the dressing?" she asked as Helen closed the toilet lid and sat.

"No, that was just an excuse. Did you find out anything?"

"Actually, I did better than that. I got Mr. Nieves' phone number and called him. He said he'd been out of his mind with worry about Ivy and couldn't understand why she'd just disappeared. He's hired a private detective to find her. When I told him you'd like to meet him, he jumped at the chance and said he could come by this evening."

"Can you call him back and tell him yes?"

"Of course I can."

"Thank — " Helen realized there was a hurdle she hadn't considered. Ed. "Wait, I haven't told my husband and don't want to until I speak with Mr. Nieves. Is there any way I could meet him in private?"

Isabelle pursed her lips and her eyes moved to one side as if she was in deep thought. Finally, she smiled. "Here's what we can do. I'll tell him to meet us at the visitors' lounge down the hall, and when he gets here, I'll come get you and say the doctor wants one more scan of your arm and shoulder, just to make sure nothing was overlooked."

"Thank you so much, Isabelle. What time?"

"I'll tell him to come around six. That way, your husband and his friends will be busy with dinner."

"Perfect. I can't thank you enough."

"My pleasure, Mrs. McCoy. Now, you better get back out there."

"Yes, of course."

They left the bathroom, and Helen headed for the table. "Thank you again, Isabelle. It feels much better."

"Glad to help. Call if you need anything."

"I will. Thank you."

Helen reclaimed her seat at the table. "Everything okay, babe?" Ed asked.

"Just fine. It's healing well, just itchy. Isabelle put something on it and the itching stopped."

"I don't remember seeing her before," Lena commented. "Is she new?"

"She said she was filling in for someone," Helen replied.

"Wonder who?" Bill asked. "I don't recall any of the regular nurses being out."

Helen shrugged. "She didn't say. All I know is it's nice not to have a perpetual itch. And," she smiled at Lena. "This sub is divine. Thank you."

"My pleasure. Are you guy up for some cards this afternoon? Bill has PT in an hour but is free after that."

"I'm game," Ed said and looked at Helen.

"Count me in," she replied. Playing cards would help pass the time and maybe while they played, she'd figure whether to tell Ed that his only daughter was engaged to a man they'd never met.

Chapter Twenty

The ring of the phone woke Judson. He was shocked he'd fallen asleep. That wasn't common for him. But then, having a gorgeous woman who'd worn him out sexually in the afternoon wasn't common either. And definitely inspired an afternoon nap with that woman snuggled contentedly against him.

He felt around on the nightstand and located his phone. "Hey, Pop, what's up?" he answered.

"Have you and Ivy finished the cabins?"

"Almost."

There was a long pause before Clayton spoke again. “Good. We’re due to call her folks and I know they and she are eager for the call.”

“Give us half an hour?”

“Take all the time you need. I told them we’d call after supper.”

Judson slid the phone onto the nightstand and turned his head to find Ivy watching. “Is everything okay?”

“Yes. He wanted to let us know that you’re going to be able to speak with your folks.”

“Now?” She sat straight up, seemingly unconcerned she was not dressed.

For a woman who didn’t flaunt her sexuality, she sure was sexy. Judson would have preferred to roll over on top of her than get out of the bed, but knew she was eager to speak with her parents, so he just smiled. “After supper, which is…” he checked the time “in a little over an hour. Think we can get finished before then?

“You bet’cha,” she grinned and threw herself down to deliver a noisy kiss. “Let’s get to it.”

Amidst more kissing, laughing and teasing, they dressed, redid the bed and finished tidying up the cabin and then hurried to the next one. If everyone moved as quickly as Ivy, work would get done a lot faster. She ran circles around Judson, and he enjoyed watching.

Once finished, they headed for the main house. She was almost skipping; she was so excited. As they neared the house, the front screen opened, and Face bounded out. Ivy stopped and braced herself as he launched himself at her.

It surprised Judson she stayed on her feet as the dog’s front legs went on top of her shoulders and he started licking her face like they’d been parted for a lot longer than a couple of hours.

She didn't seem to mind and spent a good five minutes giving Face attention before saying, "okay, buddy, we need to get moving."

He yipped, dropped onto all four paws and walked along beside her; his shoulder almost constantly pressed against her hip. Judson was pretty sure he'd never seen such devotion between an animal and a human before and enjoyed watching.

"Hey Mr. Clayton," Ivy chirped as they reached the steps leading up to the front porch. "The cabins are ship-shape. I didn't know what to do with the sheets. Should I put them in a washing machine in one of the cabins?"

"No need. We'll fetch them and do them at the laundry for the ranch over at the supply cabin."

"I can run get them now."

"That can wait until morning. Your folks and the Gordons won't be arriving until afternoon."

"Are you sure?"

"I am."

"Okay, so can I help with fixing dinner?"

"Can you cook?"

"You better believe it."

"Then let's get in that kitchen and get to it."

"Yes, sir!" she agreed and headed up the steps. "Come on Face, you can be in charge of whatever hits the floor."

Judson smiled, as did his father, and watched Ivy go inside. "She's something," Clayton commented, then turned to follow Ivy.

"That she is," Judson agreed, which had his father stopping to look at him.

"Am I detecting a note of interest in your tone?"

Judson shrugged. "Maybe. Would that be an issue?"

"Not for me."

No more was said. Not that anything more needed to be said about the matter. Clayton had never horned in on any of his son's relationships. He'd only let them know, repeatedly, that he'd like to have some grandchildren before he got too old to enjoy them.

Until recently, Judson had given no thought to being a father. Hell, until recently, he never believed he'd find a woman who'd want him for anything, must less as a partner to have children with.

Now, he hoped he wasn't wrong about Ivy and that what was happening between them might be the start of a real relationship. But he reminded himself not to put the cart before the horse. One afternoon of sex didn't make a relationship, and they still had irons in the fire to deal with.

Not only did they have to find and stop whoever wanted to kill Ivy, but they still hadn't discovered who was responsible for Jack's death, and none of them would rest until they did.

*****

Helen McCoy felt like someone out of a novel, trying to behave normally as she waited for Isabelle to come deliver the fake scan order. Ed, Bill, and Lena sat at the table, playing cards, talking and laughing. Helen tried to join in, but her stomach was in a knot, and she feared any moment Ed would realize she was hiding something.

As she obsessed over the situation and whether she was making a mistake, Isabelle entered the room. "Mrs. McCoy?"

"Hi, Isabelle."

"I'm sorry to interrupt, but your orthopedic physician wants to get one more scan of your arm now that the swelling has subsided, just to make sure there is nothing that was hidden or overlooked. Would you mind terribly doing that now? I have a wheelchair outside."

"Of course, and I can walk."

"I'm sure you're capable, but hospital orders require me to push you in the chair."

"Okay. Will it take long?"

"I'll have you back before dinner."

"I ordered delivery from a steakhouse for everyone," Ed announced.

"Then I will definitely be back on time," Helen smiled, gave him a kiss and turned to Isabelle. "Okay, let's do this."

Once they were outside the room, Isabelle gestured to the wheelchair. "Let's make this as believable as possible, shall we?"

"Sure." Helen took a seat and Isabelle pushed her down to the end of the hallway, made a right turn and took that passageway to double doors at the end of the hall with a sign on the wall that read "Visitor's Waiting Room."

Isabelle pressed the button beneath the sign, and the doors opened. She then pushed Helen inside. A very handsome Latin man seated near the window stood. The same Latin man who was featured in the photos with Ivy on her social media pages.

"Mrs. McCoy?"

"Yes," Helen replied.

"I'll just step outside and give you some privacy," Isabelle said. "I'd suggest you keep this to no more than half an hour."

"Okay, thank you," Helen gave her a smile. Once Isabelle left, Helen turned her attention to the man still standing. "Mr. Nieves?"

"Roberto, please."

Helen stood and walked over to him, extending her hand. "Helen McCoy."

"It's such an honor to meet you, Mrs. McCoy. Ivy speaks so highly of you." He chuckled like someone remembering something amusing. "Actually, she talks about you all the time. I'm guessing the two of you are quite close."

Something about what he said struck Helen as dishonest. First, she and Ivy had never really been close. They loved one another but were as opposite as two people could be. Ivy had always been her father's daughter, and still was. If she talked about anyone, it would be Ed. She filed away that tidbit and took a seat.

"Care to tell me why you showed up at our hotel the night I was shot?" Helen saw surprise register on his face. Did he think she wouldn't recognize him from the hotel room?

"I imagine that must seem confusing, to say the least. The truth is, a contact in the police department contacted me and claimed that it was Mitch Burman who killed detective Gordon. He said Mr. Burman planned on torturing you to find out Ivy's whereabouts, and once he knew where to find her, he was going to kill you and your husband to cover his tracks. I persuaded my contact to introduce me to Mr. Burman as an agent with the Federal Bureau of Investigation in order to gain access to his operation."

Helen didn't know whether to believe him. As she stewed on what he'd said, he continued. "I'm sorry for the confusion. I was desperate to find Ivy. I still am. I just want to protect her and our unborn child."

"Your what?" Helen blurted.

"I'm sorry, this isn't how you should find out. Ivy's pregnant. She got the test results back the day before she found the dead man. She called me that morning to give me the news, and I proposed that same evening."

He paused and pulled out a cell phone. "Here," he tapped on the phone for a few moments and then turned it for Helen to see. "This is the night we became engaged."

"I saw that photo on her Instagram account," Helen said.

"I'm desperate to find her," he said in halting words, as if he were holding back tears. "As you are, I imagine."

"Yes, you're right. We are. And I appreciate you taking time to come see me, Mr. Nieves."

"Have you heard from her? Do you have any idea where she is?"

If it were not for a small voice in her mind urging her to keep the information to herself, she might have told him. But she wouldn't. Not until she'd told Ed and maybe even the Gordons about the meeting.

"I wish I had something for you, Mr. Nieves, but I'm as in the dark as you. Hopefully, one of us will hear from her soon."

"Let me give you my number," he said and looked around. "Perhaps I can leave it with the nurse? She surely will have something I can write on."

"I'm sure she does." Helen rose and walked over to take hold of the handles of the wheelchair. "Again, thank you for coming to see me."

With that, she pushed the chair to the door and pressed the button on the wall to open the doors.

"Mrs. McCoy, you're not supposed to be pushing that thing," Isabelle protested. "Now sit and let me push you back to your room."

"Thank you, Isabelle." As she walked around to the front of the chair, she noticed the look Isabelle gave to Roberto Nieves. What kind of expression was that? She glanced at Roberto to find a glare on his face that quickly vanished when she looked at him.

"Good evening, Mr. Nieves," Helen said, and took a seat. "I'm ready, Isabelle."

When she returned to her room, the delivery of food had just arrived. Ed and Lena were unpacking it. "Just in time," Ed said, and pulled out her chair at the table. "When will you hear about the scan?"

Helen hesitated only a second before responding, but it wasn't in answer to his question. "There was no scan."

"Pardon?" His expression showed his confusion.

She quickly told him about Isabelle finding Ivy's Instagram page and Isabelle getting in touch with Roberto Nieves, who paid her a visit.

"Only I don't believe him, no matter how many photos on are that social media page," she finished with.

"Could we see the photos?" Bill asked.

"Sure," she fetched her phone from the table beside the bed, accessed the page and handed Bill the phone when she returned to the table.

He looked, and his face paled. "Bill? Are you okay, honey?" Lena put her hand on his arm.

"He told you his name is Roberto Nieves?" He asked of Helen.

"Yes, why?"

"That's not his name. These photos are of Rafael Martinez, a notorious drug kingpin who operates out of Cuba. Martinez is the man who killed Mitch Burman, and the man who wants to kill Ivy." He showed the screen of the phone to Ed.

Ed glanced at it and then at Helen. "This is the same man from our hotel room. What did he want?"

"To know where Ivy is."

"Please tell me you didn't reveal that information," Bill said.

"Of course not," Helen spoke sharper than intended. "I'm sorry, Bill. No, I got a bad feeling from him, so I listened but didn't share any information. He said he'd leave his number with the nurse Isabelle in case I spoke with Ivy, I could call and let him know."

Bill nodded. "And this nurse—I don't remember her. Is she new?"

"She said she was filling in."

Bill looked at Ed and then back at Helen. "She's working for him."

"Then what do we do?" Ed asked.

Bill smiled. "First, we eat this delicious dinner. Afterwards, you'll get a chance to speak with your daughter and I'll talk to Clayton Blackstone."

"About what?" Helen asked.

"About setting a trap for Rafael Martinez."

Ivy threw back the bedcovers and rolled over onto her back. Two seconds later she felt the bed shift with Face's weight. A moment later his head plunked down on her belly. She smiled and started rubbing him. He could always sense when she was upset, and she'd barely slept last night. The phone conversation with her parents, particularly her mother, had left her out of sorts and feeling that something was wrong, and she was not being told.

For what must have been the hundredth time, she replayed the conversation in her mind.

Ivy sat on the steps of the back porch, watching the seconds tick by on her watch. She clutched the cordless phone from the house, willing it to ring. Her parents were scheduled to call the ranch number at seven. It was seven now.

When the phone rang, she quickly answered. "Hello?"

"Ivy?"

"Dad?"

"Hold on."

He must have covered the phone because Ivy couldn't hear what was being said. Finally, someone came back on the line. Bill Gordon. "Ivy? Hey, it's Bill."

"Oh, Mr. Bill, are you okay? I'm so sorry about—"

"It wasn't your fault, Ivy, and thanks to your quick action in calling 911, I was saved, so I owe you a debt of thanks."

"No, you don't. You're my friend, and that means more than anything to me. I was just so terrified you'd die, but I did what you told me to do. I just hope you don't hate me for what happened."

"Never. Like you said, friendship is more important. But back to why I horned in on your conversation with your folks. Clayton is going to explain everything to you in the morning. Tonight, he and I are going to put our heads together with his boys and come up with a plan."

"A plan for what?"

"Clayton will tell you everything. For now, get some rest. This is all going to work out and soon, you'll be reunited with your folks."

"And you? You're coming too, right? You and Mrs. Gordon?"

"Yes, we are."

"I can't wait to see you."

"Same here. Now, I'll turn the phone back over. See you on Saturday."

"I will be so happy to see you. See you then."

A moment later, Ivy's dad came back on the line. "You have no idea what it means to hear your voice, honey. We were so worried. Are you all right?"

"I am. The Blackstone's have been so kind to me. And Judson saved me. Did Mr. Bill tell you that?"

"Yes, he and Mr. Blackstone filled us in on what has happened. I can only thank God that you're okay. And Face?"

"He's okay, and he was so brave, Dad. He put himself between me and the man trying to shoot me."

"And I'm betting you didn't let that stand."

"I couldn't let him sacrifice himself for me. But he was willing. He's such a sweet, devoted boy, Dad. I wish Mom could make friends with him, but that's not important now. How are you and Mom? Are you really okay? When are you coming here?"

"We're fine, honey. Even in the middle of all this fear and uncertainty, we were blessed. Bill and Lena Gordon are fine people, and we've already become good friends. I'm grateful Bill was looking out for you during all that mess, but sure hate what he suffered for his generosity."

"Me too, Dad. I wish there was a way I could pay him back. And I'll try to find one, no matter how long it takes. I haven't forgotten what you taught me."

"I didn't think you had. Well, listen, I better turn the phone over to your Mom or she's likely to put me in a hospital bed. We'll see you this weekend, baby girl. I love you."

"To infinity and beyond," she quoted the line from the old kid's movie.

"See you soon."

A few seconds later, her mother's voice came on the line. "Girl, you're going to give me a heart attack."

"Hey, Mom," Ivy smiled at the greeting she received. Growing up, she'd always wondered why her mother wasn't like

those of her friends. She wasn't overly affectionate, rarely gave compliments, and was quick to criticize. There was a time, when she was young, that Ivy thought her mother hated her.

It wasn't until she was grown that she realized. Her mother was only affectionate with Ivy's dad and babies. Once you were old enough to walk and talk well, the pampering, affection, and smiles came few and far in-between. It wasn't that she didn't love, she just didn't know how or wasn't comfortable being demonstrative of her affection.

But there was never a doubt in Ivy's mind that her mother loved her. Not once. Her mother might not have hugged her a dozen time since she was five, but she'd lay down her life to protect Ivy and go without to provide Ivy with what she needed and a lot of what she wanted.

All in all, Helen McCoy was a remarkable woman, and Ivy loved her.

"We were so worried, Ivy. I know you weren't in a position to get in touch, but I wish you'd let us know you were okay."

"I'm sorry. I did what Mr. Blackstone told me to do, and he seems knowledgeable and experienced in this sort of thing. Did Mr. Bill tell you about Blackstone Security and what they do?"

"He did. They sound like wonderful people."

"They are. They even let Face stay inside with me at night. And Face already is fast friends with Clayton—Mr. Blackstone."

"You and that beast."

There was no heat in the words, so Ivy didn't take offense. "I'm so glad you and Dad are coming here this weekend. I was terrified something would happen to you."

"You don't know terror until your child goes missing."

Ivy knew the words weren't intended as a reprimand, but it still stung a little to have her fears dismissed or one-upped. "I know you and Dad were probably scared to death, and I'm sorry.

Believe me, I never imagined something like this could happen to me.

"Mom, if you'd been at that house where this all started, you'd have had a duck. There was this giant python, swallowing a man. Literally eating him. I threw up all over the yard. It was horrible."

"I don't even want to think about that."

"Neither do I. But I was lucky. Mr. Bill came to my rescue and then he gave me Mr. Clayton's number to call if anything happened and he and one of his sons, Judson, saved me."

"Not your fiancé, obviously."

"My what?"

"You neglected to mention that bit of information."

"I don't know what you're talking about. I don't have a fiancé."

"That's what people keep telling me, and yet I see on Instagram all these photos of you and a handsome Latin man."

"What? No. I haven't even posted to Insta in months, and I sure haven't posted any photos of me and a Latin man, heck of any man."

"Well, I—hold on."

Ivy could hear her father scolding her mother about bringing up the Instagram account, especially after what Bill had told them about the man."

"What did Mr. Bill tell you?" Ivy asked. "Mom?"

"We'll talk it all out when we see you. We love you."

"Tell me now."

"I said when we see you."

Ivy knew when to argue with her mother and when not to. Her mother's tone said this fell into the latter category, so Ivy didn't press.

"Okay. I love you, Mom. See you soon."

Now, she lay in bed, wondering what Mr. Clayton was going to tell her and whether it was too early to get up and go in search of him. She'd spent a lonely evening wandering the house alone while Clayton and Judson were in Clayton's office. Several times she thought about knocking on the door, and each time dismissed the idea. If they'd wanted to include her in whatever discussion they were having, they would have invited her to participate.

That had not happened, so she'd logged onto the internet on the secure connection Judson had set up for her and tried to log onto her Instagram account. Each time she received a message saying there was no such account.

What in the world was her mother talking about? Ivy ran a search on her own name. Nothing popped up. But then, why would it? She wasn't exactly noteworthy and wasn't into all the social media stuff.

Still, it bugged her and was part of the reason she hadn't slept.

When Face's ears perked up and he raised his head, it was a clear signal that someone else was awake. Ivy rose, quickly made the bed, took care of her morning ritual in the bathroom, dressed and headed for the kitchen.

There, she found Clayton and Judson sitting at the table with steaming mugs of coffee on the table in front of them. "Good morning," she greeted them and skirted the table to open the back door to let Face out.

Then she turned and went straight for the coffeepot. Once, she had a full mug; she opened the screen door. A few seconds passed before Face bounded it and made the rounds, giving the men at the table some good-morning affection.

It touched Ivy to watch how caring and kind they were to Face. Finally, Face settled in front of the door, gazing out through the screen. For a few moments, everyone was silent, then Ivy spoke. "Mr. Bill said you all were going to put together a plan?"

"Yes," Clayton replied. "We made a dent in it last night. And before you ask, we checked out that Instagram account your mother mentioned."

He pulled out his cell phone, and after tapping on it for a few seconds, slid it over to her. Ivy gasped when she saw the screen. "What the hell is this?"

"Supposedly, you and your fiancé," Clayton replied. "The man in these photos got in to see your mother and claimed to be your fiancé, a fiancé who is sick with worry over your well-being."

"That's the man in the video, the one who was talking with Detective Burman."

"Rafael Martinez," Judson spoke up. "Drug lord and murderer."

"And he has seen my mother?"

"He has. According to what we've been able to piece together in a short amount of time, he gained access to your parents' location. We suspect that knowledge came from Mitch Burman's wife."

"How would she know?"

"She didn't. But she could have gotten it from one of the other detectives. There is one who has gone missing."

"Still, how or why would she be involved?"

"We'll never know the answer to that," Clayton said. "Her body washed up on shore around Vero Beach. From the initial coroner's report, it appears she was suffocated and dumped into the ocean."

"Oh my god, that's awful. But it doesn't explain how the Martinez man found my parents."

"This is where is gets interesting," Judson said. "A woman claiming to be a fill-in nurse approached your mother. She showed your mother that Instagram account and said your fiancé was frantic to find you and asked if your mother would meet with him."

"And Mom said yes?"

Judson nodded. "Only when the man showed up, she knew something wasn't kosher, because he was one of the men who came to their hotel room the night Burman was killed."

"And Mom recognized him."

"She did, and finally revealed the information to your father and Bill Gordon. Bill immediately recognized Martinez from the video you found of him and Burman at the press conference."

"But why pretend to be my fiancé?"

"So your mother would tell him how to find you."

Fear shot through Ivy like a hot spike. "Please tell me she didn't let him know."

"No, she didn't."

"Well, what now? Ivy looked from Judson to Clayton.

"Now we set a trap."

There was a few moments of silence before Ivy spoke, voicing her fear. "And I'm guessing I'm the bait?"

Judson nodded. "You won't be alone. We won't let anyone hurt you. You have my word on that."

Had it been anyone else, she might have doubted it. She had no doubts about Judson, and maybe that was foolish. It was all too easy to trust someone you love.

And it was then she realized that foolish or not, she was falling in love with Judson Blackstone.

Chapter Twenty-Two

"I'll head up to help as soon as I clean the kitchen," Ivy said as Judson leaned down and gave her a soft kiss.

"You don't have to do that."

"Sure, I do. I'm the one who kept you in bed later than normal, thus causing you to miss breakfast, and I'm the one who made the mess cooking for us."

"I'd gladly clean those dishes for being able to spend an extra hour in bed with you in the morning."

That statement thrilled Ivy. She turned and looped her arms around his neck. "You sure know how to make a woman feel good."

"Baby, we've just gotten started."

She wanted to be flirtatious in return, but something that'd been gnawing at her took precedent. "Is this moving too fast?"

His smile faded. "You tell me. Is it making you uncomfortable?"

"No. No, not at all. Well, maybe a little scared."

"Scared? Why?"

"Never mind," she tried to turn back to the sink, but he stopped her.

"Tell me."

She felt terribly uncomfortable but sucked in a breath and let the words out. "Because I'm scared you'll break my heart." Ivy couldn't look at him while the confession poured out. "I'm already in love with this place and the people who call it home and if you get tired of me, then…"

"In love?" he asked and put one finger under her chin to lift her head up.

Ivy nodded. "I know. I know. It's too soon. I get that. But I–I have feelings for you that go beyond friendship or gratitude for saving me. You make me feel…"

She couldn't continue for fear he'd turn away from her.

"Make you feel what?"

"Whole."

There, she'd said it. Dread over how he would respond had her closing her eyes.

"Look at me, sweetheart," he whispered. "Please."

She opened her eyes to see him smiling sweetly. "I'm crazy about you, Ivy McCoy, and I don't mind admitting that I've been falling in love with you since I saw you standing up to that gunman to protect Face."

"Please don't feel you have to say—"

"I never say anything I don't mean."

A sudden burst of happiness had her throwing her arms around him. Within a couple of seconds, he had her in his arms, twirling her around as she hung on.

"Okay, I gotta get to it. Come to the barn when you finish here?"

"Give me fifteen minutes." She gave him a noisy kiss.

Judson smiled and headed out. She found it odd, and sad that the moment he left, her fears resurfaced. Damn, what's wrong with you? Can't you enjoy a moment of happiness without screwing it up with your damn fears?

She had no answer to that. Since the day she found the man being eaten by a snake, fear had ruled her, justified or not. Trying to dismiss such thoughts and feelings, she turned her attention to the task at hand.

Ivy was headed out of the back door when Clayton's voice stopped her. She turned to see him enter the kitchen. "Can we talk?"

"Of course," she immediately responded. "Judson took Face with him to the barn. I was just headed up to help feed the animals."

"Then we'll talk as we walk, and I'll help."

"Okay," she pushed open the door, stepped out, and held the door for him.

"It's so beautiful here," she commented as she turned and looked out over the land. "As pleasant as it can be to wear shorts in the winter, Florida's natural landscape is not exactly pretty."

"Each place has its own beauty. I'm not a fan of the summer heat, but the beaches are nice, and the Everglades are possessed of a raw and untamed beauty that is unique. Not that I'd want to live there, mind you. I could live to be a hundred and never tire of looking at this." he raised his hand up and out in a gesture she understood.

"I can understand that. What about the places you own in other states? Wyoming, Montana and Texas?"

The northern properties are magnificent—the valleys and mountains, the deep silence of winter snow and the life that awakens in spring. It's awe inspiring. Texas is just a money-making operation and a suitable location for Blackstone Security. This place, though. This is and always will be home for me. It's where I watched my kids grow up. Where I buried my wife."

"You still miss her very much, don't you?"

"Every day."

"If this is too personal a question, please say, but Judson mentioned he had a sister?"

"He did. Prettiest little girl I ever laid eyes on. Losing her almost ended us — me and her mom. But we had Judson and Brady and couldn't just crawl into a hole, so we learned to go on. You just never get over it, though."

"I'm sorry you lost her. And Jack. Judson said he was remarkable."

Clayton smiled. "From the day he was born, Jack followed Jud around like a puppy. You'd have thought Jud was his father. And maybe that's my fault. My wife took her last breath and Jack took his first, and as ashamed as I am to admit it, losing her nearly ended me. It took years for me to get myself back on track."

"I can't imagine how horrible that was. And I'm sure you did your best, Mr. Clayton."

"No, I didn't. I let Jud become the man of the house, the father to the rest of the kids. He stepped up. There's no doubt about that, but an eleven-year-old boy shouldn't have the responsibility of caring for his siblings."

"He did it out of love."

"I know," Clayton smiled. "He loves them almost like they were his own."

"I meant out of love for you, sir."

The way Clayton quickly glanced at her was a surprise. "Surely you know he sees you as a hero. You're what he's always aspired to be, so if he stepped up, he did it for you."

Clayton put his hand on her shoulder and gave it a brief squeeze. "You have no idea how much that means to me."

She smiled and nodded, not knowing what else to say. She didn't have to fill the silence. Clayton did.

"Now, it's my turn and some of what I say won't be easy to hear, but you need to listen."

"Yes, sir."

"As you know from our conversation yesterday, there have been developments. I spoke with Bill again this morning and he said that another detective he and Mitch worked with, a younger man, was found dead in a dumpster. Bullet to the back of the head. His phone was recovered and there were multiple messages from Barbie Burman. He's the one who gave her the location where your parents and Bill were."

"Oh god, so Martinez killed her and the detective? Why? If he got what he wanted from them, why kill them?"

"Because he's cleaning up, making sure nothing leads back to him. That's why he was bold enough to create a risky scenario like the one that got him in to see your mother. Bill said that the woman claiming to be a nurse who facilitated the meeting has been located and arrested. Hopefully, she'll roll over on Martinez. Personally, I doubt it."

"It might have been better for everyone if Martinez had just killed me. No one else would have had to die."

"No, that wouldn't have been better, and never say that again."

She was taken aback by the heat in his tone, and it stopped her in her tracks. "I just meant—"

“I know what you meant, and I wasn’t chastising you. It’s just important for you to know that your death wouldn’t have prevented that man from killing. He’ll continue as long as he draws breath.”

“Then what do we do?”

“We end him.”

“End? You mean kill? We can’t do that. That would make us as bad as him.”

“We don’t kill unless it’s necessary,” Clayton said in a tone that brooked no argument. “But if there’s no other way, then we’ll make sure he draws that last breath.”

Ivy was quiet for a few minutes, thinking about what was to come and wondering how they’d stop Martinez without getting killed or killing him. It all seemed like something out of a thriller novel to her. This kind of thing just didn’t happen to regular people.

But then, the Blackstone family was apparently anything but normal. That inspired a question. “Did you ever imagine that your boys would all turn out to be highly trained… warriors, I guess, is an apt term.”

“Yes, I did.”

“Why?”

“It’s in their blood. Every man in my family served his country. Correction, everyone back to my great great-great-grandfather, Nassar Khan.”

“You know, you and Judson have a hint of middle eastern in your looks. Those almost black eyes and what looks like a perpetual tan.”

Clayton smiled. “That is a perpetual tan—farmers tan.”

“Huh uh.” The moment those two syllables were out, she knew she’d stepped in it.

"Oh?" Clayton gave her a sideways glance.

Ivy's mind went into gear. How do you tell a man you've slept with his son when you've only just met him?

"I, uh…". She stopped and, after another step, so did he.

"Look, I'm a terrible liar, and I hate lies anyway, so I might as well confess. Yes, I—I—I care about him, Mr. Clayton. I know we've only just met, and I know sometimes people fall for someone who saves them. I won't say I don't see him as a hero because I do. And I feel safe when he's nearby.

"But," she paused and looked him straight in the eye. "I care about him. He doesn't realize how special he is, the way he's so gentle and kind with the animals, how he loves his family and how he will put himself in danger to protect someone else. I've never met anyone more devoted to family. He's smart and strong and brave and—and—"

"And you're in love with him."

She looked down and then back at him. "I think I'm headed there. Does that upset you?"

He shook his head. "I've prayed Jud would find someone who could recognize what a fine man he is. I think God may have just answered that prayer and there's just one thing I'd ask of you. Well, two."

"Then ask. Please."

"One. Don't say it unless you're sure. He's as tough as rawhide, but his heart can be broken. Don't do that."

"Never sir. I promise."

"I'll hold you to that."

"That's fine. You said two?"

"Yes, second. I want some grandchildren before I'm too darn old to enjoy them."

She smiled up at him. "Well, I can't promise that since Judson and I haven't gotten past the infatuation phase, but I can tell you I'd love to have a family one day and can't imagine children being luckier than to be born into this family.

"And you need to look at yourself, Mr. Clayton. You're one fine man."

Clayton laughed out loud and when he stopped, he patted her shoulder. "Flattery isn't necessary, Ivy."

"It's not flattery, and I'm serious. You're smart and strong, handsome and sexy in that cowboy kind of way. I bet there are a ton of women who'd love to hook up with you. So please, don't call yourself old or act like you have nothing to offer. If the right woman comes along, she's going to be very lucky to end up with you."

"You're a kind woman, Ivy McCoy. I hope things work out with you and Jud."

"So, do I. But as he mentioned last night, I guess what we have to focus on right now is setting a trap for Martinez."

"And do you understand what that means for you?"

She nodded and broke into an altered version of an old Jimmy Buffett song. "Fins to the left, fins to the right, and I'm the only bait in town."

Clayton smiled and put his arm around her shoulders. "You're my kinda gal, Ivy."

She smiled, wishing she felt as brave as she pretended. The truth was, she was scared out of her mind and wished this could all be over. As much as she tried to pretend she was brave, she wasn't. She couldn't find a way to do as Judson suggested and get to the other side of her fear.

What worried her even more was that her fear would be a hindrance to whatever plan they came up with and she'd end up getting someone killed.

Chapter Twenty-Three

Helen moved out of Ed's embrace and looked from him to Bill and Lena Gordon. "Are we sure this is the right thing to do? We're about to provide a sadistic killer with a breadcrumb trail that leads straight to our daughter."

"She'll be protected every moment," Bill assured her, then added, "Look, I know you have no reason to put faith in what I say, but I swear to you on my life that there's no one I trust more that Clayton Blackstone. If he says he'll do a thing, it gets done. So, when he tells us he and his men would put a stop to this murderer, I'll take that as a given—enough that I'll put my life right there on the line with you."

Helen looked at Lena. "And how about you? Do you have that kind of faith in this Clayton Blackstone?"

"No, but I have it in Bill."

Lena could have said anything else, and Helen would still be indecisive, but those words struck something inside she could identify with. She'd put little trust in people during her life. Many of those she had trusted had let her down. Not Ed. No matter what, she could count on and trust him.

"Then I will, too."

"That's my girl," Ed smiled at her. "So, you ready to make the call?

"As I'll get."

"Put it on speaker and I'll record it," Bill said and pulled out his phone.

"Okay." Helen fetched her phone and sat down beside Bill. She put her phone on the table, as did he.

She placed a call to the number she'd been given and after two rings, it was answered. "Mrs. McCoy?"

"Mr. Nieves, hello, yes, it's Helen McCoy. I wanted to let you know that we just found out that Ivy is safe and unharmed."

He said something in Spanish she didn't understand, so she kept quiet, and he continued. "I am so relieved. I have been sick with worry. Where is she?"

Helen looked at Ed, who nodded. "She's in North Carolina. We're headed there tomorrow morning to be reunited with her."

"I am so relieved. Will you please let me know when you have arrived safely?"

"Yes, of course."

"Thank you, Mrs. McCoy. I hope to meet you soon and thank you in person."

“Yes, of course,” she wasn’t sure what to say. “Well, I better go.”

“Very well. We’ll talk soon?”

“Yes, soon. Goodbye.”

The moment she hung up, Helen blew out a breath and looked around at the others. “Now what?”

“Now we follow the plan,” Bill answered.

“And you think he’ll have us followed?”

“I do.”

“Then I suppose you should let Mr. Blackstone know.”

“I will.”

She nodded and stood. “I need a moment.”

With that, she headed for the bathroom. Ed followed to find her crying. “Helen, honey, it’s okay.” He gathered her into his arms. “It’s going to be okay.”

“But what if it isn’t? What if I just handed that madman what he needed to find and kill our daughter? What if I just signed her death warrant?”

“You can’t think that way. We have to believe the plan will work and soon everyone will be free of that evil man.”

“I just want our daughter to be safe. I want her to come home.”

“Well, that might be asking more than she’s willing to give. You know how independent she is.”

“And look what that’s gotten her!” Helen was suddenly filled with anger and had no idea what had brought it on. “First, she marries that—that cheater and loses everything she worked for, after she did everything for him. Then she spends years on end just scraping by, refusing help and barely making ends meet, all alone in Mama’s house with that beast of hers. That’s no life, Ed. None.”

“It’s her choice, honey, and we must respect that. Not everyone is as lucky as we are. But there’s still time for Ivy to get her degree and fulfill that dream, and there’s also time for her to find a good man who will love her.”

“From your lips to God’s ears,” Helen grumbled.

Ed chuckled. “You just need something to be mad at and I understand, but please don’t direct it at Ivy. She’s been through enough and right now, she just needs our love.

Helen felt ashamed for her outburst. “I’m sorry.”

“I know you didn’t mean it. Tell you what, let’s turn our attention to seeing her tomorrow. I can’t tell you how eager I am to hug her and see for myself that she’s okay.”

“I feel exactly the same.”

“And tomorrow that’s what will happen. But right now, how about we set up the iPad and all watch a movie or play some cards?”

“Cards,” she replied and headed out of the bathroom. “And today it’s gals against guys.”

“I’m in,” Lena chimed up. “And you fellas are going down.”

Everyone laughed, all of them relieved that the tense moment had passed. Helen knew the cheer was forced, but didn’t fault them for it. Tomorrow they’d all leave to go to a place they’d never been, with only the word of Bill Gordon that they’d be safe.

She sure hoped he was right. She’d not voiced her concerns and wished she had. Helen had a strong feeling that things would not go as planned. She couldn’t attribute that feeling to anything that had been said or done. It was just there, a perpetual scratch at her brain, begging for attention.

“Hey, earth to Helen,” Lena’s voice had Helen snapping to attention.

"I'm sorry," she apologized. "I just—never mind."

"No, not never mind," Ed put his cards on the table. "Talk to me, hon."

"It's probably nothing," she insisted.

"Tell me anyway."

She looked around at everyone, then again at Ed. "I feel like this plan won't work."

"Why?" Bill asked.

"I don't know. I can't give you a reason. It's just a feeling."

"And have you had this kind of feeling before?"

She looked at Ed, and he answered for her. "She has. Once when I was headed out with an old trailer to pick up a bull. she said she had a bad feeling about it and maybe I should wait until later in the week."

He looked at Helen and then continued. "That afternoon, a tornado touched down and destroyed the farm where the bull was. Every person in the family was killed and every building on the place was flattened. If I hadn't listened to her, I probably would have been killed as well."

Bill and Lena looked at one another and she put her hand on Bill's arm. "You should call Clayton. I don't know about anyone else, but I'd feel better if our plan was something that didn't make Helen's psychic sense ping."

"I'm not psychic," Helen argued. "I can't tell what might happen or even for sure that it will. It's just—"

"Psychic vibe," Lena argued. "Honey, my mother was the same way, and you can take it to the bank that if she ever said she had a bad feeling about anything, we all listened. I think we'd be smart to do that now."

She looked at Bill. "Don't you?"

"I do. If you all will excuse me, I think I'll ask Ed to accompany me down the hall and we'll give Clayton a call."

Lena smiled up at him, and he leaned over to give her a kiss before rising. "Ed?"

"Right behind you." Ed gave Helen's hand a squeeze, then followed Bill from the room.

Lena looked over at Helen. "They'll figure it out. I have faith."

"And I have fear. Want to trade?"

Lena reached across the table for Helen's hand. "No, but I'll share my faith."

Helen nodded. "I should have been kinder."

"To whom?"

"Ivy. You know, I wouldn't let her come visit because of her dog. He's this massive beast."

"Face? Bill talked about him. Said he's the biggest dog he'd ever seen and sweet as the day is long. Completely devoted to Ivy, and she to him."

"And a mother who wouldn't let the dog in her house." Helen stood and hurried to the nightstand for a tissue. She pressed it to her eyes, fighting tears. "What kind of mother does that? What if I never get the chance…"

She couldn't finish the sentence and wished the thought would leave her mind, but all she could think was that there was a very good possibility that she'd never get the chance to make amends with Ivy. That her daughter would die not realizing how much Helen loved her.

And that was a grief she didn't know if she could bear.

Chapter Twenty-Four

Clayton walked over to the fence where Judson stood with his forearms on the top rail, watching Ivy on the stallion, Whiskey, they'd just purchased. "Would you look at that," Clayton said as he reached Judson. "I wasn't aware she's proficient in reining."

"She wasn't either, but she's been watching and learning and damn if that horse won't do anything she asks of it."

"Shame she's not on the show team," Clayton commented as he watched Ivy guide the horse through a precise pattern of spins, circles, and stops. Few people realized the training that went into the art of reining. A western riding competition, reining is sometimes considered to be a lot like figure skating, or a Western form of dressage riding because it requires the horse to be responsive and in tune with its rider.

"Damn shame," Judson agreed. "She's a natural and look there," he pointed toward the gate where Face sat watching. Just watch."

"Well, I'll be damned," Clayton exclaimed after watching Ivy finish taking Whiskey through a perfectly executed sliding stop. As soon as she and the horse moved out of the slide and stopped, Face gave a big bark and thumped his tail on the ground like he was cheering. Almost immediately, Whiskey whinnied and nodded his head.

"Yeah, those two have formed a connection. I don't think I've ever seen anything like it. But you didn't show up to talk about this, so what's up?"

"Change in plans. Our people will appear to pick the McCoys and Gordons up at the hospital. In reality, they will leave with four people posing as the McCoys and Gordons. Ah hour later, two ambulances will leave the hospital on what appears to be a traffic fatality call. The Gordons and McCoys will be in those ambulances and will be taken to a private airport in Kissimmee, where they'll board a private jet and be transported to Ashville where our people will be waiting to bring them here."

"Okay, why the change?"

"Ivy's mother had a bad feeling about the previous plan."

"A bad feeling?"

"A psychic hunch that something was going to go wrong."

"Psychic?" Judson kept his eyes on Ivy, who continued to practice with Whiskey.

"Seems she's had them before."

"Whatever. If you're not upset about the change, then neither am I."

"Bill said he thinks she's overreacting because she and Ivy haven't been on the best of terms the last few years."

“It happens,” Judson said, then glanced at his father. “I’m not being dismissive, simply stating a fact. Some parents and children don’t get along. Sad, but it happens. I know from what Ivy’s said that she loves her mother but feels like she’d been a disappointment, quitting school to put her husband through college and law school, then getting divorced and deciding to get into vet school.”

Clayton nodded. “I remember how it surprised Ivy that we’d let Face sleep in the house. She said she couldn’t visit her folks because her mother wouldn’t allow Face in the house, and he wasn’t accustomed to being without Ivy. He was a week away from being put down when she adopted him and, according to her, they’ve been together every day since.”

“She loves him,” Judson smiled.

“He’s a remarkable creature.”

“That he is.”

“And she’s just full of surprises. I can count on one hand the number of riders I know who can do what she’s doing right now. It’s like she was born in the saddle.”

“And has a real affinity with Whiskey.”

“Well, maybe we can talk her into going on the road with you when you take him out.”

Judson cut a quick look at his father. “What about that guy from Texas, Earl something?”

“I think she’d do better.”

“Then let’s give it some thought and once this mess is behind us, we’ll talk with her about it.”

“Sounds like a plan. You want to tell her about the change in travel arrangements for her folks? "

Judson shook his head. “She’ll just worry because there was a change. And it won’t matter once they’re here.”

“I think you should tell her, son.”

"Why?"

"Because you and she won't have a relationship that will amount to a hill of beans if you're not completely honest with her. And not telling her will be perceived as either a lie or something you're hiding from her. Neither of which bodes well in a relationship."

Judson was quiet for a few moments, then nodded. "You're right. Thanks, Dad."

Clayton patted him on the shoulder and then threw up his hand to Ivy, who grinned and waved back. "I have some calls to make. See you at lunch?"

"Yes, sir."

Clayton headed back to the house, thinking about the change in plans. He held little stock in psychic stuff, but apparently Helen McCoy had convinced Bill that her hunch had enough merit to warrant the change.

There was nothing psychic about Clayton, and he wouldn't admit it to anyone but Bill that her request had triggered a red flag for him. The original plan had been worked out carefully. He couldn't see any weakness or flaw.

So why did Helen McCoy want them to change the plan? He had no answer, but sure was starting to get that itch on the back of his neck. And that only spelled one thing.

Trouble.

*****

With an hour to go before they were due to leave, the McCoys and the Gordons sat in the hospital room, watching the time and trying to come up with idle chatter. When Helen's phone chimed, she jumped and pulled it from her purse.

The text was from Roberto Nieves. *Tell the officer at your door and he'll escort you to me. If you want to see your daughter alive, you'll do as I say.*

Helen read it quickly, then looked at Ed. "A reminder that the house insurance is due. I need to call and tell them I'll make an electronic payment, but it takes a day or so for it to go through. Excuse me?"

"You don't have to leave," Lena said.

"It's fine. I'll just step outside and sit with the patrolman on duty."

"Okay," Ed agreed.

Helen gave him a quick kiss and left the room. The moment she stepped out, the uniformed police officer sitting beside the door stood. "Please come with me."

She nodded and accompanied him to the elevator. They rode it in silence to the parking garage level and when the doors open; he gestured for her to precede him. Helen exited the elevator and, after a moment, turned to look at the officer.

Had she been able to find her voice, she would have screamed. He was holding his weapon, pointing it straight at her. "Walk," he ordered.

"I—I don't understand." She remained motionless. She'd obviously made a terrible mistake. She should have known better. What was wrong with her to have believed that man? What was going to happen to her? If only she could turn the clock back five minutes.

"I said walk." The man's voice was harsher this time, and he took a step toward her, which made her quickly step back.

Helen was afraid to comply and afraid not to, but being shot in a parking deck was more frightening, so she turned around and started walking. They reached the first line of cars and the man barked, "Stop!"

Fear was making her queasy, and she felt like she was about to scream, but she did as she was told. The man pulled out a phone and made a call. He spoke only three words. “Ready for pickup.”

“Pickup?” she blurted. “I thought we were all traveling together.”

“No.”

“Why?”

“It’s not for me to say.”

“Then who do I ask?”

He pointed to a dark Mercedes headed their way. It stopped and, keeping his weapon trained on her, he opened the rear door. “Get in.”

“It’s not for me to say.”

“Then who do I ask?”

He pointed to a dark Mercedes headed their way. It stopped and, keeping his weapon trained on her, he opened the rear door. “Get in.”

Helen nearly screamed when she saw Roberto Nieves sitting on the back seat.

“Get in,” he commanded.

Helen slid into the car. “Why are you here? We’re supposed to—”

“Shut up,” he interrupted, then addressed the driver. “Let’s go.”

“Go where?” Helen asked.

“Where I choose.”

Helen was completely confused and becoming more worried with each passing second. “What do you mean?”

"Let me spell it out for you. When we arrive at our destination, you'll call your daughter and tell her to buy a ticket on the first flight she can get to Miami. We will have someone pick her up at the airport."

"Why?" That made no sense to Helen. "Why would she come here after we made plans?"

"She'll come to save her mother."

"Save…" It took Helen a couple of seconds for his statement to register. When it did, fear seized her in such a tight grip she could barely breathe. "Why?" She finally found her voice. "Why would you do that?"

He smiled and looked away. Helen leaned forward to exclaim to the driver. "Stop the car. Now. Stop."

His gaze moved to the rearview mirror, and a moment later Roberto looked at her. "Let me explain things to you, Mrs. McCoy. You have no choice in this matter. You will go wherever I decide and there will be no argument. When the time comes, you *will* call your daughter and you'll do everything in your power to convince her to come to Miami."

"And if I don't?" She wished she sounded braver.

"Then you will meet the same unfortunate end as Barbie Burman. Only this time, I think instead of strangulation, I'll cut you from pelvis to diaphragm and dump you overboard as chum. I enjoy watching sharks during a feeding frenzy."

For the first time in her life, Helen was rendered mute and immobile by fear. It took her a long time to find her voice. "Why?"

"Come now, Mrs. McCoy, you can't be that stupid."

"But—I—I don't understand. " She stared at him in dread, afraid to ask, but desperately needing assurance. "Why would you do this?"

He laughed and even the driver joined in. Helen was confused and afraid and didn't understand any of what was happening.

“Because I don’t like loose ends.” he said in a suddenly amiable tone.

It took only a split second for Helen to recognize the name. Rafael Martinez was the man who was responsible for Bill Gordon being shot, for detective Burman being killed and for Barbie Burman being strangled and dumped into the ocean.

The severity of the situation hit her like a physical blow. She was being taken somewhere and would most likely be held hostage and forced to call Ivy to convince her to come back to Florida.

Since the moment Ivy was born, Helen had prided herself on believing that she would do anything for her child. She’d give up everything she owned. She’d sacrifice anything for Ivy, including her own stop what you're doinglife.

Now she faced doing just that and, to her shame, she wondered if she had the courage.

Chapter Twenty-Five

Clayton sat at the table, finishing his iced tea and watching as Ivy and Judson cleaned up after lunch. It was a comfortable, homey moment that reminded him of years past when he and his wife would do the same. Only then, their children would be sitting at the table, coloring or playing.

He wished his sons would find love, get married and bring new life to this place. Having grandchildren was his fondest wish.

His phone rang, and he pulled it from his pocket. “Hey Bill, are you all ready to head out?”

“Are you somewhere private?”

It took only that question to have Clayton rising and speaking to Judson and Ivy. "Thanks for fixing lunch and cleaning up. I'm going to step outside and take this call."

"You're welcome," Ivy said with a smile.

Clayton walked outside, down the steps of the porch and into the backyard. "I'm guessing you've hit a snag?"

"Far more," Bill replied. "Helen McCoy has vanished."

"What do you mean, vanished?"

"She received a call and said she was going to step out into the hallway to take it — something about the house insurance payment. When she didn't return after fifteen minutes, Ed stepped out to check on her and couldn't find her."

"What about the guard? I was under the impression there would be a constant police presence."

"The officer is missing as well."

"Have you requested video footage from hospital security?"

"I have. They require a court order, so I called the Chief, and he's having a judge issue the order. We should have it within the hour."

Clayton was quiet for a minute, thinking about what Bill had told him. "Do you think her disappearance is willing or forced?"

"To be honest, I don't know, but I don't have a good feeling about it. She's not answering her phone."

"Has she had any more communication with Martinez?"

"Not that I'm aware." There was a brief pause before Bill added, "What's our next move?"

"I still think it's a good idea for you, Lena and Ed to follow the original plan and come on up."

"So, do I. I'll talk him into it. I'll call you when we're in the air."

"I'll be waiting to hear from you."

Clayton slid his phone into his pocket and started walking across the yard. He did his best thinking while outside, walking his land. This problem was one he wasn't sure how to tackle. If Helen McCoy had willingly left her husband, then chances were, she thought she had come up with a way to help Ivy.

At least that'd be his guess based on what he might do. He could be way off base. But something had made her leave the room. He'd bet the phone call was not from her insurance company.

No, she wouldn't have taken another call from Rafael Martinez. Then it hit him like the proverbial bolt out of the blue. There was one sure way to get a parent to cooperate. Threaten their child. And that meant before long they'd be hearing from Helen or from Martinez, and he'd want Helen to convince Ivy to turn herself over to him. If she didn't, Martinez would kill her mother.

Which meant that unless his people could figure out where Martinez was taking Helen McCoy and come up with a plan, in the next few days, Ed McCoy would either lose a wife or a daughter. No, he corrected himself. With a man like Martinez, Ed would lose both.

He turned and headed back to the house, trying to decide whether to tell Ivy what had happened, or wait until her father arrived. As yet, there was no proof that Helen was even with Rafael Martinez, which meant it would be cruel to scare Ivy with news that might not be true.

The problem was, when everyone arrived and Helen wasn't with them, Ivy would want to know why and Clayton didn't have a clue what to tell her except what he knew for a fact—that her mother received a call, stepped out into the hall to talk and never returned.

Hell, fire and damnation. There was just no easy way for Ivy to hear the truth or any speculation they might have about her mother's whereabouts. No matter what they said, she was going to fear that her mother was in grave danger.

And his gut told him she would be right.

Judson watched his father from where he stood at the kitchen sink, drying dishes as Ivy washed. Something in Clayton's posture struck a chord of worry in Judson. His father was not a man to let his posture slump, to round his shoulders or adjust his stance, no matter what the obstacle, issue, or pain.

The only time Judson had seen his father display any kind of weakness was when his youngest son told him he loved him a minute before he died. That nearly broke Clayton. For a month he walked like a man carrying a heavy weight, his back bent and eyes looking downward.

His current posture reminded Judson of that, but he said nothing about it. He just finished drying the dishes and then gave Ivy a kiss. "I have some things to take care of in the office. I should be done in an hour if you want to work with Whiskey."

"I'd love that," she gave him a smile that had him thinking he'd enjoy having her smile at him like that every day. "I told Mr. Clayton I'd fix a cake for tonight's dessert. He said my folks and the Gordon's should be here by dinner."

"You don't have to cook. We have Louise for that, you know. And Herbert."

"And they're wonderful," Ivy replied. "But it's the weekend and they deserve time off, so I thought we could just cook out. You have that wonderful grill area near the lake. I can get everything ready ahead of time and all we have to do is load up one of the golf-carts and ferry it to the lake. If that's okay."

"Sounds great. And I'll get out of your hair and let you get busy with that cake. I'll head on back when I'm finished."

"Works for me," she said and grabbed his shirt to pull him to her.

The kiss she delivered had him wanting to do something other than paperwork. "A man could get used to this," he remarked.

"But would a man like it?"

Judson smiled. "No, he'd love it."

Her smile lit something inside him. Maybe it was because he was flattered by her attention and the attraction she seemed to have for him. That was more comfortable than admitting he had fallen for her; despite the short time they'd known one another.

"See you soon, beautiful."

"I'll be waiting."

After one more kiss, Judson plucked his hat off the rack by the door and headed outside. His father was walking slowly in the direction of the barn, so Judson hurried to catch up. "You look like a man with a problem," he said as he drew alongside his father.

"Just trying to make a decision and having a tough time with it."

"Need an ear?"

"I do."

"Well, I have two."

Clayton patted Judson's shoulder. "I received a call from Bill."

"Everything on schedule?"

"No, son, it's not."

"Damn, Ivy will be disappointed. She's in the kitchen now baking a cake and planning on what to gather up or prepare to have a cookout for everyone."

"Actually, she's going to be more than disappointed."

"Why?"

"Her mother has disappeared."

"Disappeared? How the hell could she disappear from a hospital room being guarded by armed police officers?"

Clayton filled him in on what happened. "So," he finished with, "Bill, Lena and Ed will arrive together while we try to piece together what happened."

"Damn." Things had just taken a turn for the worst and when Ivy found out, she was going to be out of her mind with worry. "I reckon we ought to tell Ivy."

"I was trying to find words for that, but—"

They both stopped dead in their tracks at the scream that came from the house, followed by the back door banging open and Face rushing out. He galloped to them, grabbed Judson's arm and tugged.

Neither of them questioned nor hesitated. They just broke into a run and followed Face back to the kitchen door. When they entered, they found Ivy standing at the kitchen counter, tears streaming down her face and her hands gripping the edge of the countertop like she could barely stand.

"Ivy!"

The moment Judson said her name, she turned and flew into his arms. "He has her. He has my mother."

It was hard to make out the words due to her sobs, but Judson and Clayton looked at one another and a silent communication passed between them. Either Martinez had kidnapped Helen, or she'd taken it upon herself to cut a deal with him.

Either way, the outlook was grim.

"How do you know?" Judson pushed Ivy to arm's length so he could make eye contact.

She pointed to the phone on the counter. "A video. Someone texted it."

Clayton hurried to pick up the phone. Helen's face was frozen on the screen and to say she looked worse for wear was an understatement. She looked like she'd been beaten. Her right eye was swollen shut, crusted with blood and already black and purple. Both her lips were split and there was a gash on her left cheek and what looked like road rash on her chin and forehead.

Based on what Bill told them, and now this, led to one conclusion. There was going to be an offer of exchange. Helen for Ivy. Clayton felt that in his gut. But before he voiced it, he rewound the video.

Now he could see that Helen was tied to a chair, and the ropes were so tight that her arms were rubbed raw and bleeding.

"Ivy, please listen to me. I love you. I know I haven't always made you feel it, but you are more important than anything in the world and I'm so proud of the woman you've become. Please forgive me if I ever made you feel different."

A fist shot out from off camera and slammed into the side of Helen's head. She would have toppled over had it not been for being tied to the chair.

When Helen could speak again, it was heartbreaking to watch. "He said that if you come to him, he'll let me go. If not…". She paused and choked back tears. "If not, he said he'd cut me from pelvis to diaphragm and toss me into the ocean for the sharks."

Helen leaned forward as much as she could, which wasn't much more than a thrust of her chin. "Don't do it, Ivy. Please. I love you."

The video ended with a scream and the sight of that fist pounding on her face.

Clayton hit stop and lay the phone on the counter. He then looked at Ivy. "I need to speak with your father. If he gives permission, we can get the records from their mobile carrier and find out her location. Once we have that, we'll mobilize our people and go in for her."

Ivy shook her head. "No. He'll kill her."

“We won’t let that happen,” Judson argued.

“But you can’t stop it. He’ll do it out of spite if I defy him.”

Judson looked at his father. “I’d bet on her being right.”

“Sadly, so would I.”

“Then what’s our move?”

Clayton leaned back against the counter, and for a couple of minutes, there was silence. Then he straightened. “Here’s my initial suggestion. Ivy replies to the text, asking when and where. Once she gets a response, she says she’ll comply but will fly there on a private plane. We’ll get Brady here and he’ll fly, but not one of our planes. We’ll charter one. Jud, you’ll pose as first officer. I’ll have Blackstone operatives on site, ready to follow once Ivy’s picked up. If we can nail down Helen’s location, we’ll have people ready to move on it.”

He fell silent and looked at Judson, who nodded, and then at Ivy. She swiped her hand over her eyes and sucked in a breath. “Fine, as long as we save my mom, that’s all that matters.”

“Is it?” Judson asked, and she turned her attention to him.

“No, but I’ve never killed anyone and don’t know if I can, no matter how much I want to.”

“I don’t have that problem and will be with you every step of the way.”

“Then we’ll win,” she said and reached for his hand.

Judson didn’t comment. He didn’t know how to tell Ivy that no matter how strong your team or how trained, you didn’t always win. Sometimes the bad guys won.

What scared him the most was that he’d lose Ivy if they weren’t able to save her mother, and he’d realized fully that he didn’t know if he could bear to lose her.

Chapter Twenty-Six

Judson ended the call and stood at the porch railing, looking out at the long expanse of lawn, not really seeing it or the beauty of the mountains that rose majestically in three directions. He couldn't remember a time he'd looked at the mountains and not felt a sense of awe and gratitude for having been lucky enough to grow up here. There was a peace here, a sense of serenity and continuity, as if these mountains and valleys would endure when humanity fell. The land would survive, heal and flourish to nourish new life, even if humanity vanished.

At the moment, that didn't hold any comfort for him, and the reason was the woman sitting on the grass in the backyard with Face. He couldn't find fault in her fear. Had it been him and he'd seen someone brutalize a member of his family, he'd be ripe for war, and wouldn't give a care about collateral damage.

He wondered if Ivy felt that way, or if she was still held prisoner by the fear. It was easy to do. Had he not been trained, first by his father and later by the Marines, he might feel the same.

His father walked out onto the porch, holding two mugs of steaming coffee. He offered one to Judson, who accepted it with a grateful "thanks."

"She any better?" Clayton nodded in Ivy's direction.

"Nope."

"You going to just leave her out there?"

"She said she wanted privacy. I'm just honoring her request. When she needs me, I'll go out there."

"How will you know?"

"He'll tell me," Judson pointed to Face.

Clayton nodded. "The family will be here by dinner. I asked Gladys and Fred if they'd come in and cook for tonight. Don't let me forget to give them a bonus."

"I'll take care of it. I have cash in the vet office."

"If you don't mind, I'd appreciate it. I swore I'd never be one of those people and yet here I am, not a red-hot-cent in my pocket, but my American Express card is always with me."

Judson smiled briefly. "I know the feeling. Did you arrange for a charter?"

"Brady is taking care of it, and asked that you act as his first officer, which I assured him would happen. He said he'd have your back when it's time for the assault. Cal said he would be here for dinner but wants Ellis to fly them to Miami tonight since he's using a company plane to deliver Mr. McCoy and the Gordons. That way, if we have a location on Helen by then, they can do some recon tonight."

“Sounds good. What time will Bill and the others arrive?”

“They should be here in about two hours.”

Judson nodded, swallowed the last of his coffee and stared out at Ivy and Face. As if in answer to an unspoken question, Face turned his head and yipped. “There’s my cue,” Judson added.

“Give me your cup,” Clayton held out his hand and Judson passed the mug to him. “Try to strengthen her a little, or at least prepare her for her father seeing the video. It’s going to be hard on him, and thus on her, too.”

“I’ll do what I can. Thanks, Pop.”

Judson walked down the porch steps and out into the yard. He’d taken no more than half a dozen steps when Face turned to look, and his tail thumped on the ground. Judson smiled and when he reached them, he looked down at Ivy and offered his hand.

“Walk with me?”

“Please tell me it’s not more bad news.”

“It’s not, but we need to talk before your father arrives.”

She grasped his hand and let him pull her to her feet. He held her hand and started slowly wandering toward the lake. Neither of them spoke. When they reached the beach area on the lake shore, Judson took a seat on the top of a picnic table and patted the wood beside him.

They both laughed when Face jumped up and lay down beside Judson, taking up half the tabletop. Judson scooted over to make room for Ivy on the other side. Once she sat, he took her hand again. “We need to talk before your father arrives.”

“About?”

“The video. Do you think it’s wise to show it to him?”

“That’s his wife. Doesn’t he deserve to know? I mean—oh God! My brother! He doesn’t know what’s happened.”

“And doesn’t need to until the dust settles, and your mother is home and safe.”

"How can you sound so sure that's going to happen?"

He shrugged. "One thing you learn in my previous line of work is that doubt gets you killed. You have to believe, and I don't mean hope. I mean believe. Believe that you shoot faster and more accurately, that your fist does more damage than the other guy's and that you *are* going to win. You think any other way and all it gets you is a one-way ticket to the grave."

"I wish I believed she was going to be okay."

"You need to try harder." He purposely spoke a bit harshly, making his words sound like a reprimand.

"Did you just tell me what to do?"

He liked the fact there was a little anger and a lot of indignation in her question. "Yes."

"And you think that just because you're some trained killing machine, I'll listen and do what you say?"

"No. I think you will because you love your father and don't want to make this worse for him. If he sees that video, he won't be able to think about anything else. He'll see her when he closes his eyes and it won't be her smile—no, he'll see how battered and afraid she is and it will gnaw a hole in him."

"But—but we have to tell him something."

"Yes, we do. We'll say there was a video, and it's been turned over to the team we've assembled. You don't have to admit you saw it. Just try to convince him to let us do what we're trained for. And please, look at me and listen."

When she turned her head to look at him, he continued. "I'll save her, Ivy. No matter the cost to me, I'll save her."

That must have struck something inside her because she burst into tears. Judson gathered her in his arms while she cried. When she finished, she pulled back. "Please don't."

"Don't what?"

“Don’t let the cost be your life. She’s my mom and I love her, but…” she looked away for a few seconds then back at him. “I love you and the thought of something happening to you cuts with just as must pain as the worry about my mom. So, please, if it comes to fight and die or run and survive, please promise me you’ll run.”

“No.” He saw surprise register on her face, so tried to explain. “Running rarely saves you. You either outsmart or outfight and I’ve got a hell of a team backing me up. If our recon tonight suggests we need more men, we’ll bring in more Blackstone operatives. And…”

“And what?” she asked when he looked away.

“And if she’s alive when we arrive, I’ll bring her home that way.”

She nodded. “Can you at least promise you’ll be careful?”

“I vow to you I’m going to use every skill, resource and weapon at my disposal to stay alive, and my principal aim will be to get back here to you.”

“Promise?”

“Scout’s honor.” He held up one hand with the first two fingers extended and the others curled into his palm.

“Where you even a scout?”

“Eagle scout.”

“Well, in that case, I guess I have to trust you.”

“You don’t have to, but Face thinks you should.”

Ivy smiled, and this time the smile didn’t seem so forced. “He already loves you, too.”

“The feeling is mutual,” he leaned over and kissed her cheek. What he didn’t say but would if he made it back was that he was pretty sure she was going to turn out to be the love of his life. That gave him all the reason and determination he needed to go to war.

And win.

Chapter Twenty-Seven

Ivy was out of the door and running across the front porch by the time the car came to a stop in front of the house. The front passenger door opened, and her father stepped out. He barely had time to close the door before she had her arms wrapped around his neck, hanging on as if her life depended on it.

It took a minute before he could gently push her back and look at her. “I’m sorry, Dad,” she said, fighting tears. “I know it’s my fault and—and—do you hate me?”

“Oh honey,” he pulled her back in and hugged her tightly. “I could never hate you and don’t you ever let me hear you say that again. It's not your fault. None of it. It's that SOB Martinez—this is all on him."

Just then, Face reached them. Ed released Ivy and turned his attention to the dog. "Well, hey there buddy, it's been a while and whoa, you've gotten big."

Ivy smiled and wiped away her tears. "He remembers you."

Ed smiled at her. "Yeah, well, I reckon I'm just unforgettable." He looked behind him as the back passenger door opened. "Kinda like this guy."

"Mr. Bill!" Ivy hurried to hug Bill. "I'm so sorry. I hope you can forgive me. I would never have left — "

"Hush, now," he returned the hug. "If it weren't for you calling for help, I wouldn't be standing here today."

"Still, it was your kindness that got you into this whole mess, and I want you to know that I'll do everything I can to repay you for all you've done for me."

"Nonsense," he passed it off and then looked to the beautiful woman getting out of the SUV. "Ivy, this is my wife, Lena. Honey, this is Ivy."

Ivy was shocked when Lena hugged her. "Honey, I'm so sorry we dropped the ball and didn't keep a close enough eye on your mother. I've been kicking my butt ever since she vanished."

"It's not your fault, Mrs. Gordon. And I appreciate you and Mr. Bill looking out for her and my dad."

"Well, if Bill is right, and he usually is, between him, Clayton Blackstone, and his sons and operatives, you'll have your mom back in no time."

Ivy nodded. "I sure hope so."

The driver of the SUV got out of the vehicle as everyone headed for the house. Ivy got a look at him, stopped, and frowned. She'd seen him before. But where? Then it came to her. "Hi, I'm Ivy," she held out her hand. "I didn't get a chance to thank you the night Jud, and I showed up to get the horse, so thank you. I'm sorry I caused you trouble."

"Ellis," he shook her hand. "And you didn't. The sorry SOBs who wanted to kill you were to blame."

"Still, I owe you my thanks and if there's any way I can make it up to you, say the word."

"Well, you could ditch that old man and choose a younger and much better looking Blackstone," he quipped with a smile, then looked over her shoulder.

She looked and there was Judson, standing behind her. Ivy smiled at him, then returned her attention to Ellis. "To tell you the truth, I think he's pretty hot."

Ellis shook his head. "Not a word I'd use to describe him, but hey, what do I know? And besides, Jud's the biggest bad ass of us all, so I reckon that's something."

"Indeed it is," Ivy agreed and reached for Judson's hand. "Come on, I want you to meet my dad."

Jud took her hand, and they followed the Gordons and Ivy's father to the house where Clayton waited.

By the time the introductions were done, Brady and Calvin, Clayton's remaining two sons arrived. They all settled on the big back patio where two enormous tables had been set and a fire burned in the firepit.

Ivy wasn't surprised that talk turned almost immediately to the situation that had prompted the gathering. She stayed quiet unless asked a question. It didn't take long for it to be clear that the Blackstone family was an impressive group of men. Highly trained and skilled, they were all military. Jud and Brady were retired, Calvin and Ellis were on leave. All of Clayton's sons were in special forces and all were committed to helping those who couldn't defend themselves.

She didn't think she'd ever met a more remarkable family. And watching them, Mr. Bill and her dad made her realize he had a lot in common with them. Her dad left the military when she was five, after twenty years as an Marines Ranger.

Ivy remembered little about the time when he was in the service, but now, listening to the talk, she realized like the Blackstones, her dad was also a warrior and a hero. It made her proud of him in a new way.

As they ate, Clayton explained the strategy he, Bill and Clayton's sons had devised. Ed asked a few questions, as did Bill. For clarification, Jud and Cal made a couple of suggestions, and by the time dinner was over, everyone seemed to be on the same page.

All except Ivy. She'd been quite the entire meal, but now spoke up. "Can I say something?"

"Of course," Clayton immediately responded.

"Thank you. First, thank you all for what you're doing for me and my family. You don't know us and it's incredibly kind of you to put yourself in harm's way to help us get my mom back. Second, and I know I will hit opposition to this, so let me say up front, I won't give in on this. I'm going with you—to wherever they have my mom. I know the plan was for me to go to Miami and call Martinez on a Facetime call to show I'm in Florida, but I want to be there when you save my mom. I need to be there. I think it will make it easier if I'm involved."

"How so?" her dad asked.

"Martinez wants to kill me and if I don't show up, he'll hurt or kill mom out of sheer spite, so I have to go. And I know all of you will find this funny or dismiss it entirely, but I need to go. I need to get past this consuming fear and face the monster who is trying to destroy my family. I need to see him pay and know that I helped to make that happen."

There was a long moment of silence before Bill spoke, and his words surprised her. "She's right. She deserves to be part of the mission that puts an end to Martinez. And she deserves a chance to face her fear. We can't deny her that."

“I agree,” Brady spoke up, surprising her, since she’d never met him until tonight. “If it were any of us, no one would deny us.”

“No offense, Ivy,” Cal said, “and not that I don’t think you deserve all you and Bill said, but the truth is, you’re not trained or equipped for this kind of mission and if we say yes, you might get yourself killed.”

“Better than being a coward my whole life,” she looked at Judson as she spoke. “I need to do this. Me and Face.”

“You’d put your dog’s life at risk?” Lena asked.

“No, of course not,” Ivy looked again at Judson. “I know I’ll be safe with the Blackstone men there.”

“Bravo, girl,” Ellis said and grinned. “No way we can say no now.”

She tried not to smile but couldn’t contain it. “So?” she asked of Clayton.

He shrugged. “Like Ellis said, how can I say no?”

“Thank you,” she replied and looked at her dad. “Dad?”

“I agree—on one condition.”

“What?”

“That I accompany you.”

She looked at Jud, who glanced at Clayton. “I assumed as much, Ed. Are you partial to any particular weapon?”

“Just one that’s accurate and lethal.”

“Oh, we’ve got you covered on that,” Brady said, and earned a chuckle from the other men.

“There is one more thing,” Clayton looked around at everyone. “Ivy needs to contact Martinez and tell him she’s coming to Florida. Only she can’t be there until Sunday afternoon. He’ll agree and use the time between now and then to prepare.”

“Should you allow that?” Lena asked. “Giving him time to prepare?”

“No, and we won’t. We’re leaving tonight. Ellis, Jud and Ivy will take the plane back to the airport in Melbourne. They’ll drive to Miami and check in at the Blackstone compound outside of Miami. The rest of us will fly straight to Miami and finalize plans with our operatives there. We’ll move on Martinez just before dawn on Sunday

Lena \reached for Bill’s hand. “Tell me you won’t be joining any assault team?”

“Not a chance. I’ll stay in the communication center. And yes, sweetheart, you are welcome to join.”

“Then we’re agreed?” Jud looked around at everyone. A chorus of “yes’s” rang out, and he turned his attention to Ivy. “Then I reckon it’s time for you to make that call.”

She nodded and rose. “Jud, would you go with me to my room? I’d feel better doing this in private.”

“You sure you want me there?”

“Yes.”

He stood and gestured for her to precede him. Face rose from where he lay behind her chair and followed them. Once they were in her room, Jud put his hands on top of her shoulders. “Are you sure about all this? No one will find fault with you if you decide to sit this out. And it could be dangerous. Chances are that people are going to die.”

“Not our people? Right?” His statement scared her even more. “Do you think we’ll lose?”

His bark of a laugh didn’t sound at all like a man amused. It had a much darker ring to it. “No, we won’t lose.”

She nodded and wrapped her arms around his waist, leaning in on him with her face against his chest. “Just make sure my folks stay safe.”

"I will."

"And you," she pulled back to look up at him.

"Don't worry, baby."

Ivy didn't comment, she just pressed into him again, praying that when the dust settled on all this awfulness, they would return with everyone safe and unharmed. Including her mother.

Chapter Twenty-Eight

The time on her watch read one-thirty in the morning when the SUV Judson drove pulled up in front of the Miami headquarters of Blackstone, a stucco and tile two-storied building that stretched almost half a block. There was no name on the building, nothing to identify it.

Ivy, Judson, and Ellis found everyone else in the conference room. A cafeteria operated twenty-four hours a day. There was a gym, theater, offices, a lavish state-of-the-art training center, and suites where some operatives lived, others for visitors or clients.

She hadn't known what to expect, but never imagined such a high-tech, well-appointed or massive place. The conference room looked like something out of a movie. There was an eight-foot electronic "board" on one wall, allowing input from consoles set into the table at each seat. The table could accommodate twenty people, but at present, the Gordons, her father, Clayton, and his sons, along with her, were the only people seated in the heavily cushioned chairs.

"Now that we're all here, let's review," Clayton said and tapped on the console. "According to our intel, Martinez's yacht is anchored offshore, manned by a skeleton crew." He gestured to the massive electronic board and a picture displayed of a yacht.

"The Exito was built by an Italian yard in 2018. She can accommodate up to 24 guests, 52 crew, and boasts of over 4000 meters of interior space. She has seven decks, two helipads, and a hangar. It also carries a custom submarine certified to one-hundred-meter depth.

"Powered by a diesel engine, she can reach a top speed of twenty knots and has a maximum cruising range of six thousand nautical miles. From what we've been able to discern since we identified Martinez, there is a skeleton crew on board, and Intel suggests this is probably where he is holding Mrs. McCoy."

He looked around, and Cal spoke up. "I'll say it since the rest of you won't. Fifty-four crew is a lot. Obviously, not all will be trained, but I'm betting two-thirds will be. A man in Martinez's position will want to surround himself with as much protection as possible."

"Your point?" Ed asked.

"Look around this table. If everyone sitting here, excluding the women—and no offense, gals, but this has to do with training, not gender—so no offense, but we'll be out-manned. No way of telling if that means outgunned, but it wouldn't surprise me."

Ivy looked around at everyone. Judson was the first to speak. "I agree, but..." he held up a hand. "... we have six operatives at this table. No offense Officer Gordon, but we need someone at Com, and you're recuperating, so you are the obvious choice for that. We can easily have a dozen men here before dawn if you want to go in heavy."

"What do you suggest?" Clayton asked.

"Us and six more hand-picked operatives with combat experience. Brady? Any of your SEAL buddies in the area?"

Brady grinned. "Three or four."

"Think they'd be on board for a rescue operation—off the books?"

"Always."

"Then, when we finish here, get up with them. We need them here for a briefing as fast as possible."

"They're expecting Ivy on Sunday," Ed pointed out. "It's Friday night—pardon, Saturday morning. Why do they need to be here so quickly?"

"Because we're going in before dawn Sunday morning and have a lot to do."

"Is that enough time?"

"It has to be," Jud replied and turned his gaze to Clayton. "Don't we have a demolition expert in residence?"

"We do."

"I want to talk to him when we finish here."

"About?" Bill asked.

Judson typed on his console for a moment. The window on the planning board with the photo of the yacht and its specs slid to one side, and another window opened, this one displaying a massive house.

"This is Martinez's home on Star Island. Twenty-six thousand square feet with a protection detail of twenty-four."

"And?" Ed asked.

"We're going to blow it up."

"What? Why?"

"Because we want Martinez on the yacht, and the moment he realizes he's under attack, he'll take the speedboat docked at his house to the yacht, having given orders that as soon as he's on board, he's ready to head for Cuba."

"And we'll be waiting for him," Ellis added.

"Indeed, we will," Jud agreed.

"Sounds like you've covered all the bases except one," Ed spoke up, and when everyone looked at him, continued. "How do we get Helen safely off the yacht?"

"That's where Ivy comes in. We'll equip her with a comm unit—an earpiece, so she can communicate. She's going to call Martinez before we blow his house, and he'll take her with him to the yacht. She'll demand to see her mother, and when we hear that she and Helen are together, we take the ship."

"And Martinez?" Ed asked.

"You tell us," Clayton answered. "He took your wife. How do you want him to pay?"

"I want the bastard dead."

"So be it," Clayton agreed. "Okay, that's it for tonight. Jud? Brady? We need to get a demo team in and ensure we have what's needed to take down the house."

"And the ship?" Ivy added.

"And the ship," Judson agreed. "Eliminate all trace of him, and the investigation can look like a rival drug lord took Martinez out to take over his territory."

Clayton nodded and stood. "Breakfast at seven. Get some rest while you can."

Ivy rose, but Judson stayed seated. He reached for her hand, and she leaned down to hear him speak. "There are some things we need to take care of tonight. We'll have someone show you to quarters—give you a chance to spend some time with your dad."

"How long will you be?"

"Don't know."

"Will you come find me when you're done?"

"Do you want me to?"

"Please. I know chances are it will all work out, but in the off-chance I'm wrong, I'd like to wake up beside you in the morning."

"Nothing would make me happier," he smiled at her. "I'll come find you when we finish."

She smiled and surprised him by giving him a soft kiss. Then she straightened, touched Face on the head, and together they followed her dad, Bill, and Lena from the room. "Do you need to stay?" she asked Bill.

"Honestly, right now, I think I need to sleep more. Try to get some rest, Ivy."

"You too," she kissed him on the cheek and then stuck out her hand to Lena. When they clasped hands, Ivy pulled Lena in for a hug. "Rest well."

"You too, sweetheart."

"Mr. Gordon?" A tall, dark-skinned man approached. "May I show you to your accommodations?"

"Lead the way," Bill said, and then nodded to Ed. "See you in the morning."

"Yes, sir," Ed replied, and then turned when a voice sounded behind him.

"This way, sir."

Ivy and her father followed the short, wiry-built man and were shown to a suite with two bedrooms, separated by a large living space. Each bedroom had its own private bath.

Her father opted for the couch. Face flopped down on the floor in front of the sofa, and Ivy settled beside him. He heaved a breath when he sat, and she turned her head to look at him. "Are you okay, dad?"

"As I can be under the circumstances."

"We'll get her back, Dad."

"I have hopes, honey, but we also have to be realistic. We're dealing with people who obviously have no qualms about killing."

"I know, but I need to believe it will be okay. Otherwise…". Tears welled up in her eyes. "I just need to believe. And I do, Dad. Jud will make it happen. I know he will."

"You're in love with him, aren't you?"

"I think I'm getting there. Does that bother you?"

"Not in the least. I hope a week from now, we're all enjoying one another's company, celebrating defeating the enemy and the fact that you found a good man to love. At least I hope he's a good man."

"I think so. He's going to let me intern with him. He's also a large animal vet, so if I work for him while I take the rest of my classes, it will be an enormous help in my education."

"That sounds good, doodlebug. I hope it all works out."

"Me too."

There was a protracted silence, with only the sounds of Face cleaning his paws. Finally, Ivy looked back at her dad. "She shouldn't have put herself in danger for me."

"I know, but…"

"But what?" Ivy asked when his voice trailed off.

"I don't know for sure what made her sneak out to meet that man. I know it's been bothering her for a while that you and she have had a few—let's call them less than comfortable years—you know, her being so rigid about Face and upset because you wanted to stay in Florida and live in my mom's house. She felt like you cut her out of your life after that."

“But I didn’t. I don’t have any downtime with work and school, taking care of Face, and volunteering at the shelter. I tried to tell her and asked if we could come home for Easter, but she said I could come, not Face, so I had to say no.”

“I know, Ivy, I know. And when your mother is back with us, safe and sound, maybe it’s time for you and her to spend some time together and patch things up.”

Ivy nodded. “I guess so.”

“And on that note, I’m calling it a night.” He rose.

Ivy stood and gave him a long hug. “I love you, Dad.”

“And I love you, baby girl. Sleep well.”

“You too.”

After he went into one of the bedrooms and closed the door, she lay on the thick carpet beside Face, who rolled over and put his head on her belly. Two hours later, that’s how Judson found them. Sound asleep on the floor.

Chapter Twenty-Nine

This felt like the longest day of her life, and it was barely eight in the morning. Everyone at the Blackstone complex had been up since four a.m., which meant they had only a few hours of sleep.

She woke, confused about how she'd gotten undressed, and into bed. When Judson came to wake her, he told her he'd put her in bed, then left with his brothers and two demolition experts to set explosives on Martinez's home. They'd just returned. She hurried to shower and dress, and they then met everyone for breakfast in the big cafeteria.

Bill and Lena were staying at the complex, helping to man communications. Judson was headed to Martinez's yacht with

Brady, Calvin, Ellis, and four other Blackstone operatives. Clayton and Ivy's father would be on a separate boat and board the yacht once the operatives had secured it.

Before she left to be driven to the docks, she asked Judson for a moment alone. They walked outside onto a large, covered patio, and she turned to him. "First, thank you. I'm terrified of what's coming. If anything happened to you—"

"It won't."

"How can you know that?"

He shrugged. "It's part of the training. You have to believe you're bigger, badder, meaner, and more skilled and can't be beaten. I'm good at what I do. So are all the others."

She nodded, feeling that he was only saying what he thought she needed to hear. "And something else. I need you to do something for me."

"Name it."

"If it comes to a choice — if you can only save one of us— my mom or me, please save her."

"No."

"No?"

"No."

"Why?"

"Because I'm not going to let either of you be harmed, and because I love you."

Ivy burst into tears and threw her arms around him. "I love you. Please don't die."

"Not today, beautiful." He hugged her and then pushed her to arm's length. "Now, I need to say something to you. He will try and terrify you – he'll have something planned, something that will horrify you and tempt you to do whatever he says to avoid his threat. Don't let him see that you're afraid. We'll be coming aboard to take over the moment you board."

"I'll try."

"That's my girl." He gave her another hug. "Now, I have to go."

Ivy watched him leave with the other men, then hurried to find her dad. He was with Clayton and Bill in the communication center. "Promise me you'll be careful?" Ivy asked.

"Only if you will," he said with a smile.

She nodded. "I love you, Dad."

"I love you, baby girl. Now let's go save your mom."

She swiped away tears, smiled, and hugged him. "Ready?" Clayton asked.

"As I'll get."

He gestured to a man off to one side. "Randy will drive you. Remember what Jud told you."

"I will," she said and, on impulse, hugged him. "Be safe, please?"

"Always."

It was harder than she anticipated to leave the complex. The moment she was in the car, the fears returned, all the what-ifs piled in on her until she felt like she was going to have a heart attack, her heart was racing so, and her stomach felt like something was churning inside it. She tried the exercises Jud had taught her, slowing her breathing and trying to blank her mind of everything but an image of a lone cloud floating in an endless blue sky.

Surprisingly, it helped a little, at least enough, so she could get her heart rate slowed. When they reached the docks, Randy stopped and looked over at her. "Don't worry, Miss. They're the best. They'll get your mother back and keep you safe."

"Thanks," she smiled, exited the car, and stood there for a few moments, fighting back nausea. She was so scared that she felt like she was going to vomit. For a few seconds, she just stood there, taking long slow breaths as Jud had shown her. She figured she must be the most chicken person on the planet.

It didn't work. She still felt like she would spew at any moment. *Please don't let me screw up,* she prayed. Her mother's life was on the line. She had to suck it up, find her courage, and follow the plan.

With one more deep breath, she pulled out her cell phone and texted Martinez. "I'm here."

Only a moment passed before there was a response. "A boat will be there shortly to fetch you."

"He said a boat will be here soon for me," she spoke aloud, hoping the communication bud Judson put in her ear would pick up her words. She'd never worn anything like it before and was terrified it wouldn't work.

"Hang tough, baby. We're in position."

"Can't you just go onto the yacht, grab my mom and leave?"

"We won't get Martinez if we move now. And we can't be sure your mother is on the yacht. He'll take her with him if she's being held at his estate. We'll know momentarily. Wait… hold on."

She did as he said, and a few seconds later he was speaking in her ear again. "We just detonated the first explosive. Let's see what he does."

Ivy waited, and after a few minutes Judson spoke again. "He's on the dock at the estate, getting into a speedboat with a driver and four armed men. Your mother must be on the yacht."

"There's a boat pulling up now," she said. "A man is waving at me."

"Showtime. Just follow the plan."

"Don't let them kill my folks. Promise me."

"I'll do everything in my power. Again, just follow the plan."

“I will.” She slid her phone into her pocket and walked down the pier to the boat, wondering if she’d live long enough to step back onto dry land.

*****

When the first explosion shook the house, Rafael Martinez stood on the patio overlooking the infinity pool, where half a dozen nude women lay on lounge chairs or pool floats. There was a chorus of screams and women scrambling for towels.

Before he could make it into the house, another explosion rocked the house, this time raining sheetrock down from the ceiling in the room he was entering. He cursed and continued, running through the spacious salon.

Another explosion had him rethinking his direction. He grabbed his phone from his pocket and ran out onto the patio and down the steps, headed for the pool. Screams from people inside the house, groans and cracks from the structure, and more explosions turned the sunny morning into a nightmare.

As he reached the pool, the water shot up in a geyser of plaster, tile and water. The concrete under his feet shook and quaked, forcing him to fight for balance. Cracks appeared in the surface that quickly widened.

That did it. His house was blowing up around him, and he wasn’t going to become one of the casualties. He turned and ran for the dock at the seawall. It was no shock to find five of his men doing the same.

“To the yacht!” he yelled and climbed in.

In seconds, they were speeding away. Rafael watched the house. Before they were a half mile from shore, it was a pile of burning rubble. Sirens screamed as fire crews responded. He watched with narrowed eyes and clenched jaws. Whoever was responsible was going to die, and it would not be a quick death.

Rage bubbled up and out in a howl, followed by cursing that lasted a solid two minutes. His face flushed deep red. The men in the boat with him kept their mouths shut and their eyes averted. No one wanted to mess with Martinez when he was enraged. That was the surest way to a short life.

They all saw the destruction as the lavish mansion was destroyed. It took less than five minutes for the entire structure to be transformed into a pile of rubble. Martinez finally stopped cursing, grabbed his phone and placed a call.

"Find whoever is responsible! Do you hear me? No, I don't want you to kill them. I'll do that myself. Just find them."

He then texted Ivy. "Where are you?"

"With your man in a speedboat. We're almost to your yacht."

He didn't bother responding. He'd be there soon enough and take care of Ivy McCoy and her mother. It wasn't lost on Rafael that nothing had gone smoothly since the day Ivy McCoy arrived to clean the pool at Frederick Ortiz's house. It was time for that problem to be resolved.

A smile split his face as he thought about what he had planned for Ivy and her mother. Neither of them would survive the day, and neither would die easily. Once he finished with them, he'd return to Cuba for a while where he had more security. He'd find out who'd destroyed his house and deal with them.

Then he'd have his estate rebuilt – bigger and more lavish than before. And this time, he'd make sure he had those extras he'd been dreaming off, like the old-fashioned medieval torture dungeon he'd seen drawings of.

That thought made him smile. It was a shame he didn't have something like that now. He could have had hours of pleasure, torturing the McCoy women. But he'd make do with what he had on hand, and when the sun set on this day, they'd be fish food, and he would still be the king of Miami.

Chapter Thirty

Ivy slid on sunglasses as soon as she stepped into the speedboat. As they drew near the gigantic yacht, she scanned the water. Where were Judson and the rest of the team? All she'd seen thus far was two guys in a fishing boat hauling in a net weighted with fish, and another trawler sitting idle.

Had something gone wrong? Jud said they'd find a way on board ahead of her arrival. Simmering fear heated to a boiling point in a flash, and she felt sweat pop out on her skin. Had she not been afraid her mother would die; she'd jump off the moving boat and try to swim to shore.

But they were already slowing to pull alongside the yacht. Just as the driver killed the engine, a hatch opened in the bulwark and an accommodating ladder slid out, rotated, and unfolded, creating a kind of boarding walkway that fit tight against the side of the ship, with a railing on the water side.

Ivy quickly texted Clayton. *About to board.*

The driver motioned to the ladder, and Ivy carefully moved to the side of the boat. She leaned out to take hold of the railing and then dropped her phone into the water, as Judson had instructed. She stepped out of the speedboat and onto the ladder. When she reached the top, she was stopped. Facing her was Martinez and two men behind him, standing in a triangle formation.

"I appreciate punctuality," Martinez commented. "Now, ask permission to board."

That struck Ivy as supercilious. Had she not been using all her strength to keep from trembling in fear, she might have issued a pithy reply. But fear won. "Permission to board?"

"Sir."

"Sir," she added.

"Permission granted."

"May I see my mother?"

"Do you have a phone on you?"

"No."

"Check her," he ordered the men standing behind him.

The two stepped from behind him and took positions, one behind and one in front of her. They patted her down, checked her pockets, and then reported she was clean.

"Can I see my mother, please?" she asked again.

"Of course."

Martinez led the way, with Ivy behind him and the two men following. She had no clue where they were headed, but when the passageway opened in what appeared to be a four-story court, she gasped.

She'd never seen anything like it. Marble covered the floors and the walls, with immense seating areas along each side and across the back, each with its own bar and gigantic flat screen televisions.

But the centerpiece of the colossal space was the three story, round aquarium. Ivy's heart nearly stopped when she first saw it. She wasn't expert at determining size, but it had to be at least fifty feet. It was filled with water. And a shark that had to be at least fifteen feet long.

"Come, let's go upstairs where you can get a better look and join your mother."

Martinez's tone was reminiscent of a tour guide. Ivy was willing to bet he wasn't trying to impress her unless fear fit into that category. She didn't want a better look, but there was no way to refuse, so she followed him to the back wall, which meant circling the thick glass cylinder.

Despite knowing she was in no danger, she cut a wide berth around the cylinder and felt relieved when she stepped into the elevator. It stopped, and she followed Martinez. He led her down a short corridor and opened a door.

Ivy couldn't stop the gasp that escaped when she looked inside the room. Her head swam with sudden dizziness, and her eyes blurred from the rush of tears. She tried to run across the room on rubbery legs, but one of Martinez's men grabbed her around the waist from behind and stopped her.

"Let go of me!" Ivy found her voice and her mettle. She fought, kicked, scratched, hit, and squirmed, trying to break free, and finally managed to tear away. The momentum robbed her of balance, and she fell, but quickly bounded to her feet and raced across the room. "Mom!"

Helen McCoy was strapped to a metal table, the thick leather biting into her flesh. Three thick straps held her arms immobile at the wrists, just above the elbows and biceps. Likewise, thicker straps imprisoned her legs at ankles, above the knees and high on her thighs.

The strap across her forehead prevented her from turning her head, and one secure around her neck added an extra layer of immobility.

Ivy's hands trembled as she fumbled with the buckle on one of the straps. "Don't," her mother whispered. "Ivy don't."

"No!" Ivy looked at Martinez and screamed. "Let her go, you monster!"

He laughed. "Gladly. If you take her place."

Ivy released one buckle and started on another. "No. I'm taking my mother and we're leaving."

"I don't think so."

"And I don't care what you think!" She continued her efforts until Martinez rattled off something in Spanish to his men, and they hurried to her. One grabbed a handful of her hair with one hand and her throat with the other. She screamed and fought as long and hard as she could, but it wasn't long before black spots danced in front of her eyes from lack of oxygen.

The other man released Helen's restraints and pulled her from the table. She fell and he kicked at her. "Get up, *puta.*"

"Fuck you," Helen retorted, and then groaned when the man kicked her again. He grabbed her by the hair and hauled her to her feet, then looked at Martinez.

"I think a lesson in good behavior is in order," he said and pulled out his phone. "Bring him to the feeding platform."

Ivy didn't know what he meant, but it made a cold chill slide over her skin. Martinez motioned to his men. They bullied the women from the room, down the hall, and to what was basically a gate in the railing that overlooked the shark tank. They were shoved over next to the railing.

Ivy would have stepped back if she hadn't had a man standing behind her, keeping her pinned to the railing. She wasn't sure what was about to happen, but it couldn't be good. A few seconds later, three men emerged from the elevator. Two of them were basically dragging the third man between them. His hands were cuffed, and his feet were bare.

The two muscled him to the gate, opened it and pushed him out onto the platform that extended from the floor, over the water. "Jump," Martinez ordered the man.

Since she didn't speak Spanish, Ivy had no idea what the man was saying, but it sounded like he was begging. Tears streamed down his face, and he held his cuffed hands up in a prayer-like position.

Martinez looked at Ivy. "When I give an order, I expect it to be followed to the letter. I do not tolerate failure, and betrayal is a capital offense. This man stole from me and then lied about it. His punishment is death.

He then pressed a button Ivy hadn't noticed mounted on the support pole of the gate. One touch and the platform began to retract. The man screamed, looking around wildly, begging for help.

Ivy cut a look at her mom. Helen's eyes were closed. Ivy leaned over and whispered. "Open your eyes."

"No."

"Mom, open your eyes. You can't let him see your fear."

"No."

Fear and frustration got the best of her, and Ivy screamed. "Open your damn eyes!"

Helen's eyes flew open at the same moment the platform slid into its housing, and the terrified man standing on it fell. He thrashed around in the water, kicking as hard as possible and trying without success to find something to grab hold of.

A scream ripped from Helen as the shark shot upward, covering the two-story distance in seconds. Ivy felt like screaming but bit her lip hard enough to pierce the soft tissue in her mouth. She wanted to close her eyes, didn't want to see what was about to happen, but feared showing weakness would only make things worse.

If only the poor man in the water wasn't crying and thrashing, pleading for help. "I'm sorry," she said a split second before the shark reached him. One bite and a wrench of its head, and the man was torn in half.

But not dead. It was a scene from a nightmare. The water boiled with movement and blood, the shark biting and tearing, and the man flailing, eyes wide with terror and pain. She wished he would drown, pass out – something to escape the horror and agony.

It was over in seconds, and while she and her mother stood there trembling, Martinez clapped and laughed. "Well, that was exciting. Who's next?" He tapped his upper lip with his index finger. "The mother, I think." He pressed the button to extend the platform.

The man behind Helen grabbed hold of her and started muscling her toward the gate. "No!" Ivy flew at him, punching and kicking with every bit of energy she could muster. "Leave her alone!"

The second man tried to restrain her, but the way she was twisting and jerking, he had trouble holding onto her. Finally, he managed to get her right arm wrenched up behind her, forcing her into a bend to relieve the pressure and pain.

Ivy screamed as Martinez opened the gate, and the man holding onto Helen shoved her onto the platform, then slammed the gate. Helen screamed and tried to climb over the gate, but Martinez kicked her, and she lost her grip.

The next few seconds were moments out of sync with time in Ivy's perception, with multiple things happening simultaneously. The sound of gunfire came from the decks below them, along with shouts and screams. Two explosions rocked the ship, and Helen fell back, splashing into the water.

A split second later, the man holding Ivy lurched forward with blood bursting from his chest. Before that grizzly sight could register in Ivy's brain, her father was there, leaping the railing and into the water.

There were more explosions and gunfire. It sounded like war had broken out on the ship. She could only pray that all the people who were trying to help her would be safe, but at the moment she could only focus on the predicament she and her mother faced.

Martinez turned toward her, and Ivy screamed right before he grabbed her. They struggled, and his foot slid in a puddle of water. When that happened, she saw her chance and pushed him as hard as she could.

He went backwards over the railing, and since he had a death-grip on her, he took her with him. Ivy landed on top of him, and he lost his grip on her. Not that holding onto her was a priority anymore. Martinez was looking around wildly, trying to push Ivy away so he could get to the platform.

She kicked at him and spun around in the water. Her father had one arm around her mother's chest, keeping her back to him as he kicked for the platform. In his other hand was a big handgun. The shark had abandoned the carcass of the man and was now headed back toward Ivy's parents.

Ed kept moving but aimed at the shark and fired. The bullet missed, and he fired again. This time, a blossom of blood appeared in the water on the shark's left side. Ed kept swimming, backing away from the shark, keeping the gun trained on it.

Ivy cut a glance to see Martinez had reached the platform and was trying to crawl up on it. Just as he hoisted himself up, a big foot came down on his hand. If she hadn't been so terrified, she would have cheered when she saw who the foot belonged to. Judson.

Judson kicked Martinez from the platform and yelled to Ivy, "Swim!"

That's what Ivy did, but not toward the platform. Maybe she'd just grown numb to the fear, but at present she didn't care if the shark got her, she had to save her parents. She made it to them and wrapped one arm around her dad. "Come on!"

That's what he and her mother did. They made it to the platform where Martinez was trying to climb onto the platform. Every time he tried; Judson would kick him back into the water.

Judson knelt onto one knee and extended his hand. Ed and Ivy pushed Helen to him, and he hauled her onto the platform. As he helped her up, Martinez attacked Ed, grabbing him from behind. It looked as if he was trying to climb Ed like a ladder, but the reality was, he was trying to shove Ed down.

Ivy screamed and dove at them. She pushed down on the top of his shoulders as hard as she could, and he released Ed to try and get her off his back. "Dad go!" Ivy yelled. He ignored her and helped her push Martinez beneath the surface of the water.

"Ed! Ivy, get out of the water!" Helen yelled.

Ivy looked around them and saw the shark headed toward them. "Dad go!" she screamed and pushed away from Martinez.

Ed shoved Martinez as hard as he could, and then dove toward the platform. Judson pulled Ivy onto the platform as Ed reached it. "Ed!" Helen screamed, which made Judson and Ivy both look.

It looked like Martinez was trying to climb Ed's back. Each time he threw his body up and forward, Ed went under the water and the shark got closer. Judson pulled his gun and fired. Blood blossomed in the water from the side of the shark's head, but it kept coming.

Ivy lay on the platform with her body from the chest up, stretched out over the water with her arms extended toward her father. "Come on Dad!!"

Ed kicked as hard as he could for the platform. His fingers touched Ivy's but couldn't grip. She screamed a warning as Martinez grabbed the back of Ed's shirt. The shark was getting closer, with blood staining the water around it. Judson pulled his weapon again and fired. Another bloom of blood appeared on the shark's side, and it jerked. Ed reached the platform, digging at the water with both arms, with Martinez still hanging onto him.

Helen was screaming, and Ivy yelled at her. "For God's sake, shut up!"

Judson knelt to extend his hand to Ed, and Martinez roared and tried to pull Ed back. The shark was only feet away. A teeming wave of terror engulfed Ivy, and she acted without thinking, grabbed Judson's gun and pointed.

The rapport when she fired was deafening, and the recoil had her losing her grip on the weapon. It hit the surface of the platform and slid, but she didn't watch to see where it stopped. Her heart was beating so fast she was sure it would explode from her chest.

Judson pulled Ed onto the platform just as the shark struck. Ed grabbed Helen and she wrapped her arms around him, crying and shaking, blubbering incoherently. Jud just knelt there, watching impassively.

Martinez was still alive, bleeding profusely from the gunshot high on the left side of his chest. He had only enough time to look back before he was caught in the shark's jaws and propelled up, out of the water and then down. Bubbles surrounded his face from the oxygen, escaping his lungs as he howled in agony.

"Dear Lord," Helen breathed.

Ed pulled her closer. "Don't look, baby. Just hold onto me."

It took Ivy two tries to stand, but she got her feet beneath her and used her hand to push herself up. Jud stood and took her hand to pull her close. “It’s over,” he said softly. “Now you have your life back.”

“How many people died today?” she asked.

He shrugged. “I don’t know.”

“What do we do now?”

“Sink the ship and call it a day.”

“Is it necessary to sink it?”

“It is.”

“Then let’s do it. I want to go home.”

“To your house in Florida?”

“No. It’s time my folks sold that place.”

“Are you sure?”

“I am.”

“Then where do you want to go?”

“What would you think about me and Face going home with you.”

“I think that sounds perfect.”

“So do I.”

He smiled at her. “You’re not the same woman I met a lifetime ago, Ivy McCoy.”

She managed a smile. “It feels like the night we met was a lifetime ago, but I’m still the same.”

“I have to disagree with that.”

“Why?”

“I saw what you did – how you saved your father. You stayed in the water with a shark to save your folks, and you did it without hesitation.”

He hugged her close for a moment. "I'm proud of you. You made it where you wanted to be."

"And where exactly is that?"

"The other side of fear."

Ivy smiled up at him. "Let's blow this tub, go find our dog and go home. I think it's time to start a new story for our lives."

"Yeah? And what will you call it?"

"Happiness."

The End

Excerpt from

WHERE THE MOUNTAINS KISS THE SKY

Chapter One

Caught up in the view from the window seat in first class, Rylee was startled when the flight attendant leaned in over the empty aisle seat to speak with her. "We'll arrive on time if you have someone meeting you."

"Oh, thank you," Rylee smiled.

"Is this your first time visiting Wyoming?"

"Yes, it is. The view from here is stunning."

"Isn't it? Are you visiting family or on vacation?"

"Starting a new job." Rylee still had a little trouble believing she was moving to Brickton, Wyoming.

"Well, congratulations, I hope you'll be happy."

"Thank you, so do I."

As the flight attendant moved away, Rylee turned her attention back to the window. Her mind moved away from marveling over the sights to what led her to be on this flight.

No Limits Cyber Security Systems Integration, or No Limits, as it was most often referred to, was the second job she'd held since graduate school. They tempted her away from a job with the government with a salary that was like a dream to a young woman with a mountain of student loans. Things were definitely more profitable in the private sector. In the nine years she'd worked for them, she'd not only paid off her loans but also her house.

At thirty-seven, she was debt-free and eager for advancement so that she could save for a bigger home. The small home she'd purchased in Orlando, Florida, where she worked, was okay, but she wanted something in a more upscale community, with perhaps a pool.

Rylee didn't anticipate significant advancement with No Limits, but last year was given control of the team in charge of all the websites, webcams, and live feeds from the big resorts, amusement parks, and some beaches. She loved what she did and worked hard to ensure the systems operated flawlessly, with failsafe backups, generators in case of power failures, and daily diagnostics to ensure no interruptions.

She'd never imagined how successful the company actually was, but during her time with them, she'd watched them grow into a corporation now traded on the American stock exchange and one who'd gained a monopoly in the type of services they offered.

Last week, her boss called her in for a meeting. Since it was unscheduled, she was perplexed why he'd take her away from her work. Not that she questioned him, she simply showed up on time.

Ian Grant, her boss, made a name for himself in the United Kingdom, working for the government on internet security. He married an American and moved to the states, where he went into business with two other men and formed No Limits.

Rylee saw him sitting at his desk on the phone and knocked on the glass of his door. He motioned for her to enter, and she did so but remained just inside the door as he finished his conversation, which only took seconds.

"Rylee, have a seat." He gestured to the seating area on the other side of the room, came around from behind his desk, and sat on one of the big leather wing chairs. She opted for a seat on the sofa adjacent to him.

"You wanted to see me, sir?"

"I did. Do you remember Brent Corsa? He's been heading the team up in Wyoming for the last couple of years."

"Yes, I do. We had a couple of interesting conversations about the importance of developing more vendor-agnostic middleware to act as mediators between software from numerous vendors rather than between two specific applications. He has some compelling and brilliant ideas."

"Had," Ian's smile faded. "Brent was killed in an auto accident yesterday."

"Oh no." Rylee hated hearing that news. Brent was a genuinely nice person with a brilliant mind. "What about his partner, Dennis?"

"In critical condition."

"I'm so sorry."

"We all are, but like it or not, we still have a contract to honor, and the Board met last night to decide what to do. It's been decided. We're sending you to Brickton, Wyoming, to take over for Brent."

"Me?" She was stunned. "But what about–"

"Louis is ready to move up. He's been your second in command for three years, and we believe he's ready to take the reins. You've got two days to get him up to speed. We're booking you on a flight to Brickton on Thursday. You'll meet the team, have the weekend to get settled, and then jump in on Monday."

"But...". She didn't know what to say, her mind was in a whirl. "But what about my house? And I don't have –"

"The company will buy your house for above market value. We can close in under a week. We'll have your belongings put into an environmentally controlled storage unit until you decide what you want to do with everything.

"Alternatively, if you prefer, we'll secure a service to keep the house maintained inside and out until you decide what to do with it. The choice is up to you. Oh, and since your car is a compact and not a new model, we'll buy it from you and have a terrain safe SUV waiting for you in Brickton. We're arranging to purchase you a place to live, and the company will pay for all your living expenses."

"Hold on," Rylee raised a hand. "What does that mean?"

"It means it won't cost you a dime to live there."

"Do I still get paid the same?" She was already calculating how much she could save.

"No."

Her heart sank. It was wonderful to get free housing, but that didn't move her closer to her goal, which was to save and invest wisely enough that she could retire by the time she was fifty. "Oh, well…"

Ian rose and walked back to his desk. He picked up an iPad, did something on it, and then replaced it on the desk. A moment later, her phone pinged. "Open that," he directed.

Rylee opened the messenger app and lost her breath when she read the text. "Are you serious?" She reread it. "Did you mistype? This says–"

"And that's the starting salary. We're also giving you stock options and a bonus based on system performance."

"Oh, my –" she looked up from her phone. "Are you sure? There are people in the company with more seniority and–"

"But not half as good." Ian reclaimed his seat. "We recognize talent, Rylee, as well as loyalty, and you demonstrate both in spades daily. This is our way of rewarding that dedication."

She had to smile. "Well, this is one heck of a reward, but couldn't it have been attached to – oh, I don't know – Hawaii? I mean, what's in Brickton, Wyoming?"

"Only one of the highest concentrations of wealth in the country. Consider this. Why would live streaming from the center of a town with a population of under ten thousand, views of parks and stores, bars, and shops, of Yellowstone and Granite Lake, dude ranches and other things, be important?"

"I don't know."

He leaned back in his chair. "Money. Since the implementation of the system there, tourism in the state has risen nearly fifty percent. Because of that, Yellowstone has been granted an enormous influx of cash, making it the most well-maintained national park in the country. Hunting and fishing licenses cost ten times more.

"And believe it or not, since Brent started the subscription service, the revenue it's generated pays for nearly half of our fees. It is, in a word, a gold mine, and thus the salary package we're offering you is a bargain. We want our best there because what they're doing in Wyoming is being noticed and becoming the benchmark. We're already in talks with groups from Montana, the Dakotas, Iowa, and Nebraska for similar systems. Not to mention Los Angeles, New Orleans, Dallas, and New York."

"Wow," Rylee was shocked. "That's amazing."

"Indeed. Thanks to the work that you and others have done. Your agnostic approach has opened eyes to new ways of making technology not simply part of people's lives but a way for them to truly view the world without stepping outside their homes. And those who do step outside, head straight for the places they've been watching online."

Rylee knew the business was flourishing and was proud of the work they'd done but had no idea it was this much of a revenue generator. "Well, there is one other thing."

"What might that be?"

She tugged the hem of the short sleeve shirt she wore. "I don't exactly have the wardrobe for Montana."

"No, but if you have a coat that will suffice long enough for you to get from the airport to Brickton, you'll have two days on the company's dime to shop and outfit yourself."

"This is – unbelievable," she admitted. "Seriously. It's –"

"It's us affirming you're part of our family and making it official. So? Will you say yes?"

"How could I not? It's a dream come true. I can't wait to tell my–my brother. Thank you, Ian. Thank you so much. I won't let you down."

"There was never a doubt about that. Now, get cracking. You have two days until the next chapter of your life begins."

Rylee came back to the present with a smile on her face. A new chapter? Yes, it was that. If she did well in Wyoming, she would not just meet her savings goal but surpass it. Which meant she might end up retiring in her forties.

And then what? Her inner voice asked. Rylee tried not to consider the question because she knew what she secretly wished. She wanted to fall in love, to meet someone she could feel about the way her parents felt about one another. They'd married right out of high school, raised two kids, and were crazy about one another for as long as Rylee could remember.

She wanted that. Unfortunately, she'd never fallen in love and was starting to wonder if she ever would. What sort of man was it going to take to knock her off her feet?

The answer to that was a mystery and one she didn't like to contemplate because she truly feared she might be incapable of falling in love. Maybe her brain was wired for the work she did, not for matters of the heart. She had no real problems establishing casual relationships and wasn't in the least shy about letting a man know she was interested. But nothing ever progressed beyond exciting sex at the beginning that lost its appeal when she realized that's all the relationship ever would be.

She was thirty-seven and had never been in love. Maybe the problem wasn't with men but with her. Would she always be alone? Just as she felt herself starting to slide into the fear that inspired, the captain's voice sounded in the cabin, announcing the temperature of Wyoming, and informing the passengers they'd be landing on time.

Shortly after, the announcement was made for everyone to fasten their seat belts. Rylee followed the procedure, eager to land and get a look at the place she was about to call home.

Chapter Two

In her online research, she checked the average temperature in this part of Wyoming in April. The average daytime highs hovered in the fifties and nighttime lows were as far down as twenty-five. Just the thought made her want to tug her jacket closer around her.

The so-called winter coat she thought she had, ended up having two missing buttons and a frayed hem. She didn't have time to go on a coat search before she left, so hoped it would be sunny and in the high fifties when she arrived.

Those thoughts were swept away when she stepped into the terminal. The Jackson Hole, Wyoming, airport must have been designed to stun travelers with the vista beyond the windows. It was breathtaking. There was glass everywhere, presenting a nearly panoramic view of the area. Rylee got so caught up in the scenery as she made her way toward baggage claim, it caught her off guard to see an attractive, middle-aged woman waiting for her at the carousel. The woman held a piece of paper bearing Rylee's name. Rylee walked over to the woman. "Hi, I'm Rylee Monroe."

The woman smiled and extended a hand in greeting. "Well, hello, Rylee Monroe, I'm pleased to meet you. You're much younger than I anticipated but pretty as a picture. I'm Sharon Dillard, Mayor of Brickton, Wyoming."

"Mayor?"

"Is that a surprise?"

"Well, yes and no. Yes, because you're very pretty for a mayor, and I guess I always imagined one as old, male, and bald. But aside from that, as mayor, I imagine you have much more important things to do than greet me."

"Well, honey, I'm also the owner of the condo your company bought for you, so who better to show you around the town and where you'll be calling home?"

"That's very kind of you. I need to claim my luggage, and I'll be ready."

"I can help with that. It should be showing up momentarily."

Rylee followed Mrs. Dillard over to the carousel. "I'm very sorry for your loss, by the way," Mrs. Dillard started another conversation as they waited. "Your colleague, Mr. Corsa, and his partner were lovely people."

"Yes, they were," Rylee had only found out this morning that Brent's partner didn't survive.

"And now here you are, ready to jump in and take over, yes?"

"Yes, ma'am."

"Well, good. You'll be hearing from and seeing me often. I do like to drop in and check to make sure everything's on track, particularly at the change of seasons. You know, we have folks coming here for vacations all year round."

"From what little I saw from the air, and just looking outside now – oh, and the live stream I watched during the flight, I can understand why. It's breathtaking."

"Coming to us from Florida, I imagine you'll feel a bit short of breath once you're out and about. Florida is what, a hundred feet above sea level?"

"Give or take twenty feet, yes."

"Well, here you're six thousand, two hundred feet in elevation. You may feel a bit short of breath or winded at first until you become acclimated."

"Thanks for the heads up. I won't jump out and go for a long run until I acclimate."

"You're a runner?"

"Some. Mostly I bike, and rollerblade, and kayak when I can. Are there places to kayak here?"

"Honey, when you see our lakes and rivers, you'll positively swoon. I'm something of a kayaking fan, myself. You'll have to let me take you out one day."

Rylee smiled and shifted the case with her electronics from one shoulder to the other. "Thank you, I'd love that. Oh there, that's me." She pointed to her luggage.

"Call me Sharon and let me grab that. You're loaded already." Sharon lifted the piece of luggage off the conveyor belt like it was as light as a handbag. "Is this all?"

"Well, my wardrobe isn't exactly suitable for this climate, so I had most of my stuff shipped. It should be arriving this coming week. Until then, my boss said there were places in town where I could find what I needed. I hope he was right."

"He was indeed. Oh, and your vehicle arrived this morning." Sharon slid the strap of her oversized handbag from her shoulder and dug around in it. "Ha, got it." She pulled out a key fob, and on it were two keys.

"The key to the condo and your office. What do you want to see first?"

"The condo, if that's okay."

"Perfect. Here we go."

On the way out of the airport and during the drive, Sharon told Rylee about the town, the area, the people and answered all the questions Rylee asked. Rylee felt like she was receiving a thorough crash course in everything that was Brickton, Wyoming. Surprisingly, she found herself enjoying the conversation and the drive.

She also found herself liking Sharon Dillard, who was, by all accounts, an open book when it came to her own life. Before they reached Brickton, Rylee knew that Sharon and her husband, Earl, had been married for thirty-five years, had three grown boys who all still lived in Brickton, and one daughter who lived in Iowa with her husband and three daughters.

Sharon had been mayor for a decade, she and Earl owned a hotel and several condos in town, and she loved to fish and hunt, kayak, and camp. She grew up on a ranch, but now two of her sons lived there and ran it. Sharon's father died five years ago, and she moved her mother to a place near town, next door to her and Earl.

It was clear the woman had a big heart, loved her family and town, and was kind to strangers. "What do you think so far?" She interrupted Rylee's thoughts. "Pretty spectacular, isn't it?

Rylee turned her attention back to Sharon. "Honestly, it's like something you'd see in a magazine or a movie, almost too beautiful to be real."

Sharon grinned. "You know, oddly enough, I still get that feeling when I walk outside and look around, and I've been here my entire life."

"Where is your ranch?"

Sharon pointed. "About twelve miles that way. Prettiest land you've ever seen. I'll take you out there sometime if you like. We still have horses if you like to ride."

"I haven't ever ridden a horse, so I don't know."

"Well, we'll teach you. And here we are, Brickton, Wyoming."

"Oh my, it's like riding through the videos I've been watching. What a lovely town."

"Isn't it?" Sharon pointed ahead and to the left. "See right there, that group of buildings that look like a cluster of little houses? That's the condo complex. Each garage creates a barrier between buildings and allows for every unit to have a nice, screened patio and small back yard."

"It's within walking distance of everything," Rylee said excitedly. She hated having to drive everywhere and had often wished she could live somewhere she could ride her bike or walk to a store or restaurant. It looked as if that dream had become a reality.

She pulled out her phone, took a photo, and texted it to her mother. *Would you look at this, mom? It's incredible. I still can't believe I got this promotion. I wish you were here. I bet you'd love it. Will text again later. I love you.*

"Boyfriend?" Sharon asked.

"Mother," Rylee replied as she put her phone away. "I couldn't resist saying how beautiful it is here."

"You'll have to invite her for a visit soon."

"How is the town set for organic produce?" Rylee changed the subject. She liked Sharon, but she didn't talk about her family or personal life to people until she was confident they were trustworthy.

Once they reached the condo, she found herself delighted with the place. It had a window looking out toward the road, affording her a view of the mountains towering in the distance. In the back was a screened patio, and in the common area, a pool, gym, and an outdoor pavilion with chairs for relaxing.

The interior was furnished with comfortable furniture in the living area, a good solid wood desk where she could set up her home office, a gas fireplace, fully outfitted kitchen, right down to pots, pans, and dishware, and a master bath that boasted of a walk-in shower big enough for two people with double water jets.

The bedroom featured a king-size bed and a big window looking out in the same direction as the one in the living area, only giving more of a view of the mountains than the town due to it being upstairs.

There was also a guest room with a queen-size bed and its own bathroom.

"This is beautiful," she said as she put her carry-on and shoulder bag on the bed. "I appreciate you being willing to sell it."

"I made a tidy profit, so I'm not complaining." Sharon smiled and hefted the big suitcase onto the bed. "So, do you want to unpack or grab some lunch and shop? I set aside the rest of the day in case you want a guide and some company."

"I'd love that. Thank you, Sharon. You're so kind to give up your time like this."

"It's what friends do, and I believe that's what we're becoming."

That touched Rylee, and before she considered her actions, she clasped the mayor's hand. "Thank you. I sure hope so."

"No hope to it, it's already happening," Sharon gave Rylee's hand a squeeze before releasing it. "So, the next and one of the most important questions I'll ever ask. Do you eat meat?"

"Is the Pope Catholic?" Rylee quipped and headed downstairs.

Sharon grinned. "Then get ready for some of the best food you've ever had in your life. My brother Jim and his wife, Kate, own and run the best restaurant in town – well, in my opinion, I should add. It's not a fancy place, but you won't find better food anywhere, and the price won't give you indigestion."

"Sounds like my kind of place. Let's go." She opened the front door and held it for Sharon. "Can we walk?"

"Or you could try out your new wheels."

Rylee had completely forgotten about the vehicle. "Oh, I forgot, where is it?"

"See that pretty blue Subaru Outback beside my truck?"

"That's mine?"

"It is. Ready to go try it out?"

"No, I think I'd rather wait until I have a chance to read the manual."

"Ah, one of those, eh?" Sharon chuckled.

"What can I say? I'm a geek," Rylee wasn't offended.

"Then I'll drive. Besides, you might need space for all that stuff you're going to buy."

Rylee laughed. "Well, considering that I work long hours and have one friend, I don't reckon I'm going to need much. My work clothes will be fine with a sweater or jacket, and my boss said those things were being shipped today by the people packing up my house in Orlando. I should have everything in a few days."

"Oh, you'll need new stuff, child. And trust me, you'll make friends here. How could you not with me as your friend?"

"Good point. Okay, let's go stuff our faces then shop 'till we drop. I just need to call No Limits and let them know I'm here and will meet with them on Monday."

"Have at it."

Rylee quickly placed the call, spoke with a woman named Lynda, who was quite friendly, then slid her phone into her handbag. "I'm ready. Let's do this."

"That's my girl. Let's go."

When they stepped outside, Rylee stopped and looked around. She'd never considered herself as anything special, but today she sure felt blessed. She hated that her good fortune came at the cost of someone else's life but was determined to do such a good job that her big fat salary ended up being just a starting place.

And like her parents always told her, everything begins in the mind. If you can see it and you work for it, you can make it happen. That's what she was going to do. Here in, of all places, Wyoming.

Chapter Three

A chorus of greetings rang out the moment Rylee and Sharon entered The Eatery surprised Rylee. It'd been a while since she spent time in a small town. She spent most of her adult life in Orlando, which was, by-and-large, a tourist city. Since she lived just outside the city, the little Mom-and-Pop restaurants in the small towns had been steadily disappearing. There were local restaurants the natives frequented, but no places the tourists didn't find, so this hometown friendliness had become a thing of the past, except in rural areas.

"Well, hey there," an attractive woman with brown hair pulled back into a long-braided ponytail, hurried over and hugged Sharon. "I wasn't expecting to see you today."

"Today's a special day," Sharon ended the embrace and gestured toward Rylee. "This is Rylee Monroe, she's taking over for Mr. Corsa."

"Oh, I am so sorry about Brent," the woman said. "He was a nice man, always so polite and with a pocket full of silly jokes."

Rylee smiled. She'd forgotten that trait of Brent's, and was grateful to be reminded. It said something about this woman that she considered his jokes silly, but obviously endearing. "He was a good person," Rylee replied. "And it's nice to meet you…"

"Kate," The woman filled in the missing information. "Sharon's sister-in-law. My other half is in the kitchen right now. It's good to meet you and I hope we'll be seeing a lot of you. If there's anything you need help with to get settled, just give a yell."

"Thank you, that's kind. And oh, my goodness, what is that smell, and can I get a vat of it?"

Kate laughed. "That's Jim's pulled chicken, the special of the day, and I'm sure a half dozen steaks on the grill."

"I'm getting weak," Sharon cut in. "Give us a table, and feed us."

"Yes, you look a bit feeble," Kate teased. "Take that table by the window. What do you want to drink?"

"You know I want a diet coke," Sharon replied. "What about you, Rylee?"

"Do you have bottled water?"

Kate and Sharon both laughed, and Rylee realized people were paying attention, which made her feel a bit ill at ease. "I don't get it."

"Nothing says tourist or "not from here" like asking for bottled water," Kate answered.

"Oh, yes, I understand. Still, do you have bottled water?"

"Yeah, we have it. Tourists, you know." Kate rattled off the brands of water, and Rylee made her selection.

As she and Sharon made their way through the restaurant to the table by the window, Rylee couldn't help but notice how many people watched them. She bet they were locals curious about the strange woman with the mayor.

Tourists wouldn't care one way or another. She learned that working at the theme parks in Florida during the summers while she was home from college. Locals, however, in a place with as small a population as Brickton, would be understandably curious.

She spent her childhood in small towns, in North Carolina and Georgia, and there she learned how much attention newcomers received from the people who still lived in the old sections of town. In the places she'd seen since then, she realized that people who lived in small congregations tended to be more of a closed society. They were leery of outsiders, and only placed trust in those they'd known all their lives.

That wasn't a criticism as far as she was concerned. She understood the comfort that lifestyle could provide. That sense of belonging and community had its appeal. And she also understood the people who couldn't remain in the small town once they were grown and ready to build their own lives.

Opportunities weren't always plentiful in a small town. People took jobs in the closest cities, and either spent their days grumbling over having to "fight traffic" to and from work, or stopped battling the aggravation and moved closer to the city. They became part of a different social arena, where you develop a network or circle of associates and friends, but you might also not know the names of the people who live four houses down from you.

Rylee wasn't sure what appealed to her. Right now, she felt like she had a big sign on her forehead that flashed "outsider" and she wasn't enjoying it. She caught herself right before she looked at the floor, because she literally heard her mother's voice in her head. *Who doesn't appreciate someone giving them a friendly smile and asking about their day?*

That brought about the shift in attitude she needed to navigate this part of her adventure. One day the locals would see her and say, "oh yeah, that's that girl who works over at the video place, you know, the one that sends out all the live video everywhere?"

But for now, she was a stranger having lunch with the mayor. So, she'd be a friendly stranger. As they passed a table of three women, she smiled and said good morning to at each of them and did that to the next person who looked directly at her. By the time she took her seat, at least three people in the place had returned the smile.

Not a bad start, she thought and looked at Sharon.

"This is such a pretty place. It feels so… welcoming."

Sharon laughed, ignoring the people who glanced her way. "Is that what you call it? I call it being eaten up with curiosity. They're all wondering who you are, and no one has figured out a way to ask, but trust me, before we leave, someone will have texted or called someone and try to figure out who the young woman is with the mayor."

Rylee smiled. "Well, you're lucky I'm female, then. If I were male, they'd think you were having a fling."

Sharon chuckled. "Now wouldn't that set tongues to wagging?"

"Here's your drinks," Kate showed up at the table. Just as she placed the drinks on the table, a voice rang out.

"Where is he? Them people said they have a new boss, who's with the mayor, so where is he?"

"Jim!" Sharon called out as she got to her feet and headed in the man's direction. At the same time, a tall, burly man stepped from behind the bar. "Get him into the office," Sharon ordered.

What in the world was going on? Rylee watched as the man Sharon called Jim approached the upset man with his arms outspread. The gesture communicated both openness and closing a passage. "Ethan, you need to settle down now. Let's go into the office and see if we can square this away."

"I know he's here, and they have footage. I need that footage to–"

"I know, I know," Jim interrupted and guided Ethan down a hallway and out of sight.

Sharon spoke with Kate, who stood watching and then hurried to Rylee. "Come with me."

Rylee didn't question, she merely rose and followed Sharon the way the two men had gone. When Sharon knocked on a door at the end of the hall, a voice sounded with an invitation to enter.

Inside were the man who'd come into the bar, Ethan, and the big man Jim, who Rylee assumed was Sharon's brother. That thought had her looking more closely at him. Sure enough, he and Sharon resembled one another. The eyes, the shape of the lips, there was a resemblance.

Sharon addressed the upset man. "Ethan, the Chief of Police told you already that as soon as we have some answers, we'll let you know. But running all over town and kicking up a ruckus isn't going to help."

"I need answers, Mayor. He was–" Ethan broke down and his tears prompted a gathering of tears in Rylee's eyes.

"He's gone. Donny's gone. He's… He was my only boy."

Those words had the tears spilling out onto her cheeks. Rylee quickly wiped her eyes. "Mr.? I'm sorry, I don't know your last name."

"Caldwell," Ethan replied, and wiped his face on the inside of the arm of his shirt.

"Mr. Caldwell, I'm Rylee Monroe and I'm so sorry for your loss. I don't understand this situation, but heard you say there's footage of something. Is that correct?"

"Yes, those cameras are on all the time, you know. So, one of them had to record what happened."

"What exactly did happen, if I can ask."

"Someone ran down my boy, Donny. Right there in the street. Ran him down like an animal and left him to–to die."

Shock had Rylee frozen in place, and for a few moments there was only the sound of Ethan's snuffles. Sharon spoke up, easing the discomfort. "Rylee, Ethan's son was killed in a hit-and-run. We reckoned the cameras would have footage of it and lead us to the identity of the driver, but No Limits says they don't have any footage for that day, not for any of the cameras."

"No, that's not possible," Rylee said. "We have redundant backups and–"

"You're the new boss?" Ethan interrupted.

The words weren't out of his mouth when the door opened, drawing everyone's attention. Before her mind could do more than register the interruption, and the way everyone stared at the man who filled the door frame, he looked at her.

Rylee wasn't much of a romantic, so when an energy crackled its way over her skin, like static electricity, she marveled at the phenomenon before recognizing the sensation for what it was. Desire.

The man looked away and the moment ended. Rylee quickly turned her attention to Sharon., who addressed the man. "Brick, this is–"

"Is it true?" He stepped into the room. Impossibly, the room felt a little smaller. Rylee made note of that and tried to focus on his question. *Is what true?* His next words ended her confusion.

"Sharon, is it true? Is there footage or not? When is the new man from No Limits going to show up? We pay those people a king's ransom. The least they could do is get a replacement out here to square away this mess."

Sharon cleared her throat before answering. "Brick, let me introduce you to Rylee Monroe, the new Director of No Limits. She's just arrived. Rylee, meet Councilman Ike Brickman, affectionally known as Brick to his friends."

When he turned his gaze on Rylee, she stepped back before realizing she'd moved. What was it about this man? It took a moment to refocus. "Mr. Brickman," she nodded in his direction to demonstrate respect and hopefully help cool his temper, which seemed to be heating up a bit.

"Sir, I'd like to tell you that I have everything under control, but the truth is, I didn't know anything about missing footage or a hit-and-run until about five minutes ago, and I still don't have the entire story.

"But what I do have is enough for me to ask Mayor Dillard's permission to leave, so I can go to No Limits and get started trying to figure out why there is no footage for a specific date. Mayor Dillard, can you text me the date and location? I'll start with the servers and tomorrow will visually inspect the cameras."

"Sounds like a sensible plan," Sharon agreed. "Brick?"

"Fine. But make it quick. Ethan deserves to know who killed his boy."

"I understand and will do my best." She turned to Ethan. "I promise."

"I'll walk out with you," Sharon said and took Rylee's arm.

Neither of them spoke until they were outside, then Rylee leaned in closer to Sharon. "Who was that?"

"Brick? I shouldn't call him that in front of you, that's a name we gave him as kids because he couldn't pass up a dare, was either fearless or dense, and so was always getting into scrapes, getting hurt or in trouble. He was as hard as a brick – physically and mentally. Anyway, he's on the city council and arguably one of the most powerful men in the county, if not the state. His family founded this town, and thus it was named after them in a fashion.

"His family has owned the most successful performance and cow horse breeding ranch in the state for five generations. It didn't start as one of the biggest, but Ike, like his father and grandfather, is an astute businessman. They all made a habit of buying up as much land as they could if it was adjacent to their own.

"He has a daughter and two sons, none of whom are married, much to his chagrin, since he'd love to have grandchildren. He's a fair man, but not a particularly patient one, and just in case you're thinking what many women before you have thought, he has his share of lady friends, but isn't in the market for a wife."

"Neither am I. I was actually curious why he issues orders, and no one objects."

Sharon shrugged. "All too often, he says what the rest of us are thinking, but hesitant to say. Ike isn't hesitant, at all. He's a straight-forward, no bullshit type of man, if you know what I mean."

Rylee nodded, thinking he was also damn hot. But she didn't share that opinion with the mayor. "Well, if you'll point me in the right direction, I'll head for No Limits and dive in. And Sharon, I honestly had no idea there was an issue with the footage. Had I known, I would have insisted on going to the office as soon as I arrived."

"No one's blaming you, Rylee. It's just odd, and maybe it's even a case of your computers being tampered with. Whatever the case, we need to get to the bottom of it."

"Yes, we do, so where am I headed?"

"Don't you want a ride?"

"No, but thanks. It's not cold and I like to walk.

"Suit yourself," Sharon pointed across the street. "Down the block on the left. How are you getting back to the condo?"

" I can walk. It can't be more than a mile. That'll give me a chance to look around and get the feel of the place. Besides, I may want to walk back and forth to work. If–" she paused, then finished around a smile. "I have the breath for it."

As hoped, Sharon grinned. "Smart ass. Fine. Take my number and call if you need me."

"Thanks, Sharon, for everything," Rylee dug her phone out of her purse. "I'll let you know as soon as I have answers. But fair warning, it could take a few days."

"Here, let me put it in." Sharon held out her hand and Rylee handed her the phone.

Sharon quickly programmed in her cell, home, and office phone numbers, along with her email and address, then returned the phone to Rylee.

"Thanks," Rylee slid the phone back into her purse. "I'll be talking to you soon."

"Yes, indeed. Take care."

"You too."

Rylee headed in the direction Sharon indicated. This certainly wasn't the way she imagined her new job starting, and she wanted to talk to her boss, Ian Grant, to find out if he'd been told anything about the missing data.

But that would have to wait until Monday. She checked her iWatch. Three o'clock. That meant she had until Monday to figure out what had gone wrong. She wasn't worried about the contract with the town. They'd salvage that if trouble rose over the missing data. Her goal was to find that data and discover who had killed Ethan Caldwell's son.

It wouldn't bring his son back, but maybe if the guilty party was made to pay, it would bring him justice. That's what she was going to try and make happen.

Chapter Four

Sharon turned and almost collided with Ike Brickman. "Where's she headed?" Ike jerked his head in Rylee's direction.

"To her office. She wants to get started trying to recover the missing data."

"Walking?"

"I offered her a ride. She said she wanted to walk."

"Isn't she a little young? The other guy was older."

"She's old enough. And brilliant. You'd know that if you'd paid attention to the copy of the dossier we received from No Limits' headquarters."

"Still, she seems… green." Ike continued to watch Rylee make her way down the sidewalk.

"Well, she's green to Wyoming, but not to the job. Give her a chance."

"Never said I wasn't going to, Sharon."

"Fine. Then I guess I'll be seeing you at the next council meeting."

"If not before, and the Cattleman's Association has a meeting coming up. I'm guessing you or Earl will be there?"

"To be honest, I've about hit my fill with those things. Too much testosterone. Earl will be there."

"I'll look forward to seeing him."

"Well, I'm headed home, so you have a good weekend."

"If you get any news from that gal–"

"Rylee. Rylee Monroe." She interrupted.

"Right. If you hear from Miss Monroe, you'll let me know?"

"You know I will. Bye, Ike."

She headed for her car. Ike stood on the sidewalk for a moment, considering the events of the last hour. He didn't know how Ethan was holding up as well as he was. Ike's kids might have made him feel like punching his fist through a wall once or twice, but God knew he'd not survive losing one of them. Parents aren't supposed to outlive their children.

And children shouldn't grow up without a mother. That voice in his head sounded an awful lot like his father. Probably because his father and mother drove him half-crazy when his wife left. They figured he needed to find another wife, a woman who'd want to be good to his kids. It took years to convince them to stop the nagging.

Ike wasn't of a mind to get married again. Once was gracious plenty. His ex-wife Glenda had made sure of that. It wasn't enough that she cheated on him. She had to add insult to injury by cheating on him with his oldest friend.

Yep, Glenda sure kicked that friendship in the teeth, along with any favorable opinion he might once have harbored about marriage.

"You have the look of someone chewing on something foal."

Ike looked around to see the Chief of Police, Joe Rogers

Joe Rogers was a big man. As tall as Ike, which put him at six feet, four, but a good fifty pounds heavier. Ike had never known a more honest man than Joe, or one with a bigger heart and sense of justice. That's why he'd campaigned for Joe every time he'd come up for re-election in the last thirty years.

Now Joe was five years away from retirement, and Ike didn't know if they could find a man as honorable to replace him. "Since when do you work weekends, Joe?"

"Since Kate called and said there was some trouble at The Eatery. Something about Ethan attempting to accost the new No Limits fellow."

"Woman."

"Pardon?"

"It's a woman, not a man. Rylee Monroe. She looks like she's eighteen and wet behind the ears."

"Is that a fact? Well, where is this gal?"

"She headed down to her office."

"The mayor leave already?"

"You just missed her."

"Well, I imagine I'll be talking to her soon enough. Maybe you can help clear up some things for me."

"Like what?"

"Jim said the gal—Miss Monroe, didn't appear to know the footage from the camera had gone missing."

"No, I don't believe she did."

"That's odd. We called the company headquarters and spoke with—dang if I can remember his name. I have it written down. Anyway, we talked with someone who assured us that if they couldn't locate the data remotely, the new person they were sending would be able to retrieve it. I took that to mean the person coming here knew about the problem."

"Apparently not."

"Strange," Joe glanced down the street, then at Ike. "Between you and me, I'm starting to wonder if that data went missing by accident."

"How else could it have disappeared? No one I know has the expertise to break into that place and just take it. Hell, how would someone even know how or where to look?"

"I don't know, Ike, but something is starting to scratch at my brain about this. I'm going to take a closer look at Ethan's son to make sure he wasn't mixed up in something we weren't aware, and if he associated with anyone who might have the skills for something like that."

"Hell, I wouldn't even know what skills it would take. Would you?"

"Not a clue, but I've got people smart enough to help me figure out what that would be."

"Then you better get after it, Joe, because Ethan's barely holding it together."

"Don't I know it. Well, I'm going to grab a sandwich, then head down to speak with Miss Monroe. Want to join?"

"Might as well. I haven't had lunch."

"Then it's on you, my friend."

Ike smiled and patted Joe's shoulder. He might not have a wife waiting on him at home, but he had family and good friends, and that had to be enough.

Now, he just had to get the vision out of his mind, of Rylee Monroe locking eyes with him when he strode into Jim's office. Ike hadn't felt anything like that in years, that punch of attraction that nailed you in the gut and spread all the way through you.

"Say, if the new No Limits lady is a looker, maybe you should introduce her to Tom," Joe said. "To hear your dad tell it, Tom forgets to come home some nights he's so caught up in cowboying. Asa thought Tom was learning to be a rancher."

"Yeah, well, so did I, and he is, just not as fast as Pop and I would like. It seems he likes the life of a cowboy over that of a rancher, and to be honest, Joe, I don't blame him. I miss being a cowboy."

"Don't we all?" Joe asked and laughed. "Yep, those were the days."

"Indeed, they were," Ike agreed, and wondered for the first time if he was letting life pass him by. Was he so focused on the family legacy and the business of ranching that he'd cut himself off from the very thing he loved so much about it? Namely, feeling that attachment to the land and the living things it nourished. That's how cowboying felt to him. It was what he missed.

But then, at his age, there were a lot of things he missed., and some of those things he'd just have to learn to be happy without.

*****

It wasn't hard to find the No Limits office. They had a street-front location, ground floor office. Rylee noticed that the large front window and the door sported decorative metal work over the glass, she assumed as a security feature.

When she opened the door, she was confronted by four people: a woman who sat at a reception desk, three men and another woman who stood in front of the desk. It wasn't hard to figure out that she'd interrupted a conversation.

"Can I help you?" The standing woman turned.

"Hi," Rylee cut straight to the point. "I'm Rylee Monroe, Brent's replacement."

The woman smiled and offered her hand. "Sheila Smith. Hi, Rylee."

"Wow, I expected you to be older." Rylee shook her hand. "It's nice to put a face to the name."

A man who looked to be in his forties, with brown hair cut short, a trimmed beard, dressed in business casual clothing, walked over to her, extending his hand. "Jack Edwards, Ms. Monroe. Software developer."

"And overall security whiz, I hear. It's an honor to meet you, Jack. I've heard good things about you. I hate that our meeting had to arise from a tragedy."

"Same here," he paused and looked at the others. "Let me introduce you. This is Kyle Haley. He's our hardware guru."

"As I hear it, he's a hardware genius," Rylee drew on all the information she'd been given about the team here in Brickton.

"I'll take that compliment," Kyle responded, and hurried to shake her hand. "I've heard about you, as well."

"Nothing horrible, I hope," she noticed his friendly demeanor, and quick smile.

"Just that you're Ian's protégé, and he's fast-tracking you so that someone else doesn't snatch you away from him."

"Wow, I wish I'd known that. I would have asked for more money."

Everyone laughed, and the third man introduced himself. "I'm Howie Evans. I'm the in-the- trenches guy." He looked like a man who spent time outdoors, with more color in his skin and a bit more casual appearance.

"You handle camera set up and maintenance, correct?"

"Yes, ma'am."

"Please, I don't believe in formality. We're a team. And I will admit I'm psyched to be selected to work with the No Limits dream team. I just wish my time here didn't have to begin this way."

She glanced at the woman seated at the desk. "Hi."

"Oh hi, I'm Lynda. Secretary slash receptionist."

"It's nice to meet you, Lynda." She paused for a moment, then jumped right in. "Home office didn't tell me about the hit-and-run, or missing data, so you can imagine my surprise when the father of the fatality tried to accost me at The Eatery.

"I still don't have the entire story, so if you have no objections, I'd suggest we call in some food and you can all bring me up to speed while we eat. Is there a place in town with delivery?"

"The Eatery has delivery," Sheila offered. "I have their takeout menu."

"Then let's get an order made up. For myself, I'd love a club sandwich, fries, and an iced tea the size of Rhode Island. Oh, wait, do they make iced tea in Wyoming?"

"Not sweet tea," Howie answered.

"Ugh, then scratch the tea. I'll take two bottles of water."

"The water is actually good here," Kyle said. "I was hesitant when I arrived, but finally broke down and tried it and stopped buying the bottles."

"Okay, I'll trust you. An extra-large ice water. Lynda, do you have a company card for office expenses?"

"I sure do."

"Then put the food on that."

"Are you sure? Brent–"

"I'm sure. If you need additional authorization, text Mr. Grant."

"No, it will be fine." Lynda wrote down everyone's order and called it in. Once she hung up the phone, Rylee looked around. "Is this the most comfortable place for us to talk and eat?"

"We have a lounge," Howie replied and smiled. "Comes in handy when you're pulling an all-nighter because an ice storm took out four cameras."

"Don't give away all the good stuff too soon, Howie," she teased. "And how about showing me around?"

Rylee was impressed with the offices. Her team gave her the tour before they all settled in the lounge. Talk about impressive. A massive room, it boasted of a fully equipped kitchen and bathroom, with an enormous walk-in shower and lockers. A long bar separated the kitchen from the seating area which was furnished with three big deep cushioned sofas, two wing chairs and a dining room table that would seat a dozen.

"Now this is a lounge," Rylee said appreciatively, and sank onto one of the wing chairs. "Okay, gang, while we wait, I need you to fill me in."

"Where do you want us to start?" Jack asked.

"The day before the event."

"What about it?" Jack asked.

"Just tell me about it. Was there anything different about that day? Anyone out of the ordinary paying a visit, asking for a meeting? Was there anything abnormal about that day?"

Everyone was silent, glancing around at one another. It was clear from the way they looked at each other, there was no fear. They simply couldn't come up with anything to say. That was fine. Rylee just wanted to get a feel for how they reacted and interacted.

"Nothing comes to mind," Jack finally answered.

"Okay, so what about the system? Any glitches, hiccups? Are the backups for that date intact and accessible?"

"No issues with the software," Jack replied immediately.

"And no problems with the hardware," Kyle added. "We run daily diagnostics, as you know. Same procedure as your office in Orlando follows. A diagnostic report is automatically generated and uploaded to home office every twelve hours."

Rylee nodded and looked at Howie. "No issues with the cameras?"

"Nothing."

"Okay, then. So, the day before was business as usual."

Everyone agreed that was a correct assessment. Rylee pulled her phone from her purse and opened a new note, starting a list of things she needed to check into. First on the list was to read the diagnostic reports to ensure nothing was missed.

"So, what about Brent and all of you? Were you all at work the day before and the day of the event? Did anyone get into an argument, a heated discussion? Did anyone talk about problems at home or something that'd happened in town?"

"Where are you going with this?" Sheila asked.

"I'm not sure yet," Rylee admitted. "But here's the deal folks. A young man was run down in the street. His life ended, and his parents' lives were destroyed. The only chance there is of finding out who did that to him could be in the video footage. If it's missing, there must be a reason, and we need to discover what happened. Let's help the Caldwell family get justice."

There was no argument to her statement, and for that, Rylee was grateful. They didn't realize, but her motives were twofold—to help the Caldwell family and to protect No Limits and its employees.

Very wily, Ian. Rylee realized her appointment to this position wasn't made simply for her skills in data mining, design, or cyber security development. She was sent here because Ian knew she'd check every line of code, analyze every report, and run diagnostics on every piece of equipment to find out what had happened to the data.

He also knew that if anyone could identify a hack, it was her. And she wouldn't stop until she found the answer. That was Rylee's Achilles' Heel. She couldn't let a mystery go unsolved, and she'd turn over every stone in the Rockies until she found the solution.

A Note from the Author

I've been a reader my entire life, finding solace, excitement, happiness, fear, and love in the pages of books. If anything has been a constant in my life, it's reading.

I also remember all of the times in my life when being able to buy a book was a luxury, a treat that I didn't get every week. I've never forgotten those times or how much those books meant to me.

That's why I am so grateful to you, the readers. Regardless of your level of income or profession, I understand how precious your reading dollars are, and I feel humbled that you've used some of those dollars to purchase my books.

I hope my stories prove worthy of your investment and thank you from the bottom of my heart.

Many blessings.

Ciana

www.ingramcontent.com/pod-product-compliance
Lightning Source LLC
Chambersburg PA
CBHW070539310726
48982CB00010B/1411/J

* 9 7 8 0 9 9 8 5 8 0 8 9 0 *